Praise for the Exponential Apocalypse Series

"This should be the next show on Adult Swim."

— lady on Amazon.com

"[*Exponential Apocalypse*] definitely owes some inspiration to Douglas Adams, albeit with more 'f-bombs' and hookers than I recall seeing in the *Hitchhiker's Guide*."

— Jason Dorough, Fandomania

"Fast, weird, and funny as hell."

— Victor David Giron, author of *Curbside Splendor*

"If *The Avengers* was written by Terry Pratchett and directed by Kevin Smith, you might end up in the same dimension as *Dead Presidents*. Eirik Gumeny's sequel to *Exponential Apocalypse* is a weird, wild ride through post-post-apocalyptic America. And it's dead funny."

— Kat Clay, Radiant Attack

Also by the Author

Exponential Apocalypse
Dead Presidents (Exponential Apocalypse #2)
High Voltage (Exponential Apocalypse #3)
Black Hole, Son! (Exponential Apocalypse #5)

Store-crossed
Quintology of Qualms
We're Going to Die Here, Aren't We?
Devil Went Down to Jersey
Screw the Universe (with Stephen Schwegler)

AN EXPONENTIAL APOCALYPSE NOVEL
BY EIRIK GUMENY

Jersey Devil Press
www.jerseydevilpress.com

REVENGE-ARONI

Jersey Devil Press
Red Bank, NJ

www.jerseydevilpress.com

1st Edition

ISBN 978-0-9859062-5-2

For Monica.

Thank you for saving my life.

Also, the transplant team at Stanford.
I'm sure you guys had something to do with that too.

"Certainly, in taking revenge, a man is but even with his enemy; but in passing it over, he is superior; for it is a prince's part to pardon. … A man that studieth revenge, keeps his own wounds green, which otherwise would heal, and do well. … Vindictive persons live the life of witches; who, as they are mischievous, so end they infortunate."

– "On Revenge," Sir Francis Bacon

"Villain, I have done thy mother."

– *Titus Andronicus*, William Shakespeare

REVENGE-ARONI

PART ONE

The End of the
End of the World
As We Know It

CHAPTER ONE

And I Feel Fine

"So, let me get this straight . . ."

"OK."

"What I'm pretty sure you're saying is that the blackout, the one we all went through, everywhere, six months ago, was caused by the sun wigging out and blowing up all of the world's electricity."

"Right."

"So you and your friends here teamed up with a mad scientist –"

"The maddest."

"– to steal a bunch of technobabble nonsense-sounding supplies and go to the state-sized electrical grid in Montana to fix the, and these are your words, 'shiny, computery stuff' that powers North America, meanwhile completely ignoring the problems of the rest of the world."

"You make it sound like that's a bad thing."

"And while you guys were doing that, buttloads of mythological creatures, hired by someone somewhere for some reason, were running around, wrecking up any alternative power sources and trying to keep the world in the dark, while you, yourself, had to fight the killer ghosts of two elderly women, who showed up in Montana expressly to keep you from repairing the electrical grid."

"That's what they said."

"And so, in order to do that, one of them possessed a gorilla you knew and proceeded to beat the ever-loving shit out of you, until a friend of your friends showed up and threw a handful of salt in their faces and re-killed the ghosts. Or whatever it is you do to ghosts."

"Bust."

"I'm sorry?"

"You bust ghosts. That's the technical term."

"OK, sure. This friend of a friend shows up and *busts* the ghosts, at which point you somehow electrocuted just everything, jump-starting the engine of the power grid and turning the lights back on across the entire continent."

"Verily."

"And because of all that," continued the waitress, her eyebrow raised in what one could conservatively call a skeptical fashion, "you want free pancakes?"

"Yes," replied Thor Odinson, former Norse God of Thunder, sitting in the booth before her.

"No."

"What? Why the hell not? Weren't you listening?"

"Well, for one thing," explained the gelatinous young woman, "I don't believe you. And, for another, you're not wearing pants."

Thor looked down at his boxer-clad crotch.

"I eat better like this," he said with a shrug.

"If you're not going to wear pants, you shouldn't even be in the diner. That's what I came over to tell you."

"I thought you were here to take our order."

"No."

"But you brought coffee …"

"You had your pants on when you ordered the coffee."

"Coffee doesn't fill me up like pancakes do."

"Put on your pants."

"I don't want to."

"Then please leave."

"What if I get my pancakes to go?"

"You're not getting any pancakes."

"Please?"

"No."

"I think I liked the old waitress better," mumbled the thunder god.

"You said she tried to poison you," explained Dennis, a burly urban lumberjack type, sitting across from Thor and furrowing his brow.

"Well, yeah, sure, but she put the poison *in* the pancakes, so at least I got the pancakes."

The waitress, a jellylike blob, took a deep breath and undulated what passed for her shoulders backward.

"Please either put your pants back on, or get up and get out," she demanded. "Now."

"Fine," huffed the bearded blonde man, sliding out of the booth. He grabbed his worn-out jeans from the duct-taped vinyl benchseat and slung the pants over his shoulder. Nodding toward the man who had been sitting across from him, Thor said: "Let's go."

"You still owe me for the coffee," said the waitress, slowly and obviously putting the bill down on the table.

"You're kicking me out *and* making me pay?"

"You're kicking yourself out, Donald Duck."

"If you really want to eat in your underwear," said Dennis, sliding out of the booth and putting a meaty hand on the Norseman's shoulder, "we can go to Denny's. They have zero standards."

Thor narrowed his eyes and gave the other flannel-clad man a look. Then he began searching for his wallet, his hands wandering from his underwear to his jeans to his shirt pocket and then back to his butt.

"Shit. Hey, man, can you –"

"You're supposed to be paying *me* to be here, remember?"

"Oh. Right."

"You're not going to, are you?"

"Uh ..."

Dennis the Lumberjack, a strictly platonic male escort hired at an hourly rate from FRIENDS – For Rude and Inimical Entities Needing Dinner companionS, Inc. – bit his lower lip and shook his chiseled, perfectly scruffy head.

"I thought you were cool, man."

Dennis the Lumberjack walked out of the diner.

The former Norse god, watching the man he paid to be his friend leave, sighed heavily, as if he were deflating. Somewhere, a sad song began playing, something dramatic and orchestral with heavy piano. Somewhere else, a movie was being filmed, and the camera pulled back for a long crane shot, leaving the hero starkly alone in a restaurant incredibly similar to this one.

The waitress, moved by the pathetic scene, slithered over and put a tentacle on Thor's shoulder.

"That was terrifically sad," said the jellylicious young woman, "honestly one of the most tragic things I've seen here – and that's saying a lot – but you still owe me for the coffee."

"Yeah …" Thor stood quietly for a moment. Then he asked: "How are you guys on electricity?"

"Self-sustaining. Sorry."

"Shit," he said. "Do you need anybody hurt?"

"Me or the diner?"

"Whichever gets me off the hook for the coffee."

Slowly, the waitress picked up the check. "Like, *anybody* anybody?"

CHAPTER TWO

Little Pink Houses

NOTHING OF ANY IMPORT WAS GOING ON IN THE WORLD.

Initially, this lack of any terrible happenings had been, in and of itself, terrifying. After twenty-seven-and-a-half apocalypses, half a lifetime of nothing but disaster on the daily, everyone everywhere was anxious all the time. But without a reason to be, without a justified outlet for that anxiety, the world kept piling up that unspecified worry, until most of society was a twitchy, half-delusional mess. Destruction had become the status quo and its six-month sabbatical had folks crapping their pants in abject, crushing boredom.

Cities had long ago become things that just went away sometimes. But now they were standing, and thriving, and, apparently, they required maintenance. Traffic lights needed to be repaired, garbage needed to be collected, sewers needed to be emptied of crocodile-men and hulking reanimated corpses. The days of setting an apartment on fire because you were tired of the paint color and then blaming it on rampaging mutant moths had come to an end.

Slowly, hesitantly, society had begun building itself back up again, the notion that everything was out to kill them all the time cautiously slinking back into the recesses of the collective consciousness where it belonged, festering as mild paranoia and traumatic memory instead of a primary survival tactic.

Crime rates had dropped across the board – vandalism, robbery, murder, double parking, supervillainy. People even stopped swearing so much.[1] Instances of crazy shit no one could explain were minimal at best. Sales of cigarettes and guns and Hot Pockets had plummeted, while drug stores found themselves having to order more and more condoms and birthday cards to keep up with demand. Shuttered gyms and La-Z-Boy outlets had reopened. Vegan restaurants had suddenly become viable. The prevailing opinion was that the endless armageddons had ultimately served some good, culling the herd as it were, and removing all the undesirables from society.

Except for the vegans, obviously.

People were even looking into purchasing honest-to-goodness real estate since it was starting to look like houses might have a real chance at still being houses come the end of the year. People like Queen Victoria XXX and Chester A. Arthur XVII, the last surviving clones of their respective namesakes, created by a German sausage manufacturer for bloodsport entertainment, before earning their freedom and becoming mercenary heroes. They'd even managed to save the world a couple times.

"Do you really think we should buy a house?" asked the raven-haired royal replica, standing in a purple sweatsuit before a two-bedroom ranch house in the lovely residential neighborhood of Edgar, a suburb of the mighty metropolis of Secaucus, New Jersey.

"We haven't had a real home since the Holiday Inn burned down," replied Chester A. Arthur XVII, taking her hand into his, his broadening, heavily-scarred belly barely held in by his polo shirt and khakis, the universal uniform of a guy who has given up giving a shit. "We can't keep living like hoboes forever."

"I don't know," countered Queen Victoria XXX, "some of those hoboes are pretty old. Murray seems to be doing all right for himself."

"He's missing his entire lower half and gets around in a shopping cart."

"Yeah, but it's a *nice* shopping cart. It's got a horn."

"This place is right down the street from Ali and Catrina."

"Is that a selling point? I know they're our friends, but they are some of the most boring people I've ever met. Can't we move to Las Vegas with Billy?"

"Do you have any idea what the property taxes are like out there?" replied the patchwork president. "I mean, good for Billy, but there's no way in hell we can afford that. Especially now that the 'hero-for-hire' business is all but done."

"We could always cause problems and then get people to pay us to fix them."

"Like common con artists?"

"We would be *exceptional* con artists."

The queen leaned her head against her boyfriend's shoulder. They stood there silently, looking at the house and contemplating their future together. After a few moments, a tracksuited, greying couple in their late fifties power-walked past the clones, waving genially and saying hello.

"Ugh," scoffed the replicated monarch, watching as the older folks turned the corner. "That's going to be us, isn't it?"

"More than likely."

"I really thought I'd have died in a chemical fire by now."

"Sorry, honey," replied the president, leaning over and kissing her forehead.

CHAPTER THREE

It's the Artisanalest

"HAVE YOU FOUND ANYTHING?" ASKED SATAN, the former Judeo-Christian boogeyman, wearing a wrinkled suit and sitting on a hand-carved milk crate, drinking terrible coffee in a pretentious café on the outskirts of the city-state of Atlanta.

"Well," began Steve Careers, former Director of Operations for WANG and even more former demon, hunched over a laptop, the light reflecting in his glasses, "I managed to pull up the security footage of the attack, but the recording was damaged in the ensuing collapse, and it wasn't the greatest to begin with …"

After a bunch of mathematicians belonging to a variety of different churches got tired of arguing amongst themselves and used hard numbers to accidentally disprove all religions everywhere and end the world for the eighteenth time, all of the former gods and angels and demons and whatever became mortal and had to find some way to fill their newfound time. Some went on murderous rampages. Others turned to alcoholism. And still others, like Satan, found their calling as high-ranking employees of large corporations.

The devil, along with just a shitload of other erstwhile evil deities, was hired by the Walt Sidney Company and put to work. In short order, Old Scratch was made director of the Sidney subsidiary Worldwide Atlanta Natural Gas and Electric, with eyes on moving farther up the corporate food chain.

Then, six months ago, after a geomagnetic superstorm blanketed the world in darkness, Satan, tasked by Walt Sidney himself with keeping it that way, finally saw his opportunity.

The devil failed. He failed so hard.

Partly because of Thor and Chester A. Arthur XVII and their friends, but mostly because of his own hubris, Satan did not succeed in keeping the lights turned off. The god and the clones, and some other clones and a couple scientists, repaired the North American electrical grid, thwarting the devil's plans. As an insult to this already grievous injury, WANG's corporate campus was then destroyed by assailants unknown. The Father of All Lies was summarily called into Walt Sidney's office and fired.

On his way out of the office, Satan got into a spat with his direct supervisor, Loki Laufeyjarson, the former Norse God of Mischief and current COO of the Walt Sidney Company. Entertained by their bickering and not exactly a fan of Loki's, Walt Sidney made a deal with the devil: If he could find out who destroyed the WANG headquarters and exact his vengeance, without tying the Walt Sidney Company to the endeavor, he'd get his job back.

Satan threw everything he had into the effort.

"What are you saying?" asked the devil.

"The information is inconclusive at best. All I can tell with any authority is that it was a white guy. And a rat. I think," explained the man in the turtleneck.

"A white guy and a rat?"

"I'm pretty sure."

"We're never going to figure this out, are we?"

"It's not looking great, no."

The fallen angel rubbed his fingers against his forehead.

"So much for my unceasing vengeance."

"You could always get a job here."

Satan held out his mug and looked at the contents.

"This coffee is pretty awful, isn't it?"

CHAPTER FOUR

The Coupons Never Expire

CATRINA DALISAY, FORMER EMPLOYEE OF THE FORMER Secaucus Holiday Inn, and Ali Şahin, owner of the last-standing Dunkin' Donuts in the known world, wandered through the labyrinthine aisles of Bed, Unknown Kadath and Beyond, pushing their ever-filling shopping cart before them.

"These light fixtures would look great in the living room," said Catrina, stopping and admiring a display of dimmable black track lights.

"We already have lights, Cat," replied Ali wearily, leaning heavily on the shopping cart, his one non-mechanical foot sore from hours of browsing homewares.

"We have *a* light and it's not super helpful. The entire back corner of the room is always dark."

"It's not like we use it for anything."

"We *could* use it for something if there was light."

The man with the robotic arm sighed. "OK, let's get the lights."

"Thank you."

"We're going to have to stop at a hardware store after this if you want me to install them."

"You just want an excuse to buy more power tools."

"Yes. Yes, I do."

CHAPTER FIVE

Garage Sale

QUEEN VICTORIA XXX WAS STRETCHED OUT on her newly-purchased couch, screaming at the laptop perched on her legs.

"This asshole's bidding five dollars for my knives. Five dollars!"

"So set a minimum bid, honey," replied Chester A. Arthur XVII from where he was doing dishes in the kitchen.

"Is a thousand too much?" she asked. "I don't think a thousand's too much."

"A thousand's too much."

"Do you know what these knives and I have been through?"

"Yes," replied the Frankensteined president. "And I question the prudence of a paper trail connecting them to you."

"That's actually a good point," replied the cloned monarch, biting the side of her lip. "I'll use a fake email and move them over to Craigslist."

CHAPTER SIX

Do NOT Contact Me With Unsolicited Services or Offers

HIS FRIENDS PAIRED UP AND SETTLING INTO SUBURBAN LIFE, and the people he paid to be his friends not willing to do so without actual money being exchanged, Thor Odinson, former Norse God of Thunder, had returned to the only mortal avenue he enjoyed: being paid to perform wanton acts of violence.

"Can you get my cat out of this tree?"

Things were not going as well as he had hoped.

"You do know I'm a god, right?"

"It's a really big tree."

"The ad said I was available to solve problems. Specifically, problems that require excessive force."

"It's a *really* big tree."

"Sif's silken taint," mumbled the burly blonde man, shaking his head. Then he grabbed a tree limb and yanked.

CHAPTER SEVEN

That Movie from the '90s?
It Wasn't That Great

THROUGH NO FAULT OF HER OWN, QUEEN VICTORIA XXX had been roped into being civil and introducing herself to her neighbor and was now sitting in the tastefully appointed living room of Erin McCafferty, the grey-haired, track-suited, power-walking old lady she and Chester A. Arthur XVII had briefly met before moving in.

"So," asked Erin, handing the queen a glass of iced tea, "when are you two planning on having kids?"

"You mean like baby goats?" replied the replicated royal. "I don't think we really have enough of a yard for that."

CHAPTER EIGHT

What Up, My Knitta?

"WHAT DO YOU THINK OF THESE, BABE?" ASKED ALI ŞAHIN, holding up a pair of circular metal knitting needles.

"I have no opinion," replied Catrina Dalisay, several skeins of yarn under each arm. The oppressive weight of aimlessly wandering the aisles of Knit's All, Folks! was beginning to take a toll on her. Her shoulders hunched. Her vision blurred. "I don't even know what those are."

"They're for knitting that scarf I told you ab–"

"Don't you already have needles for that?"

"Yeah, but not this size. And not square."

"There are different kinds of needles?"

"Yes," he replied sternly. "You know that."

Catrina stared at her boyfriend. She stared at the needles. She blinked a few times. Then she stared at her boyfriend again.

"Look, I love you, Ali, but I'm going to be taking a nap in that discount wool bin if you need me."

CHAPTER NINE

Rent-a-Cop

BRYCE SNOOTWELL III RAN THROUGH THE MALL, a pair of video games clutched to his abdomen, his feet pounding against the vinyl floors. And then, suddenly, his feet weren't pounding anything anymore.

The teenager hung upside down, six feet in the air. The games dropped to the ground, along with his wallet, the keys to the car his parents had bought him, and a handful of half-melted candy bars he had shoved into his pockets.

"Nice try, asshole," said the psychic squirrel telekinetically holding the shoplifter aloft. His jumpsuit fluttered in the breeze coming from Grim Fandango, the fan store he was standing in front of.

"I'm sorry!" said Bryce. "I'll go back and pay for it!"

"You're damn right you will."

"Timmy?" asked a voice.

The rodent turned and, his concentration broken, dropped the teenager onto his head. Timmy the super-squirrel found Mark Hughes standing behind him, several shopping bags at the cyborg's side.

"Mark," said the squirrel with a tiny nod.

"This is what you're doing now?"

The security guard shrugged. "There aren't all that many wrongs that need righting anymore. And the pay here is pretty good. Plus I get to eat at the food court for free."

"I was worried sick, Timmy," Mark scolded. "I went to the RV after the diner that day and you were gone. No note, no anything! It's been months!"

"Sorry, chief," replied the squirrel with another tiny shrug. "I was pretty angry at you. Wasn't … all your fault, though," he conceded slowly. "I think I was going through some stuff. Mid-life crisis or whatever. I *am* five."

"I ended up going back down to Atlanta," the rodent continued, "to be sure WANG and Sidney weren't trying anything funny. Figured I'd take them on by myself if I had to, since you guys all humaned out. But it turns out you and Charlie were right. The Hollow Men – hell, the entire underground slave operation – was gone, nothing but boring office buildings and boring office workers, being boring. Nothing insidious at all. Even their tiered pricing plans were pretty fair.

"I ... well, I didn't really know *what* to do after that, so I just wandered around, helping people here and there, fighting off the occasional tobacco monster uprising, 'til eventually I found myself back in New Jersey. I was running pretty ragged by that point and the mall was hiring, so here we are." Timmy nodded at the bags full of frilly linens and things. "What the hell are you up to?"

"Opening a bed and breakfast," replied Mark, the once and future hotel owner. "I found some property not too far from where the Holiday Inn was. Historic pharmaceutical factory, great condition. Right on the swamp."

"That sounds ... kind of awful."

"The only other property I could afford was down the shore."

"OK, so maybe not *that* awful."

After Mars crashed headlong into the sun and released a massive wave of hot, solar death across the Earth, drying up a couple of oceans and ending the world for the seventeenth time, there was a mad rush to claim the new, even-more-beachfront properties before anyone else could get there.

Folks drove for days across the boiled-away oceans, looking for a shoreline. What they found instead was the towering city of Atlantis, just sitting there, hanging out and no longer underwater. Contrary to popular opinion, however, the Atlantians were not a race of technologically-advanced, peace-loving fish-people, but instead primitive, belligerent crab-people. This discovery, perhaps not surprisingly, surprised the pioneers, and they instinctively pulled out their shotguns and started shooting. Also, they were hungry and crab-people were delicious.

The Atlantians, despite being disoriented from the lack of ocean, did not take kindly to getting fired upon and slaughtered the beach-seeking invaders. A few of the settlers survived long enough to flee back to the mainland and spread the word that the Atlantians were not to be trifled with and maybe they should all just leave the desiccated Atlantic Ocean alone.

The Atlantians, however, did not receive that message and, after fundamentalist merpeople set off a hydrogen bomb under the floor of the Pacific Ocean and re-flooded the planet, ending the world for the twenty-fifth time, the crab-people seized the moment and revenged the ever-loving shit out of things. They attacked the entire North and South American waterfront, murderously evicting anyone living there and claiming the land for their own. Everyone who didn't die was surprisingly OK with this turn of events.

As a result, the Jersey Shore – and almost all other shores of note – were nothing but blood-soaked graveyards of what they once were, littered with busted arcades and collapsed taffy shops and splintered boardwalks, and absolutely crawling with homicidal, grudge-holding crab-people.

"You know," said Mark, pointing with his chin, "that kid hasn't moved since we started talking."

"Shit," said Timmy, turning toward the teenager, "not again. If I killed another one I might get written up."

CHAPTER TEN

Invasion of the Body Snatchers

"HEY, BABE," SAID CHESTER A. ARTHUR XVII, LEANING AGAINST the door jamb of their guest bedroom, wearing a bathrobe and the same pair of workout pants he'd had on all week. "You think you want to, maybe, fool around later?"

"No, not tonight, Charlie," replied Queen Victoria XXX, sitting cross-legged on the floor in a pair of sweatpants and an ill-fitting t-shirt, an open scrapbook in front of her, photos and stickers surrounding her. "I think I'd rather —" Suddenly, immediately, abruptly, she stopped. Her entire body seemed surprised.

"Holy shit," she said, "did I just —"

Chester A. Arthur XVII threw an elbow into the glass fire box in the hallway and wrenched the axe free.

"Who are you and what did you do with my girlfriend?" he shouted.

"Yeah, very funny," replied the lady in sweatpants. "You know we have to pay to replace that glass, right?"

"*I am not fucking around, lady!*" The cloned president stepped into the room, hauling the axe over his shoulder. "*Where is Vicky?*"

CHAPTER ELEVEN

Invasion of the Booty Snatchers

CATRINA DALISAY STRADDLED ALI ŞAHIN, NAKED, SWEATING, smiling. The brown-skinned man grabbed her by the shoulders and rolled her onto her back. She gasped happily. Ali lifted himself on top of Catrina, his hands pressing her wrists into the mattress.

"I'm going to put a BABY in you," he said.

"That is such a terrible name for a dildo," she replied, shaking her head.

"You're the one who bought it."

"I didn't think you'd *announce* it."

"I'm not just gonna stick something into you without asking first."

"And I appreciate that. But maybe don't call it by its name next time."

"OK." He held up the 'Brator Activated By Yelping sex toy. "So … do you want me to use this or not right now?"

"Well, yeah," she replied. "That's why I bought it."

CHAPTER TWELVE

Invasion of the 404 Not Found

THOR ODINSON SCROLLED HAPHAZARDLY THROUGH the Library of Congress's public archives of vintage hardcore pornography, eventually clicking on a screenshot that seemed promising and settling into his chair. The movie opened on screen, lighting up the darkened room. Thor undid his belt. He slid lower in his seat. And then … the unthinkable happened.

"What the fuck?" he shouted, clicking impotently on the play/pause button, over and over. "No … No! Not now!"

The video had frozen, and not even on a good part.

"Come on …" he whined.

Thor closed the window the movie had been playing in and clicked on one of the others he had open.

"What is going on?"

He closed and clicked. Closed and clicked.

"Where …?" he stammered. "Where'd the naked people go?"

He opened a few more videos and then, with a more profound disappointment than any other man had ever mustered in the history of time, he leaned his head against the keyboard and gave up.

CHAPTER THIRTEEN
Another Sunny Afternoon

"THE BACKYARD'S ON FIRE," SAID QUEEN VICTORIA XXX matter-of-factly, walking into the house and sliding the glass door shut.

"You said you were going out there to weed," replied Chester A. Arthur XVII, looking up from his computer.

"I did."

"And now the backyard is on fire."

"Yes."

"Why is the backyard on fire, Vicky?"

"Do you know an easier way to get rid of weeds?"

The calico clone closed his eyes, sighed, and pinched the bridge of his nose.

"You are going to put it out, right?"

"Eventually," she replied, turning and looking out the door. "Those morning glories are fucking *resilient*."

PART TWO

Send Lawyers, Guns, and Money

CHAPTER FOURTEEN

Come Sail Away

AMEN-RA, FORMER EGYPTIAN GOD-KING OF THE SUN – fully healed from the attack on Heliopolis and heavily scarred, as well as just heavy, after all the surgeries – stood in line at the counter of the Carny Cruise Lines customer service desk, tapping his foot impatiently.

"Next!"

"It is about time," Ra mumbled, stepping up to the counter. "I need a ticket, please."

"And what is your destination, sir?" asked the cornrowed white woman standing before him, her fingers poised over the keyboard, tingling with anticipation. And meth.

The bald Egyptian man lowered his eyes, his face set like an iron mask. Slowly, intimidatingly, his voice a sledgehammer dragging across pavement, he said: "America."

"OK, that's great, sir, but can you be more specific?"

"To avenge my pet lioness, Bambi."

"I'm sorry?"

"To kill the man who ruined my life," he rumbled, "to eviscerate the cowardly son of a bitch that sent his officially licensed Lindsey Louse special ops dragoons to do his dirty work and destroy my company after I refused to let him take it over."

"OK, whatever," replied the ticket lady. "Let's try this again: Do you have a city-state in mind, sir? A territory? Corporate province?"

"The Walt Sidney Corporation."

"That is none of those things."

"You said corporate."

"Province."

"Province?"

"Corporate province."

"Right. And I said —"

"The Walt Sidney Corporation. Which is not even a thing. I assume you meant the Walt Sidney *Company* —"

"I did."

"— but they do not technically own their own province."

"So?"

"So we can't just sail you to their door. We have ports of call. Carny Cruise Lines cruise ships are built from the recycled bodies of fighting robots and war machines, and ports need to meet certain spatial and anti-radiation requirements."

"Well, do you know where they are?"

"The ports? Yes," she said, her tone somehow becoming even snarkier. "They're on a list on the board behind my head."

"No," thundered Ra, "the Walt Sidney Corporation."

"Oh." She tapped repeatedly on the keyboard in front of her. "Their headquarters is on a private island in the chain of islands that comprise Sidneyworld, in the Gulf of Sidney."

"Then that is where I want to go."

"*But we don't sail there, sir.* You think we can afford the rights to sail into Sidneyworld?"

"Well," said the former Egyptian god, stifling several stockpots worth of rage, "do you sail near there?"

"Carny Cruise Lines can get you to Atlanta. You can rent or steal a car and drive to the Sidney Company headquarters from there."

"How am I supposed to drive to an island?! You just said it was an island! What kind of nonsense are you peddling here, you —"

"There's a very, very long bridge in the southeastern corner of Atlanta that spans the endless, bubbling, waterlogged swamp that was once the state of Florida and brings you right to the main entrance of Sidneyworld. It's a very popular and picturesque bridge. It's been on the cover of magazines."

"I don't read magazines," Ra seethed.

"That … OK, sure," replied the woman, shaking her head.

"Well …"

"Well what, sir?"

"Well what are you waiting for? Do that," he demanded, slamming his fist onto the counter.

"Do what?"

"Everything you were just saying!"

"About sailing to Atlanta and renting a car?"

"Yes."

"I can't rent you a car, sir. We're a cruise line."

"Then do what you can do! Get me on a boat that will get me to Atlanta!" he shouted. "We are wasting time here. I don't understand why you're making this so difficult."

"Me, sir?"

"Yes, you."

"I think you're mistaken."

"Do you know who I am?!" the sun god boomed. Light poured in through the glass walls surrounding the lobby. Several of the customers in line turned their heads or shielded their eyes.

"I can assure you that I don't care. At all." The clerk took his ticket from the printer, placed it in a cardboard sleeve, and handed it to him. "Sincerely. From the bottom of my heart."

CHAPTER FIFTEEN

7 Problems Only Redheads Understand That Can't Be Solved by Ghosts

PIOTR PUSHKARYOV SAT AT HIS DESK, EMPTY CANS of energy drinks everywhere, hunched over his laptop and scouring the seediest subthreads of the internet, in search of a new story for *The Daily Butt Trumpet*, North America's most trusted source for inconsequential news and stolen pictures of celebrity boobs. It had been nearly six hours since the site last updated. Things were looking grim.

There was a knock on the editor's door.

"Come in," he said.

A disheveled young man in a blazer and thrift store t-shirt entered. "Mr. Pushkaryov?"

"McGuire." The editor sighed and leaned back in his chair. "Vhat is it this time?"

"I've been told that there's a psychic squirrel working security at Willowbrook Mall."

"So? That is not story."

"Well, rumor is he's kind of super reckless. He's killed a couple of kids."

"Kids die all the time, McGuire."

"Rich white kids."

"Vell, shit," said Piotr, leaning forward, "vhy did you not open vith that?"

"Because it seemed crass and terrible. And, honestly, irrelevant. Kids are dying. It shouldn't –"

"Crass and terrible is vhat ve do, McGuire. Do you not read emails I send?"

"I try not to. They're usually pretty offensive. To, like, everyone."

"Such thin skin you have."

"I think I can get a story out of this, Mr. Pushkaryov. A real one. Something that will give *The Daily Butt Trumpet* credibility and expose –"

"No. You know that is not of interest to us. You vill give me a sensationalistic list of crimes of squirrel," said Piotr. "You have got two hours, McGuire. I vant it up on front page of site before lunch."

"But –"

"And see Debbie. Get her started on headline."

"Before I even have the article?"

"Of course. Vhat does article have to do vith headline?"

CHAPTER SIXTEEN

Fresh Squeezed from a Civet's Butthole Every Morning

SATAN AND STEVE CAREERS SAT ON REPURPOSED PORTABLE commodes in a dark café on the outskirts of the wreckage of Washington, D.C. Something that sort of resembled music played softly overhead.

The devil took a sip of coffee from his misshapen, hand-molded mug and nearly choked.

"What is so hard about making coffee?" he grumbled. "There are two steps. And one of them is 'buy coffee that isn't terrible.'"

"Found something, boss," interrupted the turtlenecked IT guy, the light of his laptop reflecting against his glasses.

Satan leaned over his shoulder and looked at the computer screen.

"Who do we know that's in the area?" he asked.

"Persephone."

"Hot damn."

CHAPTER SEVENTEEN

Hell Hath No Fury Like a Woman Denied Dental Benefits

MIKE MCGUIRE HUDDLED BEHIND A POTTED PLANT. His "10 Mind-Blowingly Illegal Things This Security Guard Did (Also He's A Psychic Squirrel)" column had gone viral almost immediately. But he knew there was more to the story, something real, something that spoke to the greater problems plaguing society, so he set out for the mall to photograph the killer squirrel in action.

What Mike found was Timmy the jumpsuit-wearing super-squirrel sitting in the food court eating the vegetables out of Mark Hughes' lo mein.

The reporter was profoundly disappointed.

Luckily for him, a busty brunette in tight pants and a fur-lined greatcoat chose that exact moment to storm into the food court, kicking open the mall's doors, a shotgun in each hand, along with a couple more strapped across her back. Mike's pants immediately got tighter.

The squirrel and the cyborg turned to see what the commotion was. They were promptly fired upon. The pair clambered underneath the table – Timmy on purpose, Mark because he had been shot in the shoulder and fell out of his chair.

"Rumpelstiltskin," grumbled the bed-and-breakfast proprietor, gripping his bleeding arm.

"I got this, buddy," replied the squirrel. Using his brain, he upended the table so the two of them were hiding behind its stainless steel surface, just as two more shots rang out. The table buckled and slid a few inches backward in response.

Timmy leaned his tiny head out from behind the table and grabbed the woman with the guns telekinetically, pinning her arms to her sides and lifting her into the air.

"What the shit, lady?" the squirrel politely inquired.

"This is all your fault!" shouted Persephone, former Greek Goddess of the Underworld, wriggling in his psychic embrace. "You're the reason I don't have a job anymore! I don't want to go back to farming meat pumpkins! I won't!"

"I have no idea what you're talking about, sweetheart."

"Fuck you."

"Look," said Mark, popping his head out from behind the table, above Timmy, "maybe we can talk this out. What exactly are we supposed to have done?"

"You helped stop the blackout and wrecked up WANG. So then Walt Sidney fired all of us. All of us! I had a corner office!"

"So Walt Sidney *was* behind the blackout?" asked Timmy.

"Well, he didn't *cause* it, if that's what you mean, but he certainly *prolonged* it. It just made good business sense."

"If we say we're sorry, will you stop trying to kill us?" asked Mark.

"Not a cracker's chance at a cocktail party in Hades," she spat.

"I don't – Do they like crackers in Hades? Is that what you're implying?"

"Like you wouldn't believe."

"Then you don't leave me any options," replied Timmy. He dismantled her guns with his mind and then dropped her hard to the floor, pinning her arms behind her back.

Persephone writhed helplessly against the tile, her fury rising with each passing second. She thrashed and thrashed against the psychic bear-hug, her cheeks beating against the floor like a short-circuiting android, her body squirming like a worm on a frying pan.

And then she was free.

"Oh shit," said the cyborg and the rodent simultaneously.

The goddess pulled herself to her feet. Timmy the super-squirrel tried to seize her psionically again, but Persephone wasn't having it.

"*Shit.*"

With a wave of her hand, Timmy collapsed like a soufflé against the floor of the food court. His fur began to wither and grey, his breathing became shallower.

"Timmy!" shouted Mark, ducking back behind the table. He pulled his rodent friend closer. "Timmy!"

"She's doing something to me, Mark," coughed the squirrel. "I don't feel right."

"Hang on, buddy."

"You're next, robot boy," said Persephone. Mark could hear her boots approaching against the tile.

The cyborg grabbed a nearby chair and snapped off two of the legs. He crouched as close as he could to the steel tabletop, using his x-ray implant to watch the former Greek goddess near. As she gripped the edge of the table to pull it away, Mark lunged upward and stabbed the pointed chair legs into her shoulders. Persephone shouted in agony. Her arms fell limp by her side. Mark grabbed the table and swung it into the woman's face. She toppled to the ground.

Mark scooped up the sputtering super-squirrel from the floor with his good arm and bolted towards the exit.

From a heap on the tile, Persephone yanked one of the chair legs from her shoulder and let loose a primal scream. A powerful pestilential curse radiated for fifty feet around her, killing plants and salads and the handful of fry cooks that had been looking on.

The edge of the curse caught Mark's calf and he tumbled into the foyer. Picking himself up, he staggered out of the mall, dragging his dying leg behind him.

Mike McGuire, safely fifty-one feet away from the furious goddess, ended the video recording and slid his cell phone back into his pocket.

"I am going to be Scottish duck levels of rich."

CHAPTER EIGHTEEN

And the Horse They Rode In On, Just In Case It Was Taking Notes or Something

"MR. SIDNEY, SIR," SAID LOKI LAUFEYJARSON, an enormous smile beaming across his skinny face, "we've got a problem."

The former Norse God of Being an Asshole stepped into the sparse, sterile, very white office and stood directly in front of an immense, semicircular plastic desk. The desk belonged to Walt Sidney, Founder and CEO of the Walt Sidney Company, the largest and most beloved multifarious conglomerate on the planet.

"Then why are you so happy?" replied the executive, his voice like gravel in a blender.

Walt Sidney was a middle-aged, balding man with a pushbroom mustache and oversized glasses, unassuming and the exact opposite of intimidating – an appearance he cultivated and often used to his advantage. Right up until he died, anyway. That was several decades ago. Walt Sidney now existed as a cryogenically frozen head, in a jar of cloudy preservation fluid, and gave pretty much everyone the willies, all the time. He used that to his advantage too.

"The Walt Sidney Company has been linked to what went on at WANG Electric. Our gremlins say there's a reporter working on the story now.[2] One of the ones with actual integrity, sir. It won't be long before the news gets out."

"That," the frozen head grumbled menacingly, "is unfortunate."

"I know, right?" replied the former Norse god, barely able to contain his glee.

"Was it Lucifer?"

"Yes, Mr. Sidney. Persephone, technically, but she was under orders from Lucy. They found the guys who totaled WANG – well, the one guy and a chinchilla or something – and she confronted them, inadvertently confirming the company's part in the blackout in the process. The guy and the furry thing managed to fight her off and get away."

"A guy and a chinchilla fought off *Persephone*," echoed the head, disbelievingly, "the former queen of the Greek underworld."

"The chinchilla has telekinetic powers," clarified Loki. "Did I not mention that?"

"You did not."

"Here's the best part, sir: it turns out they're linked with Chester A. Arthur and Thor!"

"You need to be less excited about this."

"I'm trying, Mr. Sidney. I'm sorry, Mr. Sidney."

The frozen head sighed. "Well, I guess you know what the next step is."

Loki began jumping up and down with joy.

"Kill everyone involved," snarled the jarred head of Walt Sidney.

"With gusto," replied the trickster god, a sinister grin cutting across his face.

"*Start* with the reporter."

"Aw," Loki whined. "Fine."

"You need to learn to prioritize, Loki," replied the severed head. "How else do you expect to get anywhere in this organization?"

"I'm already your right-hand man, sir, and the COO. Where else is there to go?"

"Someday I may need someone to take the reins of this company, Loki, a successor to the Walt Sidney Company crown when I'm unable to go on. I am nearly one hundred and fifty years old."

"Are – Are you serious, Mr. Sidney?" said Loki, his dreams suddenly tangible, within reach, like an all-you-can-eat Chinese buffet with steaming bins of crab Rangoon and spare ribs and no one else around. His heart pounded. "That would be an honor, sir. I'd be –"

The frozen head erupted with a very hearty laugh.

"Don't be so gullible, Loki," he said. "I'm going to live forever."

CHAPTER NINETEEN

This Is What Professional Ambition Gets You

MIKE MCGUIRE PULLED HIS RATTLETRAP SEDAN into the parking lot of *The Daily Butt Trumpet,* only to find the building – and most of his co-workers – on fire. The reporter could see his editor, Piotr Pushkaryov, completely engulfed in flames and running back and forth in front of the towering inferno. Piotr passed a burning heap that Mike was pretty sure was the payroll department.

"That's probably going to make getting my check difficult," he said to himself. Then he shrugged. "Good thing there's still *The Huffing Paint Post.*"

As Mike put his hand on the gearshift to move the car into reverse, he heard a tap against his window. He turned his head. There appeared to be an enormous, red-haired, red-eyed dog-man standing outside his car.

"Boo," said the furry monstrosity. [3]

"Ah, shit," replied Mike McGuire.

CHAPTER TWENTY

No Shirt, No Shoes, No Sandwich

WEI AND SHANNON LEBER-ZHENG SAT IN THE DINER across from their new friends, Queen Victoria XXX and Chester A. Arthur XVII, four cups of cooling coffee and two mostly eaten cheesecakes between them. The couples were having a remarkably in-depth discussion about interior decorating.

"We found these really pretty lead-lined drapes," said Shannon, "at this store right off Route 7."

"The place is haunted by the murderous ghosts of Vikings," added Wei.

"Well, yes, but the prices are amazing."

"And they're radiation-dampening?" asked the president.

"They're rated to six thousand gigabecquerels."

Chester A. Arthur XVII turned to the replica queen. "We could use something like that in the back bedroom."

"Are you guys facing that exploded factory too?" asked Wei.

"Yeah. Roger said the radiation was contained, but I'm not buying it. When the wind shifts, there is definitely the distinct odor of nuclear waste."

"Rick was there when it all went down. Swears the explosion was to blame for his impotence."

"Is he serious?"

"Yeah. He's not happy about it. Won't shut up about it either."

"So, about Rick …" began Queen Victoria XXX conspiratorially, "is he … you know …"

"A werewolf?" replied Wei. "I'm pretty sure, yeah."

"I'm not convinced," added Shannon.

"Have you seen the way the man eats steak?" asked the cloned president.

"I know," said Wei. "What else could he be?"

At that moment, Thor Odinson came crashing through the wall, and part of the roof, of the diner, clamped between the jaws of a dragon the size of a tour bus. A dragon that came crashing through the same wall, an adjoining wall, and more of the roof.

"Thank fucking Cumberbatch," said Queen Victoria XXX, grabbing a fistful of silverware and standing on the vinyl bench. "No offense to you two, but this life is as boring as watching oatmeal boil."

"You don't like oatmeal?" asked Shannon.

"It's an insult to breakfasts everywhere."

The facsimile monarch threw off her tasteful blazer, clambered over her boyfriend and out of the booth, and then ran towards the wreckage of the wall and jumped, forks blazing, at a second dragon that had landed outside.

Thor, meanwhile, was punching the first dragon in the face repeatedly. The gargantuan monster dropped the thunder god into a table, then let loose a column of flame that seared the Norseman and everything within five feet of him.

"You destroyed my *donut shop!*" shouted Thor, pulling himself free from the wreckage of the booth.

Through the hole in the ceiling, Chester A. Arthur XVII could see a sky full of dark clouds angrily rushing together.

"We should probably leave," said the artificial politician to the Leber-Zhengs. "Now." Less deftly than he imagined, the patchwork president pulled himself onto the straining table and shouted to the rest of the diner: "Everyone needs to evacuate this restaurant immediately! A good deal of destruction is imminent!"

"But I haven't gotten my BLT yet!" hollered some guy at a table in the back room.

A canyon of lightning split apart the sky, striking the dragon through its skull and sending sparks through everything metal nearby. The beast shook its head and then let loose a pants-soiling roar in reply.

"Nevermind!" shouted the BLT guy, springing from his seat and hauling ass for the door.

Several more bolts of lightning ripped through the dragon as Chester A. Arthur XVII herded the diner patrons to safety.

Once more, the dragon roared awesomely in response, rattling the very bones of the thunder god, before stomping forward, spreading its wings and taking out several support beams of the erstwhile eatery. The building began collapsing like it was in a Michael Bay movie.

"And now my diner?!" screamed Thor. "*You asshole!*"

Thunder clapped like the audience at a Who show full of people with giant hands. Cups and napkin holders and window blinds shook. A heavy rain began to fall, pouring into the building through the shattered roof. Thor stood opposite the seething monster, shaking with barely contained rage, like an off-kilter lawnmower engine. His shirt soaked to his muscular chest. His hair fell into his face, his beard began to resemble a wet puppy. He was breathing slowly, heavily, his eyes set with slaughterhouse intent.

The dragon snapped at the thunder god, just as lightning crashed down into and around the beast, again and again, faster and faster, in an increasingly erratic pattern.

"Hey, Thor? Buddy?" called Queen Victoria XXX, astride the neck of the wriggling second dragon and looking with trepidation at the lightning tearing through the air around her. "Think you could be a little more focused on what you're electrocuting?"

"They destroyed the Dunkin' Donuts, Vicky," replied the Norseman coldly.

"OK, sure, but –"

A dozen flashes of electric murder burned through the sky in quick succession, obliterating chunks of the diner and the parking lot and sending both of the dragons into a frothing fury.

"Right. I'm just gonna leave this to you then."

The queen bounded from the back of the bucking beast, forks still lodged in the monster's skull. The second dragon looked after her for a moment, then charged forward at the thunder god, joining the first one in unleashing an otherworldly fire upon the brawny blonde man.

More and more lightning crashed down recklessly, striking the dragons, the ground, the cash register, everything, the Norseman's rage overpowering his control. Swallowed by the inferno, his clothes burning away into an ashy memory, Thor began trembling like a particularly terrifying vibrator, staring with a growing berserker fury at the two creatures trying to roast him alive.

And then they stayed like that for a while.

Chester A. Arthur XVII, huddled with Queen Victoria XXX and the Leber-Zhengs behind a car in the far corner of the parking lot, looked at his watch.

"That can't be good, even for him," he said.

"Probably not," replied the made-up monarch, pulling back her wet hair.

"Should we help him?"

"Do you have a plan?"

An errant lightning bolt took out a nearby tree.

"Nope," replied the cloned president.

"What about running away?" asked Wei. "Can we run away?"

"Well ..." began the plotting president. The sedan lurched as the heat from the unrelenting flames melted one of the car's tires.

Shrugging, Chester A. Arthur XVII said, "You know what? Sure."

The foursome scurried away as the elemental standoff continued behind them — god against beast, electricity against fire, a marathon of pigheadedness to the death.

Eventually, the second dragon succumbed to the electrical onslaught and crumbled to the ground, its skin sizzling, smoke pouring from its eyeballs. The first dragon looked at its comrade and let loose a frenzied roar — the sound alone tumbling down what was left of the broken walls — before hurtling toward the thunder god, teeth first. With remarkable deftness for a man his size, especially one covered in fourth-degree burns and missing pants, Thor rolled around the creature's snapping maw and threw his arms around its enormous neck. He clamped down hard, digging his fingers into the beast's scaly flesh, straining his every muscle and pulling the struggling monster toward the ground.

The dragon thrashed and flailed, expanding its leathery wings into the rubble and shattering the glass front counter of the diner. Thor redoubled his efforts, his feet punching through the linoleum floor of the restaurant. The beast began screeching and flapping furiously, trying to lift itself free of the Norse god's grasp. But for every ounce of energy the monster expended trying to break loose, the thunder god increased his grip twofold, until, finally, Thor tore the dragon's head off.

The cumbrous reptile's body collapsed into the detritus of the diner, a cloud of dust kicking up weakly into the rain. The Norseman likewise slumped to the ground, dropping the beast's head and leaning against a slab of what used to be the wall. Above him, the clouds began to unknit, the storm to recede. As he sat breathing deeply, the dragon's blood pooled beneath the thunder god, seeping into places one generally doesn't want blood to seep.

"Well, that was a thing," Thor said, his naked, scorched body smoking profusely. "Can I get some water or something?"

Slowly, cautiously, the waitress peered over the cluttered counter behind which she was hiding.

"You're, uh, you're kind of not wearing pants again," replied the waitress, pointing a gelatinous tendril toward the naked man's blistered, blood-stained junk.

"For fuck's sake, lady."

"It's not my rule!"

CHAPTER TWENTY ONE

Bunch of Savages In This Town

THOR ODINSON, CHESTER A. ARTHUR XVII and Queen Victoria XXX raced back to the Plaza at the Meadows just in time to be just too late to help Ali Şahin. The cybernetic entrepreneur, profoundly uncomfortable and hemorrhaging more blood than a Quentin Tarantino extra, moaned and twitched from beneath the pile of rubble that used to be his Dunkin' Donuts. Several feet away, Catrina Dalisay was sprawled atop a planter of wildflowers in an unconscious heap.

Pulling his armored minivan directly onto the brick of the plaza, Chester A. Arthur XVII and a smoldering, vesicated, still-naked Thor leapt from the automobile and began digging Ali free. Queen Victoria XXX sprinted to Catrina's side.

"Hey, wake up," the queen said, shaking her friend by the shoulder. "Catrina. Come on. Catrina, wake up." Getting nowhere, the reconstituted monarch slapped her across the face. "Catrina!"

"What?" said the tiny Filipina woman dreamily, jerking her head around and blinking her eyes. "What ... what happened?"

"I was really hoping you could tell me."

"Ali!"

Catrina tumbled from the flower bed and stumbled over to her boyfriend, clambering across the debris of the donut shop and grabbing Ali's hand.

"Ali, honey ..."

"I wasn't even supposed to be here today," he coughed. "I just ... We've been spending so much money on house stuff and decorations and yarn ... So much yarn ... And it's so expensive ..."

"It shouldn't be, but you like the crazy alpaca/griffin blends."

"They're just a better quality," Ali replied. He tried to take a deep breath, his lungs wheezing like an emphysemic asthmatic.

"Oh, sweetie," Catrina replied, putting a hand against his bloodied cheek, "you'll never have to go shopping again, I promise."

"I don't think I'll be doing much of anything again, if we're being honest here."

"Don't talk like that."

"I can feel my organs failing, babe."

"That's not how organ failure works," explained Chester A. Arthur XVII.

"When they're being … squished to the point of exploding it is."

"Frigg's flaxen forelocks," mumbled Catrina. "Dig faster! Dig faster!"

Thor and Chester A. Arthur XVII did as instructed, continuing to remove chunks of Dunkin' Donuts at a literally superhuman rate, now assisted by Queen Victoria XXX as well. As the sizeable stack of spifflicated store parts subsided, the slabs of rubble immediately crushing the cyborg shifted, and not in a helpful way. A large block of concrete slid downward, landing heavily on Ali's waist and most of what was underneath his shattered ribcage.

"See?" he muttered through the increasing agony. "Whatever that organ was, it's gone now." He winced. "I'm pretty sure it was important."

"It was probably just your spleen," cooed Catrina.

"No, I had that removed years ago."

"Maybe it was a kidney then. You have three."

"Two," corrected Chester A. Arthur XVII.

"No, Ali has three," re-corrected Thor. "It's a whole thing."

The god and the presidential clone hefted an automatic cake donut machine from atop Ali's upper back. He immediately began screaming.

"Put it back! Put it back!"

The Norseman and the Frankensteined politician looked at one another, shrugged, and then dropped the immense steel contraption back down on their friend.

"Thank you," muttered Ali. "I think that's pinching the nerve that tells me how much pain I'm in."

"We'll figure out some way to get you out of here," said Chester A. Arthur XVII.

"No," he replied. "I don't think that's going to happen."

"Then we'll bring you back to life after you die," said Thor.

"OK," sputtered the man from Dunkin' Donuts, blood and other important bodily fluids dribbling from his mouth. "That … that sounds good." His eyes began to flutter.

"Ali?" said Catrina, gripping his hand tightly. "Ali?"

The cybernetic donut shop owner coughed and then, expending a tremendous amount of his dwindling energy, raised his head to look directly into his girlfriend's dark eyes.

"I love you, Catrina."

"I love you too, Ali," she replied, pressing her forehead against his. "I'll see you soon."

And with that, Ali Şahin died.

A few tears rolled down Catrina's face as she sat there, holding Ali's human hand, but, after a moment and a few deep breaths, her demeanor changed considerably. Perched atop the shattered Dunkin' Donuts, next to her mutilated boyfriend, in grey sweatpants and an old t-shirt of his, the woman was by all appearances more bummed out than devastated, looking as if the worst thing that had happened to her recently was her favorite television show being cancelled on a cliffhanger, rather than the love of her life being mangled to death by dragons.

"You don't seem particularly broken up about this," said Queen Victoria XXX, sitting down beside her.

The former hotel employee shrugged. "You heard Thor. It's not like we don't know a guy who can bring him back to life. I mean, how many times has Charlie died on you?"

"Good point."

"Although," said Catrina, turning and looking sternly at Thor, "you could've dug him out earlier. Instead of abandoning us and doing whatever it was you did after I was knocked out."

"Fighting dragons," replied the scabbing thunder god, sitting down atop the rubble, his balls swinging in the breeze. "I was avenging his death."

"He wasn't dead yet."

"Right. *Yet.*"

"You could've saved his life."

"And I still will," explained Thor. "You know, after lunch."

"You're a jerk."

"Dr. Arahami regularly spits in the face of death, for fun. What are you so mad about?"

"It's not the death I'm mad about, Thor, it's the gross negligence."

"I took a shower this morning!"

The Filipina woman shook her head.

"Is it the Freddy Krueger thing I got going on now? 'Cause that's not my fault, Catrina."

"Backtracking a little," said Chester A. Arthur XVII, "what exactly *did* happen here?"

"Those dragons from the diner," explained the Norseman.

"The three of us were hanging out in the back of the store," Catrina expounded. "Thor and I stopped by so Ali could show him how to make éclairs, so he wouldn't keep showing up at our house at three in the morning and dragging Ali's ass out here whenever he wanted one. And then the dragons showed up out of nowhere and started fucking up the Dunkin' Donuts."

"You're sure you didn't provoke them in any way?"

"I'd never even seen those assholes before," replied Thor.

"OK." The patchwork president looked around the rest of the abandoned – but undamaged – plaza. He shook his head. "I don't think this was an accident."

"Who do we know that has access to dragons?" asked Queen Victoria XXX.

CHAPTER TWENTY TWO

A Fish This Fine Belongs in a Fish Nugget-Style Chunklet

AMEN-RA WALKED BRUSQUELY DOWN THE GANGWAY of the cruise ship and onto the wooden dock.

"Welcome to Supernova Scotia!" said a cheery young woman in an ill-fitting jumpsuit, holding out a tray of complimentary fried fish.

"Is that the American way of saying 'Atlanta?'" he asked.

"I … what? No?"

Ra looked around – at the quaint seaport, at the non-polluted sky, at the strangely glowing Canadian – before shifting his eyes to his ticket, his eyebrows furrowed. The sun god growled slightly.

"I do not like that woman."

"I'm sorry," replied the woman with the fish, visibly crestfallen.

"Oh, no," countered Ra, surprisingly softly, putting a hand on her shoulder, "not you. No. You seem like a delightful young lady. I was talking about the inbred hillbilly woman who sold me this ticket."

"Oh, OK," she replied, breathing a sigh of relief. "That actually happens a lot."

"Really," replied Ra.

During the international blackout that had ended the world for the twenty-sixth time, the governor of Nova Scotia – at the time, Billy "Buzz" Bee, a grizzled longshoreman who had lost a bet – had the "brilliant" idea to coat everything in the green stuff found inside glow-in-the-dark light sticks. The "elected" official called up every party store and Halloween warehouse he could think of and then personally flew a crop-duster back-and-forth over the province until Nova Scotia no longer needed electricity.

The paint job helped the darkness situation considerably, but ruined pretty much everything else. The glow-in-the-dark substance was gumming up the water infrastructure, keeping everyone awake all the time, and killing most of the flora and fauna. Later studies determined the goop was, like, *super* carcinogenic.

Not wanting to admit defeat – or, really, be a governor in the first place – Billy Bee changed the name of the province to Supernova Scotia to reflect this newfound luminosity and attract more tourists. He also hoped this would help the people forget about the insomnia and the cancer.

For reasons unknown, his plan did not work.

"Seventy-five percent of our tourism comes from booking errors." The young Canadian lifted the tray higher. "Fish?"

Ra picked up a piece and looked at the misshapen lump, turning it back and forth.

"Can you be more specific than 'fish?'" he asked.

"For legal reasons," replied the woman, "no."

CHAPTER TWENTY THREE
Back in the Saddle Again

LEAVING HIS RV IDLING IN THE PARKING LOT, Mark Hughes limped his way across the empty plaza, an artificially-aged Timmy the super-squirrel cradled in his non-shotgunned arm. He trundled over to Thor, Catrina, Chester A. Arthur XVII, and Queen Victoria XXX, all sitting around the decimated Dunkin' Donuts and eating pizza. Also, Ali's battered corpse was there, still buried in the rubble.

"What the hell are you guys doing?" asked Mark as he approached, taking in the scene before him. "What happened to the donut shop? Is that Ali? What the fuck is going on?"

"Eating pizza," replied Thor, his mouth full. "Dragons. Yes. He's dead."

"And you're sitting here screwing around?"

"We're gonna fix him after we eat. It's a long ride to Las Máquinas. You don't seriously expect us to do it on an empty stomach, do you?"

"I hate it when the stupid things you say almost make sense."

"What's wrong with Timmy?" asked Catrina, putting down her slice. "Why does he look a giant, furry raisin?"

"A woman attacked us at the mall. She used some kind of magic or something, it really messed him up."

"Magic?" said the naked thunder god, raising an eyebrow.

"Judging by what I'm pretty sure is going on with my leg," continued Mark, limping forward, "she aged him somehow, pushed him through I don't know how many years in an instant. My leg still works, technically, but it's tired, weak. Wrinkly. And it kind of smells like mothballs. The plants she hit bloomed, withered, and then died, like that." He snapped his fingers. "That's probably what's going on with Timmy, too."

"That's not good," said Chester A. Arthur XVII. "Squirrels only have a lifespan of about twelve years, maximum."

"I know. That's why I brought him here. Which, by the way, why don't you guys answer your texts? I was driving all over the place trying to find you guys. And what the hell happened to the diner?"

"Dragons," replied Thor, answering both questions at once.

"Maybe you should have brought Timmy to a hospital first," said Queen Victoria XXX. "And, you know, yourself." She nodded toward his wounded shoulder. "You seem to be bleeding pretty profusely."

"It's just a flesh wound," replied Mark with a dismissive shake of his head. He handed the sleeping Timmy over to Catrina.

"I think I can see bone, dude," the naked Norseman.

"Really?" The cyborg craned his head to look at the damage.

"You two need medical attention," said the cloned president.

"Anything a hospital can do, I can do better, quicker, and cheaper," replied the former military medic, "and with less chance of catching some kind of super virus."

"I'm not doubting your abilities, Mark, but the mechanics of the situation leave something to be desired. I don't think you can physically stitch your own shoulder shut."

"Sure I can."

"You're right-handed."

"So?"

"So you were shot in your right shoulder."

"Oh. Yeah."

"How much blood did you lose?" asked Queen Victoria XXX.

"Look, the shoulder's not the issue. Whatever's going on with Timmy and my leg is some seriously next level shit. No mail order doctor is going to be able to do anything helpful."

Shortly after the world ended for the sixth time and the increased hostility and bureaucratization of the various insurance industries made getting dependable medical attention nearly impossible, many nurses, doctors, and surgeons – having souls and tired of the institutionalized dismissal of the Hippocratic oath – went rogue and began helping people from outside the established hospital system, generally via Craigslist ads or in roadside tents or out of the trunks of their cars.

These medical professionals were immediately hunted down by armed insurance representatives and brutally massacred. Their heads were put on pikes outside of hospitals, as a warning to anyone who might dare to help someone without first thinking about the obscene levels of profit that could be made in the process.

As a result, actual, competent, good doctors were in short supply. Not that this mattered to the insurance companies or hospitals. Using what ultimately was only a small fraction of its untold wealth, the medical-industrial complex managed to reduce the process of getting a doctoral degree to an online test that could be completed in an afternoon, thus ensuring that the only people willing to fill the positions were unskilled and desperate or unethical and horrible. Even the janitors sucked. Hospitals quickly devolved into hideous, disease-riddled cesspools of everything that was wrong with humanity.

"Why don't you come with us to Las Máquinas?" offered Catrina, gently stroking the back of Timmy's head. "Dr. Arahami or Dr. Gonzalez might be able to do, I don't know, something, right?"

"That's not a bad idea," said Chester A. Arthur XVII. "Even if they can't, I'm sure they'll know someone with expertise in artificial aging."

"Works for me," replied Mark, sitting down on a planter. "Plus mad scientists are probably going to be able to put up some defense against all the crazy being thrown at us."

"You may need to clarify that statement," said Queen Victoria XXX.

"Oh, right," said the bed-and-breakfast owner, a huge grin forming on his face. "The lady at the mall didn't attack us at random; she was hired by someone. Turns out WANG was connected to the Walt Sidney Company after all! And they're pissed off and actively trying to kill us!"

"You are way too happy about that."

"Sorry. Validation gets me sexually excited."

"That's not something anybody needed to know," replied Thor, shoving another slice of pizza into his mouth.

"Which they?" asked Chester A. Arthur XVII.

"What?" countered Mark.

"Which they? You said 'they're pissed off and actively trying to kill us.' Which one, WANG or Walt Sidney?"

"Does it matter?"

"Yes, absolutely. WANG is a shriveled nub of its former subordinate self, with limited versions of its already limited resources and manpower. The Walt Sidney Company, on the other hand, literally has more money and power than any other organization in the world. We can handle the former, but if it's the latter that's after you our best course of action would be finding an underground bunker and hiding you and Timmy away for the rest of your lives."

"You are such a fucking pansy lately," said Queen Victoria XXX.

"Satan," Timmy thought weakly, turning in the crook of Catrina's arm.

"What?" she asked, instinctively lifting the squirrel closer to her ear, despite the fact that he was talking psychically to everyone.

"Satan, the devil," continued the jumpsuited, newly elderly rodent, "he used to be in charge of WANG. When I went down to Atlanta to check on them, to make sure they were done, I heard ... after Mark and I flattened their headquarters, Walt Sidney fired everyone, including Satan, and made WANG go legit."

"So you think it was Satan that sent that woman to attack you?" asked Chester A. Arthur XVII.

"She did say she wanted her job back," said Mark.

"I can't imagine the devil *wouldn't* hold a grudge," added Timmy.

"That's fantastic," said Queen Victoria XXX.

"I can't tell if you're being sarcastic or not," said Catrina.

"I'm not really sure myself," she replied. "These last couple months of not righteously marauding have got me all turned around."

"Then I suggest we go and find out," said the patchwork president, "by beating the devil."

"This is because I called you a pansy, isn't it?"

"You mean, like, physically beat, right?" asked the thunder god through a faceful of pizza. "With fists?"

"Yes, Thor," replied the Frankensteined politician. "With fists."

"Hot damn. This is so great," said the lonely Norseman. "Do you think he'll have powers? I hope he has powers."

"You people have the weirdest priorities," replied Mark.

"Says you, Mr. Scared of Hospitals."

"I'm not *scared* ..."

"Do you think Satan sent the dragons too?" asked the reconstituted monarch. "Maybe he's coming after all of us because we effed up his plans to take over the continental grid."

"If I was a betting man," said Chester A. Arthur XVII, "that's the likelihood on which I would place my allotted stake of money."

"I don't know," said Thor, "I've pissed off a lot of people."

"That is also definitely a possibility."

"A *lot*."

"Either way," continued the president, "we need to be prepared for anything. We're going to need weapons, any and all intelligence we can find on Satan, his current whereabouts and known associates, a plan of action ..." The more he talked, the more authoritative his voice became. "Several plans of action, actually, dependent on any of myriad combinations of possible adversaries and outcomes ..." The calico clone found himself standing up straighter, his paunchy midsection becoming less pronounced, his khakis looking less boring. Synapses were firing, blood was flowing.

"There's the cold-blooded strategist I fell in love with," purred Queen Victoria XXX, her blood also flowing, albeit in a different direction.

"Hey, can we maybe, you know, bring my boyfriend back to life first?" asked Catrina. "Like we promised him on his deathbed?"

"Oh, right. Ali. Sure," replied Chester A. Arthur XVII. "You and Thor can take my other car and drive out to Las Máquinas."

"The Batmobile?" asked Thor hopefully.

"For the last time, it's not a Batmobile."

"It looks like a Batmobile."

"Bring Timmy and Mark with you," continued the president, ignoring the thunder god, "find someone to help them. Vicky and I will stay here and see if we can track down Satan."

"Among other things," cooed the queen.

"We know you guys are going to have sex," Mark grumbled, "you don't need to insinuate it every time."

"I *like* insinuating it, OK, Mark?"

"Oh. OK," replied the cyborg, taken slightly aback. "I didn't – So it's, what? Low-level exhibitionism or something?"

"Pretty much," replied the cloned monarch with a shrug. "Full-on public boning doesn't do much for me, but everyone knowing we're up to something filthy?" Queen Victoria XXX shuddered, a smile crawling seductively in its underpants across her face.

"Huh. I always figured you were doing it for our benefit. So we wouldn't walk in on you guys or something."

"Like we'd even notice."

"I can actually vouch for that," mumbled Catrina.

"Let's get going, everyone," ordered Chester A. Arthur XVII, gathering up the pizza boxes. "Every second we waste is one more second wasted."

"Was that *supposed* to sound stupid?" asked Thor, snatching the pizza from the president's hands. "Because it did."

"What about that whole 'don't get involved if we're not getting paid' thing you're always going on about, chief?" asked a very elderly-looking Timmy.

"That was before they attacked you and killed one of our friends."

"And our diner," added Thor, his mouth once again full of pizza.

"And before Vicky insulted his manhood," added Catrina.

"And before he remembered how boring settling down actually is," added the queen.

"Honestly," said Chester A. Arthur XVII, opening the driver-side door of his wood-paneled minivan and placing a foot inside, "I don't know who I was kidding."

"Yourself, mostly."

"And whoever sold you that van," added Thor.

CHAPTER TWENTY FOUR
Paging Dr. Feelgood

PERSEPHONE STAGGERED TOWARD THE ABANDONED CAFÉ on the outskirts of the literal shithole that was once Philadelphia[4]. The bell above the door jingled mightily as she stumbled inside and over to the first seat she saw. She plopped down into the faded orange mohair sofa with excruciating exhaustion. Satan and Steve Careers looked up from a nearby table.

"You didn't tell me they'd fight back," she spat, each hand covering the bleeding wound in the opposing shoulder.

"I thought that part was obvious," said Satan.

"It was not."

"The two of them destroyed WANG. On their own. They were clearly a force to be reckoned with."

"How was I supposed to know that, Lucy? All you told me was that I was going after a mall cop and a bed-and-breakfast owner. You absolutely failed to mention that they had previously caused any kind of damage or that the gerbil was telekinetic."

"Really?"

"Really," replied Persephone. "Asshole."

"You, uh, you seem to be bleeding," said Steve Careers, pointing meekly, "a lot."

"That's because I was stabbed with a pair of broken chair legs by a guy who was part robot. Something else no one felt compelled to tell me."

"Right. Sorry about that," said Satan.

"You should probably get to a doctor," said the tech entrepreneur, turning back to his laptops. "You don't want to get tetanus or something."

"Can't *you* fix me?" the former goddess of the underworld asked, nodding toward the devil's nubby horns. "Aren't you made of magic now?"

"Not exactly," said the former King of Hell, igniting a tiny fireball in his hand. "Besides," he said, extinguishing the fireball, "repairs aren't exactly in my wheelhouse."

"What about … Ta-Bitjet?" asked the IT guy, using the internet to stalk nearby gods and the like. "Think she could help?"

"Not a chance," replied the devil. "She's one of those goodie-goodie types. I highly doubt she'd be interested in helping Seph get fixed up just so she could go a-murderin' again."

"Oh." The former entrepreneur shifted his gaze from his computers. "It's just … I mean, she's a giant scorpion-lady. I figured she was one of us."

"Nope," answered Persephone. "Plus her deal is mostly poisons, healed by her menstrual blood. Which, ew."

"What about Shitala?" continued the tech-adept demon, typing furiously.

"Diseases only," explained Satan.

"Verminus?"

"Cows," replied Persephone.

"Seriously?"

"Seriously."

"Huh."

"You know," said the former goddess of the underworld, leaning forward slowly and carefully, "you'd think with the way mortal healthcare turned out, we'd really have *someone* with some kind of medical skills on our side."

"It certainly would explain a lot," said Steve Careers. "In the meantime," he continued, with no small degree of flourish, "at least we've got Bite, Pear's proprietary search engine."

"Really?" Persephone raised an eyebrow.

"Steve," Satan chided, "you've been dead for a good long while now. You don't need to keep pretending."

"Oh, thank goodness," replied the founder of Pear, deflating. "I am going to Google the crap out of this."

"You're not going to use Bing?" asked the Greek goddess. "Or Yahoo? Or … those … other ones?"

"Bing is only good for porn and hating yourself, and Yahoo's all about making rich finance fuckers richer and fuckier."

"Benedict Cumberbatch," she mumbled, "tell us how you really feel, Steve."

"Well," he began, "Bing has unbelievably poor relevancy algorithms, despite everything Microsoft says to the contrary, weighs commercial and paid results significantly higher than they should, and can be tricked by cheap SEO hacks from the late 1990s. Yahoo, on the other hand, while admittedly older and arguably briefly relevant, doesn't even run its own search engine anymore and might as well die in a garbage fire for all the good that it does."

"That was ... it was just a joke."

"Oh."

"I think I saw some twine and a tiny knife around here somewhere ..." muttered Satan, turning to rummage through the coffee shop.

"I'm going to regret this, aren't I?" asked the goddess, carefully sliding off her blood-soaked coat.

"If this were Bing," answered Steve Careers, scrolling through Google's search results, "absolutely."

The preceding chapter has been paid for by Google.*
Google: "Come on. Have you ever actually used another
search engine?"

*The preceding chapter was not actually paid for by Google.
However, if Google would like to pay for the chapter retroactively,
the author is open to that.

CHAPTER TWENTY FIVE

I Cut Down Trees
I Eat My Lunch
I Go to the Lavatory

CATRINA DALISAY PULLED THE CUSTOM-BUILT LUXURY TANK into a spot outside I'm A Lumberjack And I'm OK – a boutique specializing in denim, flannel, and silky, frilly things in big and tall sizes – and threw the gearshift into Park. She turned in her seat and said to Thor: "Get out and buy some clothes right the hell now."

"What? Why?" argued the naked Norseman sitting spread-eagled in the back seat, his skin still raw and red and revolting. "I'm fine like this. I kind of like it."

"You're a hideous eyesore," said Mark Hughes, turning in the passenger's seat, "and there's no way having all that damaged flesh exposed to the elements is good for you."

"I'm getting better."

"You look like a bunch of salami sticks tied together with slugs."

"Why don't you guys have to buy clothes?" The blonde man nodded his beard toward Mark. "You're covered in blood and Catrina's basically in pajamas."

"You're oozing on the seats," said Catrina.

Thor shrugged. "Charlie coated them with that stuff to make them super resistant to, like, everything, remember?"

"I don't care. It's disgusting."

"You mean distracting, right?" replied the thunder god, waggling his eyebrows and nodding his chin suggestively.

"No, I mean disgusting," replied the young woman, looking at his burned wang and swallowing back vomit. "I honestly don't know if I'll be able to sleep with Ali again after seeing that."

"I thought he had a robot dick."

"He does. That's how messed up yours is right now."

Thor lifted his roasted wiener and began flopping it back and forth between his hands, examining the extent of his injuries.

"I don't –"

"Get out of the car, Thor!" ordered Mark.

"OK, OK ... Benedict Cumberbatch," he mumbled. Thor threw open the door, climbed out, and began walking towards the store. After a few steps, he stopped, patted himself up and down, and then turned back around.

"Does anyone have any money?" he asked, poking his head back into the luxury tank. "I don't have any money."

CHAPTER TWENTY SIX

Megazord Sequence Has Been Initiated

AMEN-RA, THE MAN FORMERLY KNOWN AS the Creator of the Universe, was standing at the map board of a rest stop off the abandoned interstate with a pen and a Tim Horton's napkin in hand, plotting out the most efficient and least treacherous drive to Sidneyworld. Looking up and squinting, trying to convert kilometers into American Freedom Units, Ra absentmindedly took a step back, directly into someone doing the same thing as him.

"Watch it, you maple-eating –" Amen-Ra stopped abruptly, realizing he knew the man.

"Vulcan?" he asked.

"Ra!" exclaimed the bearded, grey-haired Italian man. "Hey, man!"

The two former gods, old friends and slightly less old leaders of Fortune 500 energy companies, embraced warmly.

"What in the world are you doing here, man?" asked Vulcan.

"I am going to avenge myself against Walt Sidney," rumbled Ra, his voice like a crowded bowling alley. "But the lady at the desk back in Cairo gave me the wrong ticket."

"Same thing happened to me in Genoa. That's weird, man. That's weird."

"Excuse me," said a woman who looked remarkably like Catherine the Great LXIX, the CEO and owner of Horsepower!, an energy production company based out of McMoscow[5]. "Did I hear you say something about revenging yourself against Walt Sidney?"

CHAPTER TWENTY SEVEN

When You Gotta Go...

THE FROZEN HEAD OF WALT SIDNEY FLOATED IN HIS JAR atop the end of a large white conference table, in a sparse room decorated to resemble the 1950s' version of 1990.

"Thank you, Ukko," said the CEO, nodding to the large, hirsute Director of Acquisitions, formerly the Finnish God of Storms. "And now, Loki, what's the status of our proprietary information breach?"

"Well, the reporter's dead."

"That's something. And the actual troublemakers? The ones with the capacity to be ongoing problems for us?"

"I am making their lives *extremely* difficult, sir."

***

Thor stood beside the custom-built luxury tank, bouncing from one foot to the other and staring out into the hundred miles of nothing surrounding them. Catrina waddled back from the rest stop bathroom, similarly uncomfortable.

"That one's broken too!" she shouted.

"Then fuck it," said the burly Norseman, undoing his jeans. "I'm pooping behind the picnic table. Nobody look."

***

"Why do they still have lives to make difficult?" rumbled Walt Sidney, his voice like a vacuum sucking up pennies. "I told you to kill them."

"I know, Mr. Sidney, and I am," said Loki. "But it's more fun this way."

"I didn't tell you to have *fun*. Fun has no place within the walls of the Walt Sidney Company."

"But we're an entertainment company, sir," slurred a very confused junior executive through his slobbery mandibles.

"Quiet, Alex," barked the head in the jar. He returned his glare to the skinny Norseman. "Quit screwing around, Loki."

"They're going to die *eventually*, Mr. Sidney," explained the trickster god. "And not one of them has shown even the slightest inkling that they're going to release the information publicly. In fact, they seem to think it was Satan behind everyth—"

"Get it done. Now."

"Yes, Mr. Sidney," replied Loki, sinking back into his chair. Then, nodding to the swamp monster, he added, "Although, Alex does make a good point, sir. For the head of a children's entertainment company you are, with all due respect, sir, kind of a humorless dick."

"I am well aware," replied Walt Sidney matter-of-factly. "Now, moving on to inventory issues: Who the hell is using all the copy paper? Who's using *any* copy paper? We live in the future, damn it."

CHAPTER TWENTY EIGHT

Reach Out and Stab Someone

"'GET IT DONE. NOW,'" MUMBLED LOKI LAUFEYJARSON, lowering his voice and mimicking his boss. The trickster god riffled through a box of old, pre-internet personnel files. "Fine. You want dead people, Mr. Sidney? I'll give you dead people. Sucking all the joy out of everything. You're lucky I want your job, old man. And that you pay well. And that you offer a 401K *and* a pension plan. And that the mini-fridge in my office is always stocked. And then there's the masseuse, and the foosball table in the break room ..." Loki paused. "You really do know how to run a company, Walt."

The scrawny Norseman found what he was looking for. He pulled a yellowed piece of paper from a manila folder, then entered the phone number on the paper into his cell.

"Hey, it's Loki," he said. "I need a favor."

"Yeah. A murder favor."

CHAPTER TWENTY NINE

Viva Las Vegas

AMBER GONZALEZ-PATEL, HAVING GAMBLED AWAY every last cent of the money her wife had just inherited from their dog, walked contentedly down the Las Vegas Strip and back toward their hotel. Carissa, the wife in question, was several steps behind her, decidedly less content and grumbling to herself.

"This is exactly the reason Cleo left the money to *me*," Carissa finally said. "She knew you'd do something stupid and lose it all. In less than an hour!"

"Yeah, well, *you* said it was stupid to let her invest our money in the first place," replied Amber, "so who's laughing now?"

"You. You are. You're laughing about squandering the windfall that could've gotten us a new stove and a better car and a less shitty backyard and who knows what else. That's the problem."

"I don't see how it's a *problem*."

"Losing three million dollars on a half dozen spins of roulette isn't a problem?"

"To be fair to me, I was up at one point."

"Yes. You actually doubled your money and *then lost it all again*."

"Look, we didn't have three million dollars last week and now we still don't. We're exactly where we were. I don't see why you're getting your panties all in a bunch."

"At least I'm wearing panties."

"Oh, now you're going to get on me about that?"

"There are elevated glass walkways everywhere!"

"I'm wearing jeans!"

As the women walked past the perpetually burning fire fountain of the Super Miragio, Amber was suddenly and viciously attacked by a chupacabra. The tiny, spiky-backed, lizard-like canine came tearing around the corner on all fours, before jumping and latching itself onto her face and shoulders.

"Luke fucking Skywalker!" she screamed, spinning around with the creature on her face.

"I don't see how this is a *problem* …" said Carissa.

"It's really starting to hurt, babe."

"Oh, OK."

Quickly, Carissa grabbed the chupacabra by the neck with both hands and began pulling. Amber got her hands between the miniscule monster and her shoulder and pushed.

"Get it off! Get it off!"

"What do you think I'm trying to do?!"

The two women wrestled with the creature for several minutes, circling around on the sidewalk, all elbows and shouting, before giving up.

"Man," said Carissa, catching her breath, her hands on her knees, "that thing is really on there."

"I think it's got a claw in my bones," explained Amber, futilely punching the lizard-dog in the side.

"OK, hang on," replied her wife, looking around. "You're not going to like this."

"Like what?"

Carissa threw an arm around Amber's waist and pulled her toward the fire fountain. Grabbing her roughly by her hair, Carissa managed to duck the chupacabra – and Amber's face – squarely into one of the jets of flame. The creature screeched and let go, toppling into the decorative pyre, while Amber quickly snapped her head back and out of harm's way.

"What the shit was that?" she asked, stray hairs still burning away against the purple sky beyond her.

"A chupacabra, I think," said Carissa.

"No, I meant the roasting my face."

"You're welcome."

"You could have killed me!"

"Oh, please. I would have severely disfigured you at worst. Besides, it worked, didn't it?"

"That's not the point."

"You didn't have any better ideas."

"I certainly couldn't have had any worse ones."

Carissa didn't respond. Instead, she took a few steps backwards.

"Fine, duck the issue, just like you always do," said the other woman.

"No ..." Carissa pointed behind her wife. Amber turned.

"Oh, fuck," she said.

CHAPTER THIRTY

For Every Action ...

ABYZOU, AN ERSTWHILE DEMON WITH A PREDILECTION for baby murder, stood on the side of the road, watching as the intimidating, black luxury tank rumbled toward her, the caterpillar treads churning up dirt as the car barreled forward at a, quite frankly, ludicrous speed.

"OK, Abby," she said to herself, "you can do this. Ready ... ready ..."

The dreadlocked former demon pulled back on the massive slingshot mounted into the ground, let go, and fired a jagged rock the size of an overweight kindergartener at the tank just as it passed her. The projectile bounced off the rubber-reinforced titanium body and ricocheted straight back into her face. Abyzou tumbled backward, staring dazedly at the turquoise sky overhead and watching a handful of her own bloody teeth rain down onto her face.

"If I wasn't so high right now," she said, blinking her eyes repeatedly, "I guarantee this would hurt."

CHAPTER THIRTY ONE
Office Space

CHESTER A. ARTHUR XVII SAT ON HIS COUCH in a fresh pair of boxers, leaning over his coffee table. A laptop, two tablets, three cell phones, and a mess of papers were spread out before him. As he scoured and searched, scrolling through spreadsheets and flipping through printouts, trying to pin down Satan's current location, he jotted down notes on a pad of paper resting next to him on the couch.

Queen Victoria XXX entered the living room in a bathrobe and put a cup of coffee down in front of her boyfriend.

"I'm going to go for a run," she said.

"Don't you want to help me with this?"

"I brought you coffee."

"And I appreciate that," he replied. "But there's a lot of data points and dubious sightings to go through. You don't feel like lending a hand?"

"No, not even a little." The cloned monarch continued on her way, through the living room and into the back hallway.

Chester A. Arthur XVII shrugged, then looked at his handwritten notes and reached for one of his phones. As he did, the phone immediately rang.

"Hello?" he said.

"I need help."

"How bad?"

"I'm calling you, aren't I?"

"Good point. I'll be there as soon as I can."

"Bring Vicky."

Chester A. Arthur XVII ended the call.

"Hey, babe?" he called. "Where did we put the jetpacks?"

CHAPTER THIRTY TWO

Not All Those Who Wander Are Lost, but, Yeah, Usually They Are

SATAN, A SURPRISINGLY WELL-MENDED PERSEPHONE, and Steve Careers, lugging several bags of guns and computer equipment, trudged through the radioactive wastelands that were once Pennsylvania – now the Sovereign Nation of Atomic Mutants – in search of another café, or, really, any other place that had free or easily stolen Wi-Fi and a high tolerance for dudes with horns growing out of their heads.

"Why are we walking again?" asked Persephone.

"Because we can't stay in one place too long," explained Satan. "By now they're bound to be looking for us."

"Yeah, but can't you just teleport us where we need to be?"

"I can teleport *myself*, sure," he explained, "but probably not anybody else. My powers are all pretty self-serving, even when they're at one hundred percent."

"They're not at a hundred percent?" asked the deceased tech mogul, rushing up from the rear to be part of the conversation. "But … the horns …"

"They're usually a lot bigger."

"I don't know," teased Persephone. "I don't remember anything being that big."

"Shut up," replied Satan. "Besides, it's not like you're at full strength either."

The goddess in the bloodstained greatcoat shrugged. "Something's better than nothing, right?"

"Kind of weird that you guys only got part of your powers back, though, isn't it?" asked Steve Careers. "You'd think it would be an all or nothing situation."

"Eat me, mortal."

"Look, I know I don't know a lot about religion and all, but –"

"No, you don't, Steve," bristled the former Prince of Darkness, "so shut your hole."

"OK," he meekly replied, before falling a few steps behind the fallen gods again. "Sorry."

The trio marched onward.

"So, continuing our conversation," began Persephone, shooting Steve Careers a dirty look, "I get that we have to move, and I get that teleporting is out of the question, but why are we on foot?"

"Because," replied Satan, "today is apparently some kind of mutant holiday and none of the buses and trains are running."

"OK, right," said the former Greek goddess slowly, "but I don't think you get what I'm saying. Why are we relying on public transportation at all? Not exactly the quickest way to make a getaway."

"Well, Seph," began the devil, suddenly remarkably condescendingly, "Sidney took away my car, so unless you have –"

"Why don't we steal another one?"

"Oh. Yeah. We should probably do that."

"Cinnamon toast crap, Lucy. You are not on your game lately."

"I'm a little focused on the revenging, OK?"

"Yeah?" she replied, grabbing her wounded shoulders. "How's that going for you?"

"Hey, how radioactive are these radioactive wastelands?" asked Steve Careers, stumbling up from the rear once again. "I'm not feeling so hot."

CHAPTER THIRTY THREE
Fly the Friendly Skies

CHESTER A. ARTHUR XVII AND QUEEN VICTORIA XXX roared through the air, her silk assault dress fluttering in the radioactive wake glowing dimly behind them.

"This is so fucking awesome!" screamed the queen.

CHAPTER THIRTY FOUR

... There Is an Equal and Opposite Reaction

AKA MANAH, THE FORMER ZOROASTRIAN DEMON OF ILL WILL, cautiously leaned out from behind the desiccated shrub and threw a pair of traffic spikes in front of the approaching luxury tank. The vehicle, sensing an obstacle in the road, automatically unfolded the grille into a cowcatcher and scooped up the tire shredders as it raced past, flinging them harmlessly to the side of the road.

Well, mostly harmlessly.

One of the spiked rubber strips stabbed itself into the protective guards built into the front of the old man's pants, before wrapping painfully around the back of his thigh.

"Benedict H. Cumberbatch," he grunted, hobbling backward and ripping the caltrops free from his leg. He held the three foot strip of spikes in front of him, exhaling deeply.

"That wasn't so b—"

The erstwhile demon tripped on a large branch and fell to the ground, the small of his back landing squarely on the other set of traffic spikes. Aka Manah spent the next hour screaming and swearing and trying to remove the steel points from his spine.

CHAPTER THIRTY FIVE

It's a Mad, Mad, Mad, Mad Scientist's World

ONCE UPON A TIME, DURING THE EVENTS LEADING UP TO the twenty-fifth-and-a-half end of the world, Chester A. Arthur XVII died spectacularly, his insides ending up all over his outsides after trying to catch a grenade with his stomach. Thankfully, the cloned president had been smuggling rare breeds of scrap metal to Dr. Lee Arahami, a reclusive roboticist living in a volcano in the scientist sanctuary of Las Máquinas, in what used to be New Mexico. Dr. Arahami saved the life of Chester A. Arthur XVII by cybernetically rebuilding him – better, stronger, and with a cannon in his chest.

***

During the geomagnetic solar storm that blanketed the globe in darkness and ended the world for the twenty-sixth time, the cyborg Chester A. Arthur XVII shorted out and effectively died. A few times. He was carted back to Dr. Arahami for repairs, but, this time, opted to go under the knife with the roboticist's neighbor, Dr. Joselin Gonzalez, a renegade biologist.

Dr. Gonzalez removed the electronic components from the president, replacing them with a grab-bag of all-natural body parts she happened to have on hand. The clone, despite looking like several half-finished jigsaw puzzles jammed together, had not died since.

***

Bio-Evocative Technologist X1211MR, or Bex for short, was nearly six feet of steel, circuitry, and curves, with the smartest brains her engineers could find – including those of Stephens Hawking and Colbert – uploaded into her cybercortex. Under the employ of William H. Taft XLII, mayor-king of Las Vegas, when the lights went out, she was tasked with going to Montana to fix the continental electrical grid. She did so, with the assistance of her companion, Tanner, a transgender gorilla, and Dr. Lee Arahami.

They were heroes.

Hooray.

Dr. Arahami and Bex, compelled by necessity, raced back to Las Máquinas to personally mend the fractured relations between humans and robots. By boning.

Eventually, the android and the roboticist put their genitals and sex-ports away and fell into an easy rhythm, living and sciencing and being the best thems that they could be. They would often have Dr. Gonzalez over for dinner.

Tanner, for her part, after being unceremoniously left behind at the electrical grid, began working for the newly-formed Continental Electric Company, a private corporation of recently graduated electrical engineers that had, when no one was looking, quietly taken over the grid and the need of running it. The pay was great, the breaks were plentiful, and her new bosses knew all the best video games. Tanner was thrilled.

And so it was that the doctor, the other doctor, the robot, and the gorilla all lived happily ever after.

CHAPTER THIRTY SIX

The Empire Strikes Back, or, More Accurately, the First Thirty Minutes of *A New Hope*

CATRINA DALISAY SPED THE CUSTOM-BUILT LUXURY TANK along the battered interstate until the smoking volcanoes of Las Máquinas began to rise into view.

"Aren't all the volcanoes out here dormant?" asked Mark Hughes, leaning forward from the backseat.

"Yes," replied Catrina, slowing the car and staring at the hundreds of dark plumes twisting into the sky.

"Dormant means asleep, right?" asked Thor – his skin no longer resembling pepperoni, and fully clothed in his standard denim, flannel, and silk thong uniform.

"Yes," replied Mark.

"Then that can't be good."

***

The tank pulled up in front of the volcano lair of Dr. Joselin Gonzalez. They knew it was hers because her lifeless corpse was strung up by vines across the enormous doorway. Smoke poured out from within her lair. Scattered beneath her body were the stomped and smashed bodies of her mutant plants and marsupial/flower hybrids.

"This definitely can't be good," said Thor.

***

The tank pulled up in front of the volcano lair of Dr. Lee Arahami just in time to see his torso stop crawling forward and collapse face-first into the dust. Behind him, Bex was piled in a dozen mangled pieces. Also, Dr. Arahami's legs were back there. And a lot of his blood.

"Yep," said Thor. "We're fucked."

"Oh my god," said Catrina, killing the engine and jumping from the car. "Lee!" She ran to the dead roboticist's side. "Lee!"

Mark Hughes limped after her. "This is pretty messed up," he said, looking down at the doctor.

"Lee," said the Filipina woman, stifling a good cry. She lifted his hand, then dropped it limply to the ground.

"I'm not an expert," said the thunder god, sidling up behind his former co-workers, "but I don't think he's coming back from that."

"Maybe there's …" began Catrina, before trailing off. She looked at the black smoke collecting in all corners of the sky.

"I don't think so," said the cyborg, putting what was supposed to be a comforting hand on Catrina's shoulder. "It looks like all of Las Máquinas has been taken out. All the scientists are gone."

"But … if they're … oh god," she began whimpering. "Ali …"

"Shouldn't we go knock on some volcano lairs and make sure?" asked Thor.

In the distance something large, and probably nuclear, exploded.

"I don't think we're going to like what we find," replied Mark.

"He's … Ali's dead?" continued Catrina. "Ali's actually, completely dead? Forever?"

"I'm afraid so."

Catrina dropped her head into her hands, a sobbing, hysterical mess.

"So … you need a minute or something?" asked Thor.

"Thor," scolded Mark.

"What?"

Catrina continued crying.

"Look," said Thor, feeling uncomfortable, "I'm gonna go get Ali's body out of the trunk. It's what he would've wanted. I'm assuming."

CHAPTER THIRTY SEVEN

Them!

AS QUEEN VICTORIA XXX AND CHESTER A. ARTHUR XVII defied most of the laws of physics and thermodynamics and approached Las Vegas, a terrible sight came looming into view over the city.

"What the hell is that?" asked Queen Victoria XXX, shouting over the sound of the jetpacks.

"A booger bug," replied Chester A. Arthur XVII.

"Is that ...?"

"A giant bug made out of boogers? Yes."

"That is fucking disgusting."

***

The couple touched down in the center of the Las Vegas strip moments later. They found, much to their displeasure, that aside from the giant booger bug towering over the casinos, a pair of Amish butter monsters and swarms upon swarms of chupacabra were also ransacking the city.

And that's just what they could see.

"Holy shit," said the president.

"Butter monsters," grumbled the queen, sliding the jetpack from her shoulders. "Why did it have to be butter monsters?"

CHAPTER THIRTY EIGHT

Punches with Wolves

THOR ODINSON UNCEREMONIOUSLY DROPPED ALI ŞAHIN'S BODY next to the pile of robot pieces and eviscerated doctor parts. He stood there, trying to simmer the rage boiling up inside of him, but found that the stove of his anger only went down to medium-high at best. The only man he knew who knew how to make donuts was dead at his feet, next to the man who knew how to bring him back to life. Thor could hear Catrina sobbing on the far side of the tank. The realization of the finality of Ali's death had turned her tiny human frame into a wet, snotty ball of heartache.

The thunder god wanted to punch something. Hell, he wanted to punch everything. But there was nothing to punch. Well, maybe the volcano. But that was already on fire, so it hardly seemed like a productive use of his punching. Still, there had to be something Thor could do.

"We should probably bury him, right?" he asked solemnly, looking down at his dead friend. "That's what you mortals do?"

"You should probably dig a couple extra holes while you're at it."

The beefy blonde man looked up and saw a heavily-mustachioed, naked Native American man striding from the darkened entrance to Dr. Arahami's lair. Behind him was an equally as naked woman, two long braids of hair hanging down to her waist. They were both covered in gallons of blood.

"How come they don't have to wear pants?" asked Thor.

"I assume then that you're the guys that did all this?" asked Mark Hughes, hobbling to Thor's side and indicating the butchered landscape surrounding them.

"We did," said the slight man.

"I have a hard time believing that." Mark furrowed his brow, looking the smallish, unarmed, naked folks over.

"Do you?" The woman's eyes turned black. "How about now?"

In a heartbeat, the Native American lady transformed into a gigantic, frothing black bear and let loose a roar that shook the ground. The man dropped to all fours and changed into a ravenous coyote the size of a large motorcycle.

"OK, yeah," stammered Mark, taking a few steps backward, "*now* I think I might believe it."

"Hot damn," said Thor, clenching his fists.

The coyote rushed at the Norseman, covering the distance between them in a fraction of a second and pouncing from ten feet away, tackling the thunder god to the desert floor with tremendous force.

"Damn it," shouted Thor, dust billowing up around him. "I think I landed on a cactus."

"Yeah, that'll happen," said the canine, before snapping his maw toward the Norseman's face.

The enormous bear, meanwhile, charged at Mark, who had heroically, if a bit stupidly, decided to stand his ground. The black bear rammed a razor-clawed paw into his shoulder and lifted the man up, Mark's one good leg kicking at the creature's face.

"This was a terrible idea," he moaned.

"You guys must have really pissed off the devil," replied Thor, pinned to the ground by the colossal coyote, his forearm wedged into the animal's dagger-toothed mouth.

"You guys seriously think we'd work for Satan?" asked the bear, lowering the cybernetic bed-and-breakfast owner to the ground and easing up on the stabbing ever so slightly.

"You're not?" replied Mark, likewise pausing his spastic kicking.

"I'm insulted," she spat. "That guy *sucks*."

"Oh. Well, any chance you could tell us who you *are* working for then?"

"Not really, no."

"I figured," replied Mark, wanting to shrug but deciding against it, what with the ursine hand-knives in his shoulder and everything. "Thought it couldn't hurt to ask."

"Understandably," replied the bear. "Back to the fight to the death?"

"I guess so," he said wearily, bracing himself to be hoisted back into the air by his bones and shredded muscles.

Instead, a jagged piece of Bex's leg burst through the bear's chest. The bear casually looked down at the bloody harpoon, then removed her claws from Mark, patted him on the head, and leisurely turned around to find out who exactly it was that had rammed the robot remainder through her. She found Catrina standing there.

"You stupid, shithead *motherfuckers* killed the man who could've unkilled my boyfriend!"

"It was just business, honey," replied the bear nonchalantly.

The Filipina woman screamed, grabbing another piece of android and stabbing it into the bear's massive chest. The bear sighed heavily. Catrina tilted her head slightly.

"This, uh, this doesn't seem to be bothering you."

The Native American shapeshifter shrugged.

"Shouldn't you be, like, dead or something?" asked the former hotel employee.

"Why would I be dead?" asked the bear.

"You've got two giant pieces of metal through your organs."

"What makes you think that's where I keep my organs?"

"What?"

"Oh, fuck," said Thor. Immediately, he pulled his arm from the coyote's mouth, pushed up on the bottom of his jaw, and punched his fist straight through the animal's chest. The coyote gave no indication that this was a problem.

"You too, huh?" asked the thunder god.

"Yup."

Thor set his face.

"Do you mind moving that?" asked the coyote, pointing awkwardly with his snout toward the arm through his torso. "It's starting to get a little annoying."

The former Norse God of Thunder flipped through the Rolodex of his mind.

"Coyote?" he eventually said.

"You didn't already know that?" replied the Navajo god.

"Well, it's not like we ever formally met or anything."

"I'm an immortal, shapeshifting coyote. Who else was I going to be?"

"You do realize how much crazy shit regularly goes on out here, right? Last time I visited Las Máquinas I met a half-koala/half-mushroom."

"OK, sure, but I can't help but be a *little* offended."

"Oh, come on," replied Thor, "like you'd really recognize *me* in a supermarket."

"It just … it hurts, you know?" said Coyote. "Not the arm through the chest thing, obviously, I'm talking about emotional pain, an insult to our pride. Changing Bear and I used to be such a big deal."

"Believe me, I get it."

"How did you cope with it? The Fall. Do you ever get used to it?"

"It's not easy. Drinking helps."

"Hey, if you guys are done making out," shouted Catrina, running past them with the enormous, snarling bear goddess chasing after her, "she's decided to try and murder us again."

"Oh, right," said Coyote. "That."

"You know," said Thor, removing his arm from the coyote's chest, "you didn't have to kill *everyone* out here." He tossed the animal sideways.

"Probably not," replied the Navajo god, scrambling to his feet. "But it definitely made your lives more difficult. And, honestly?" The enormous coyote lunged at Thor again, once more knocking him to the ground, his knife-like teeth inches from the Norseman's face. He snarled: "It was pretty fun."

Thor kicked his foot with tremendous force into the coyote's crotch. Coyote gave him a look.

"Those are organs too, buddy."

"You removed your testicles," Thor dead-panned.

"It was obviously the right move, wasn't it?"

"Who removes their testicles?"

"Someone who gets kicked there a fair amount more than most."

Thor grunted, punched the shapeshifter in the face, and then rolled and hurled the coyote across the scrub-strewn desert. Before the Navajo god finished skidding across the dirt, lightning tore through the sky and struck Coyote square in the cavity that would normally have been holding his heart. Shaking his head, the elephantine animal lurched back to his feet.

"That'll wake you up," he said.

"I'm assuming we've got to find your organs and squish them?" asked Thor, likewise picking himself back up.

"Generally how it goes, yeah."

"OK," replied the thunder god. "Timmy?"

"Timmy?" echoed Coyote.

"Already on it, chief," replied Timmy, the artificially-ancient, mind-reading super-squirrel, his jumpsuit tied around his shoulders like a cape.

Turning to look where Thor was looking, Coyote saw, a short distance beyond the melee, and in front of the chained caterpillar treads on the passenger side of the tank, a good-sized pile of internal organs gleaming in the sun.

"Oh shit," muttered the Navajo god.

"Sorry, man," said Thor with a shrug.

"No, you're not."

"In my defense, you were trying to eat my face."

"Hey, so, how do I move this thing?" asked Timmy psychically from the driver's seat. "I don't exactly have a driver's license."

"Can't you just push it with your mind?" asked Thor out loud.

"Not really, no. I don't have the strength. I burned myself out finding all this crap. I'm barely keeping conscious right now. This shit's going to have to be done manually."

Sensing Thor's preoccupation and seeing an opportunity, Coyote began to sprint towards the organ pile. He was immediately struck by a catastrophic thunderbolt and dropped to his knees.

"Not a chance, dude," said Thor, shaking his head.

"Turn the key," shouted Catrina, running between the two gods, the third god hot on her tail, "move the gearshift from P to D, then push down the accelerator."

"Which one's the accelerator?" asked Timmy.

"The long skinny one," said Mark, staggering forward and throwing himself into Changing Bear's knees. The massive ursine god tumbled forward and landed directly on top of him.

"That was a mistake," he grunted.

"Got it," thought Timmy. "Thanks."

The tank rumbled to life and began inching forward. Coyote once more made a desperate scramble for the viscera, but, before he could reach them, the tank ran over the organs, exploding them in a gratuitously disgusting manner and killing the Navajo gods dead.

Coyote fell mid-stride, collapsing into the desert and sliding forward in a cloud of dust.

"That was close," muttered Mark, the full weight of the now-deceased Changing Bear laying on top of him. "Can someone give me a hand? I think I broke some bones."

"One second," said Thor, wiping blood and chunks of supernatural coyote from his arm. "Who knows what kind of diseases that guy was carrying."

"That's kind of racist," said Mark.

"What? No. Like sex diseases, not smallpox."

"I don't really know if that's any better."

"Thanks, Timmy," said Catrina, hands on her knees and catching her breath.

There was no response.

"Timmy?"

The young woman ran over to the tank and found the squirrel passed out cold on the floor of the driver's seat and looking remarkably like a mummy.

"That's not good," she said.

"OK," said Mark, painfully and awkwardly attempting to shinny his way out from underneath the gargantuan black bear, "I think I might be ready to get some medical attention now."

CHAPTER THIRTY NINE

With a Little Help from My Friends

WITH ONE FOOT FIRMLY ON THE SPIKY HEAD OF THE CHUPACABRA, Chester A. Arthur XVII pulled his axe free from the creature's brain, then turned to William H. Taft XLII, an old friend and current mayor-king of Las Vegas.

"What in the holy hell is going on here, Billy?" The dead president spun around and decapitated two more chupacabra lunging toward him. "What exactly are we up against?"

"Last count," said the other dead president, tearing a goatsucker in two with his bare hands, "two Amish butter monsters, the booger bug, a cyclops, a throng of boraro,[6] at least one mothman, and, like, all the chupacabra in the world."

"How are they all working together? And why?"

"That I don't know."

"There doesn't seem to be any rhyme or reason to their attacks," added Martin Van Buren XCIX, another cloned president, heaving a chupacabra over his head and throwing it into another group of the tiny lizard-dogs. "Just random violence and disorder."

At that moment, Boudica IX, the last-surviving clone of the unstoppable Britannic warrior-queen, came flailing through the air and landed in the middle of the group.

"Holy nuts," she said, standing up and shaking her wild red mane.

"What the hell was that?" asked Queen Victoria XXX, pulling her broadsword from the abdomen of one of the lizard-dogs.

"We got a cave troll."

"Seriously?"

"Yuppers."

"Shit."

"Hey, how come my arm doesn't work?" asked Boudica IX, limply shrugging her left shoulder.

"It's probably dislocated," said William H. Taft XLII.

"Can you feel this?" asked Queen Victoria XXX. She punched Boudica IX in the bicep.

"Nope," replied the cloned Celt.

"It's broken," said Chester A. Arthur XVII.

"Well, balls."

"Less talking, more fighting, guys," said Martin Van Buren XCIX, reloading his revolver and indicating the densely packed crowd of salivating monsters closing in on them.

The group of clones constricted, back-to-back-to-back-to-back-to-back, weapons and fists out, surrounded by thousands of frothing, snarling, scaly, spiny, reptilian canines.

"This is pretty fucked, guys," said William H. Taft XLII.

"Kill count contest?" asked Queen Victoria XXX.

"You're on," replied Chester A. Arthur XVII, peeling off his wool jacket and tossing it to the side.

"Loser goes down on the winner."

"Can we all get in on this?" asked Martin Van Buren XCIX.

"Yeah, all right," replied the queen with a shrug. Then she kicked the head off a chupacabra.

CHAPTER FORTY

Eulogy

THOR PLACED THE SHOVEL OVER HIS SHOULDER and looked down at the pile of dirt now covering Ali Şahin, his oldest friend in this plane of existence.

"I think something's wrong," said the thunder god. "I've got this weird feeling in my stomach, like it's been hollowed out or something."

"You're sad, Thor," answered Catrina sadly, sitting cross-legged beside the grave and feeling even sadder.

"You're sure I'm not just hungry?"

"Do you normally feel like that when you're hungry?"

"No."

"Then you're not hungry."

"Well, if it is sadness," said the blonde man, "it sucks."

"Yeah, that's basically sad's whole deal," explained Mark, sitting on the dusty ground and leaning against the treads of the luxury tank. He pointed his chin toward the bifurcated remains of Dr. Lee Arahami. "Any particular reason you didn't bury the scientist too?"

"Odin's curly ass hairs," mumbled the Norseman, planting the shovel back into the ground.

CHAPTER FORTY ONE

Golden Showers

AFTER HEROICALLY SAVING THE DAY BY FINDING a riding lawnmower and just enough gasoline to accidentally-on-purpose cause the mass extinction of the chupacabra, Martin Van Buren XCIX ditched the sputtering farm equipment in a fountain and ran through a street littered with shredded goatsucker meat toward his friends on the tree-covered median to deal with the newest problem facing the fivesome: every other godforsaken monster attacking the city-state of Las Vegas.

"I know we were more-or-less created to deal with crap like this," said William H. Taft XLII, rolling up his shirtsleeves and eyeing the mythical beasts destroying his home, "but holy shit."

"I'm kind of with you on this one, Billy," said Queen Victoria XXX, pulling a tooth from the shoulder of her leather bolero jacket.

"That's never a good sign," said Chester A. Arthur XVII, brushing lizard-dog guts from his tweed trousers.

"Is that a banshee?" asked Martin Van Buren XCIX from where he was sitting on the ground, pointing toward an elderly Irish woman floating in the sky.

"Motherfucker," said the mayor-king.

"Somebody kill her before she opens her mouth," ordered the patchwork clone, looking around for a weapon.

"Benedict Cumberbatch, Charlie," replied the queen, throwing him an axe. "Misogynist much?"

"What? No, I –"

The thirtieth clone of the last Hanoverian monarch smiled at the seventeenth facsimile of the twenty-first American president.

"OK, I know you're messing with me, but now I feel bad," he said.

"I love killing banshees," squealed Boudica IX. "I'm on it!" The redheaded clone, her left arm hanging uselessly at her side, grabbed a spike-laden spine from the chupacabra slurry covering the boulevard and ran off toward the banshee.

"You know we have guns, right?" Martin Van Buren XCIX called after her.

The four remaining clones watched the wounded, miniskirted redhead skipping through a sea of chupacabra guts and around the corner. She appeared to be singing to herself.

"She must be amazing in bed," said Queen Victoria XXX.

"You have no idea," replied William H. Taft XLII.

Suddenly a mothman – a humanoid cryptid with moth wings and a red-eyed, buggy face – came flying in from a side street, swooping low over the boulevard and howling unintelligibly. Martin Van Buren XCIX pulled his revolver from his shoulder holster, fired a single shot into the mothman's head, and dropped the creature to the street where it crumpled into gooey dust, because mothmen are terrible, stupid, pointless fucking monsters.

"Anyone got dibs on the cyclops?" asked the Black man, holstering his gun and nodding toward the enormous one-eyed man-beast hefting a car over his head farther down the street.

"All yours, buddy," replied William H. Taft XLII. He looked up toward the giant, undulating pile of snot pounding on the upper floors of a hotel. "I'm going after the booger bug."

"I don't think we have the firepower to take down –" Chester A. Arthur XVII abruptly stopped talking and started screaming as a chimpanzee-like boraro hidden away in a nearby palm tree – its backwards feet clamped to the tree limb, its massive wang being held with both hands – had begun pissing acid on him. The president turned and hurled his axe at the forest nymph, cleaving its head in twain.

"Them," he snarled, parts of his face melting off. "I'm killing *them*."

From the trees, the remaining boraro began murmuring in fear. Then they began raining acid piss down on everyone.

"Oh, that is disgusting," said Queen Victoria XXX, backing up and lifting the bottom of her dress out of the way of the splashing urine.

SPLORCH.

"Speaking of disgusting …" Martin Van Buren XCIX, jogging backwards towards the cyclops, pointed past the boraro toward a pair of approaching butter monsters.

SPLORCH.

"Fucking great," began Chester A. Arthur XVII, trying to hold his face together. "Marty, forget the cyclops, you and –"

"No," barked Queen Victoria XXX, putting her hand on her boyfriend's chest and staring at the squelching dairy beasts bearing down on them. "Those assholes are mine." She turned to William H. Taft XLII. "Where's the nearest bakery?"

CHAPTER FORTY TWO

Hi-Diddly-Ho, Neighborino!

JORGE RAMIREZ, SITTING ON HIS COUCH AND WATCHING THE NEWS, called to his wife, Erin McCafferty.

"Hey, honey, you need to see this."

"What's going on?"

She walked in from the kitchen, tea cup in hand, and looked at the television.

"Is that ... Vicky? And Charlie?"

The television was, indeed, broadcasting their neighbors. Queen Victoria XXX was perched on the shoulder of a towering Amish butter monster, repeatedly stabbing the two-story dairy terror with loaf after loaf of freshly-baked bread, being tossed to her by a baker baking with breathtaking abandon, while, in the background, Chester A. Arthur XVII – his melted face wrapped in a souvenir scarf, his eyes barely visible through a gap in the wool – was hacking a pack of fleeing boraro into little pieces.

"Remind me never to piss them off," said Jorge.

"Do you think we should get their mail? We should probably get their mail."

CHAPTER FORTY THREE

There Really Aren't Worse Ways to Go

MARTIN VAN BUREN XCIX AND WILLIAM H. TAFT XLII, having successfully slain the cyclops and a handful of orcs and a roving pack of saber-toothed smilodons they had not previously known about, sat on the steps outside the burning New Hampshire, New Hampshire casino, bloodied and bruised, catching their breath and cannibalizing their shirts for bandages, planning their next move. That's when Martin Van Buren XCIX noticed a large bison prowling along the otherwise empty boulevard, all of the action having moved to other parts of the city.

"Great," he said, with several years' worth of exasperation. "The zoo must have been damaged. That's the last thing we need, wild animals running around with all the crazy monsters."

"Technically, the saber-toothed tigers were wild animals *and* crazy monsters," replied the mayor-king, cinching his linen shirtsleeve around his trunk-like thigh.

"Well, as long as it's not –"

The creature locked eyes with the Black man, then brayed and charged at the sitting presidents.

"Benedict Cumberbatch." Wearily, the ninety-ninth clone of the eighth president of the United States of America stood up on the stairs of the casino. "I'll get this one," he said, grabbing a bright red shawl from the nearby corpse of a tourist. "I was a professional bullfighter for a while."

As the cloned politician crossed the vast street and approached the approaching creature, something odd struck William H. Taft XLII about the animal's appearance.

"Marty! No!" shouted the clone suddenly, hefting himself from the steps. "That's not one of ours!"

But it was too late.

Before Martin Van Buren XCIX could even spread open the shawl, the creature bellowed and spun around, firing a steaming, acidic shit straight through the president's chest at four hundred miles per hour.

The bison-looking creature, was, in fact, not a bison at all, but instead a bonnacon, a mythical beast built like a buffalo, only with a more equine face and, perhaps most importantly – and in this situation most certainly – weaponized feces. But the replicated politician did not know this, and that lack of knowledge regarding ancient Macedonian legends and Pliny the Elder's *Naturalis Historia* proved to be the cloned president's doom.

"Marty!"

Martin Van Buren XCIX fell to his knees, a sizzling, poop-encrusted hole where the majority of his torso should have been. He managed one confused look down at his chest before the life left him and he toppled forward onto the street like the statue of a deposed dictator.

"I'm sorry, Billy," said Queen Victoria XXX through a mouthful of well-buttered French bread, walking down the stairs and putting a hand on the hefty man's shoulder. "That was a shitty way to go."

"Shut up, Vicky."

The cloned monarch, hearing the anger and sadness in William H. Taft XLII's voice and realizing the poor timing and terribleness of her pun, for the first time in her life obliged him.

CHAPTER FORTY FOUR

A Horse with No Name

A SHORT WHILE LATER – AFTER DRIVING BACK TO THE LAIR of Dr. Gonzalez to bury her, and then driving back again to the lair of Dr. Arahami to bury the two Navajo gods after Thor came down with a bad case of sympathy – the foursome of the god, the girl, the cyborg, and the squirrel rested inside the luxury tank, cranking the air conditioning and hoping Chester A. Arthur XVII had replaced the battery recently. Thor lay across the frontmost of the backseats, Timmy comatose and breathing weakly on his chest. Catrina was leaning her head against the driver's side window, staring out across the desert absentmindedly. Mark sat in the passenger seat fiddling with the GPS.

"There's got to be a hospital or a vet or *something* out here," he mumbled.

ZZ Top's "Sharp Dressed Man" suddenly burst through the car.

"Huh? Oh, sorry," said Catrina, roused from her daydream, "that's me." Slowly, she looked around, then pulled her cell phone from the back pocket of her jeans.

"Hello?"

There was a pause as the person on the other end of the phone spoke.

"OK, sure. We'll be there as soon as we can."

She ended the call and slid the phone back into her pants.

"That was Billy. They need us in Las Vegas."

"That's a city. Please tell me they have an actual, useful medical professional," said Mark. "Or at least more medical supplies than that box of Band-Aids I found in the trunk."

"They do," she replied. "Charlie's apparently using most of them."

"The supplies or the professionals?" asked Thor.

"Both." Catrina turned the key and the engine roared to life.

The thunder god sat up, cradling Timmy in his arm and shaking his scraggly blonde head.

"Why is he the one in charge if he's the one that's always getting maimed?"

CHAPTER FORTY FIVE

Ready to Form Voltron
Activate Interlocks

AMEN-RA PULLED HIS RENTAL SUV INTO THE REST STOP, Vulcan's busted-ass trailer rattling to a halt behind it.

"That is the last time I eat gas station sushi, man," said Vulcan, leaping from the passenger seat and speed-walking toward the propped-open door of the men's bathroom. "I won't be long," he called back, "this does *not* want to wait to get out."

"I could have lived without that information," replied Ra. He popped the hood of the SUV, stepped from the vehicle, and, locking the hood open with one hand, flipped open the lid of the deconstitution matrix[7] with the other.

"Why are you eating gas station sushi anyway?" he mumbled, emptying a nearby trash can into the fuel matrix. "You have an entire *kitchen* in the trailer you are making me tow. A trailer you have not once used ..."

Meanwhile, a few parking spots over, a tall, svelte woman in cowboy boots and a utility vest was standing in front of her rusting sedan, holding up the hood as smoke and steam poured out. She leaned over to get a better look – like, all the friggin' way – her magnificent dumper stretching her khakis tight and pointed directly at the SUV. Catherine the Great LXIX, after a good long moment and some blinking, hopped out of the SUV and headed over toward the woman.

"Something wrong with your car?" asked the cloned empress.

"I think so," replied the dark-haired woman. "I don't know what, though. I'm not exactly the best with cars."

"Let me take a look."

"Thanks."

The woman stepped to the side, still holding the hood, and the Rubenesque replica of the late Russian ruler, waving away smoke, bent over to inspect the damage. She saw asphalt.

"You seem to be missing an engine," the Horsepower! CEO explained coolly, "along with almost everything else that's supposed to be in there." Then, scrunching her brow, she said to herself: "What the hell is smoking?"

"I thought I heard a clunk."

"Just the one?"

The woman sighed heavily. "Is it bad?"

"It can be fixed," said Catherine the Great LXIX, slamming the perforated hood shut, "if you have an entire other car sitting around here somewhere."

"Yeah, I … uh, I don't."

"No, I figured that. It was …" She shook her head. "Nevermind."

The woman in the boots sat dejectedly on the hood of the car and crossed her arms across her chest.

"I don't drive much. I only rented this stupid hunk of crap after my cruise submarine got diverted to Quebec instead of Atlanta."

"Atlanta?" repeated the replicated Russian, raising an eyebrow. "You trying to kill Walt Sidney too?"

"What? Yeah. Kind of. How …? Why, are you …?"

"All of us are," she replied, indicating the sun-god standing in front of the SUV and the Roman god in the men's room. "We all run energy companies in Western Eurasica.[8] Sidney tried to forcefully take us all over six months ago, during the blackout? Because we weren't really affected and were basically making *more* money off of it. Anyway, obviously, we didn't let him. We sent back his goons in pieces, if at all. That apparently didn't sit to well with Sidney, though, and so he sent just a fucking shitload of his higher-end hired assholes to firebomb our companies off the face of the Earth. Took out most of the companies still running on the continent, actually. It was a fucking disaster. Basically blacked out all of Eurasica again. A lot of people died."

"So … you're going to avenge all those innocents?"

"What? No. Why would we do that? We're just going to fuck up Sidney the way he fucked up us."

"Oh," said the woman. Then: "That's an awful lot of information to just give out like that."

"Well, I've been cooped up in that car for a while now," said Catherine the Great LXIX, sizing up the skinny woman, "and, if we're being honest, I don't think it'll be that hard to take you down if it turns out you are on Sidney's payroll."

"I'm not," explained the woman slowly, looking down and shaking her dark head. "Trust me. My ... my girlfriend died a while back ... due to a design flaw in one of the Sidneyland rollercoasters. Apparently there was also a *maximum* height that no one felt compelled to tell us about. Her family and I ... we took the Walt Sidney Company to court, but he's been dicking us around for years." The woman looked at Catherine the Great LXIX, a thousand years of hardship and anger crossing her porcelain face. "I figured it was time to bring the matter to him directly."

"So, what I'm hearing is you don't like being dicked around?"

"What? No, of course not," said the obviously confused woman. "Who does?"

"Not me," answered the cloned empress, a gleam in her eye. "Look, come with me then. Ra over there went with the premium package for some reason. There's tons of room in that thing. And a mini-fridge."

"Wait? Ra? The Egyptian god?"

"Yeah. You know him?"

"Only in passing. I didn't realize ..." The woman stood up, taller than she had seemed before, and extended her hand. "Artemis," she said, "Greek Goddess of –"

"– the hunt and the wild and the moon," said Catherine the Great LXIX. "I'm ... I'm a fan."

"Oh, well, thanks."

"Yeah," replied the clearly starstruck CEO. She shook her head. "Look, just hurry up and get your crap," said the clone. "Vulcan's too stoned to hold up a conversation for more than a minute and Ra is just *terrible* company."

CHAPTER FORTY SIX

Sinus Infection

THE NUCLEAR JETPACKS CRANKED TO ELEVEN and their safety valves snapped off, William H. Taft XLII aimed the atomic backpacks at the heart of the booger bug tea-bagging the giant M&M's mascot atop the chocolate store and let go. The jetpacks swerved and twisted through the air, before lodging themselves inside the snot monster. The president waited with bated breath. He waited some more, this time with regular breath. He got ready to wait some more, this time while hyperventilating, maybe, just to spice things up.

Then the booger bug exploded.

A ring of atomic energy burst from the creature's chest, circumcising several nearby buildings, and raining gobs of radioactive mucus down on everything else within three miles.

"Han motherhumpin' Solo," said William H. Taft XLII, wiping the disgusting from what was left of his suit. "This was … this was a terrible idea." He began waddling away. "I think it's in my pants."

CHAPTER FORTY SEVEN

Every Breath You Take

HAVING SUCCESSFULLY STOLEN A CAR AND HEADED WEST, Satan, Persephone, and Steve Careers set up shop in a filthy warehouse passing itself off as a coffeehouse on the island of Chicago.

"Hey, boss," said Steve Careers from the reclaimed park bench he was sitting on. "I've got eyes on them again. The cyborg and the hamster are heading towards Las Vegas. There's a big blonde dude and an Asian lady with them." The tech-savvy demon studied the screens before him. "Not entirely sure what they're up to; Vegas is in a world of shit. Literally, actually. There's a herd of bonnacons tearing up the city."

"Bonnacons?" echoed the devil.

"Among other things."

"Loki must be going after them now too," grumbled the devil. "That conniving dick," he continued, pacing back and forth across the café, lost in his own obsessive thoughts. "He must have heard about Seph and those other guys and got worried I'm going to get his job after all."

"I don't —"

"We're going to have to double down." The fallen angel walked over to Steve Careers and put a hand atop either laptop. He leaned in and said, "Get everyone you can on it, Steve. *Everyone.* Call in every favor, offer whatever you need to. We're going to kill those a-holes first."

"Sure," replied the former entrepreneur with a slight nod.

Persephone, taking a seat on the large cardboard box next to them, spit out a mouthful of coffee.

"What is this made from," she asked, studying the paper cup, "feet?"

CHAPTER FORTY EIGHT

Every Move You Make

A VERY UNHAPPY-LOOKING GREMLIN TOOK UP the majority of the screen in front of an equally as unhappy Loki Laufeyjarson.

"What do you mean they're dead?" asked the trickster god. "They're *immortal*."

"Yeah, well, that was apparently more theoretical than practical," replied the gremlin, scratching an unshapely clawed finger against his cheek.

"And where are the ferret and the cyborg now?"

"The girl they're with got a call. They're going to Las Vegas."

"Why are they going to Las Vegas?"

"To gamble? Get a prostitute or three?" The gremlin shrugged his bony shoulders. "I don't know, man, I'm only telling you what I heard."

Loki tapped a few keys, pulling up a window showing the interior of a casino beset by orcs. Gamblers frantically fled, pausing only to shove piles of chips into their pockets or dodge the occasional flying roulette wheel.

"Las Vegas is under siege," explained the skinny Norseman. "How do you not know that? It's all over the news."

"When am I going to watch the news? You've got me tailing these assclowns across the entire damn country. And I only have limited data minutes, wink wink. If someone were to increase my retainer, I could maybe –"

"That's not happening," replied Loki coldly. "Goodbye, Reginald." The chaos god closed the Skype window and leaned back in his chair. He stared absentmindedly at the corner of his tiny, sterile office.

"Lucy," he snarled. "That leather-faced donkeyblower must be luring them to Las Vegas." He sat up in his chair. "Not if I can help it."

Loki grabbed his cellphone from his desk and entered a few numbers. He hit send. After a moment, someone on the other end of the line spoke.

"It's Loki," said Loki. "You guys still in Nevada?"

"Good," he continued. "I need you to do something for me."

CHAPTER FORTY NINE

Lord, What Fools These Mortals Be

PUCK, A CELTIC HOBGOBLIN, AND RHIANNON, A WELSH fairy queen, stood astride their motorcycles at the Welcome to Las Vegas sign, helmets under their arms, bags of weapons and supplies and beef jerky slung over their shoulders, staring at the explosions and the smoke and the giant mukade – a poisonous Japanese centipede the size of the Lincoln Tunnel – curled around several buildings and the general chaos reigning over the city.

"Yeah …" said Puck slowly. "I'm not going in there."

Rhiannon swung her bag forward and pulled her cell phone from an exterior pouch. She thumbed around a bit and then said, "Money's already hit the account."

"Idiot."

"Definitely wasn't the smartest thing he could've done."

The couple watched quietly as another casino collapsed in on itself, dust and smoke billowing up and blanketing half the city.

Puck started his bike's engine.

"So … want to just go fuck around San Diego instead?"

Rhiannon slid on her helmet. "Sounds like a plan."

"What?" asked the hobgoblin, shaking his head slightly.

"Oh, right." The fairy queen flipped up the shield of her helmet. "I said, 'sounds like a plan.'"

"Oh, OK. Cool."

CHAPTER FIFTY

You Shall Not Pass

THE CAVE TROLL STOOD BEFORE QUEEN VICTORIA XXX, Boudica IX, and William H. Taft XLII, nearly ten feet tall, a looming mass of muscle and moss, with skin like smoothed rock, perpetually damp and dripping with some kind of stagnant liquid. Throwing its arms back and its head high, the colossus let loose with an unearthly roar, then slammed its fists against the ground, cracking the asphalt and unleashing a tremor that crawled for blocks.

The three politicians stood their ground, chests heaving, eyes set. Boudica IX, her left arm still hanging limply, wiped the blood from her mouth with her good hand and smiled.

"Same to you, buttface," she said.

Then the redheaded Celtic queen charged at the troll, her scimitar held high. The monster bellowed, grabbing a stop sign and hurling it toward the queen's midsection. Boudica IX dropped to her knees and slid forward, bending backward, the sign sailing over her head. Immediately back on her feet, the cloned Briton kicked off the ground and jumped at the cave troll, swinging the blade down at the hulking creature's neck. As the edge closed in on its target, something like fear rising on the troll's stony countenance, Boudica IX was suddenly and fatally speared through the abdomen by an orc.

"Bo!" shouted William H. Taft XLII as the cloned Celt hung impaled and dead from the orc's lance.

"Not ... Not dead yet," she corrected, lifting her arm slightly before coughing up a mouthful of blood and adding, "Oh, no, wait ..." and dying for reals this time.

The orc roared in triumph, raising its spear – and Boudica IX – into the air. Behind it, a dozen more of the misshapen green humanoids, fresh off their pillaging of several casinos, cheered. More and more gathered by the moment.

In less time than it took a hummingbird on coffee to blink, an ancient fury rose in William H. Taft XLII – love and loss, years of torment and bottled rage and all kinds of other feelings boiling over in a scalding torrent of unbridled wrath. The orc – unaware of this and consumed by its own bloodlust – tossed the spear unceremoniously to the side and pulled a pair of daggers from its belt. The slavering beast charged at the president, several more following behind it. William H. Taft XLII, his eyes like sharpened stones, stood up straight, seeming to double in height, then, quickly, unfalteringly, stepped forward and grabbed the lead orc by the neck, stopping the creature's charge mid-stride and lifting it nearly a foot off the ground. The orc slashed fitfully at the president's arms, drawing blood but doing very little to help its situation. The creatures behind it halted and took a step back.

"Well, now you've done it," said Queen Victoria XXX.

A fist the size of an office desk slammed into her chest.

"Oh, right," she coughed, picking herself up and turning to the cave troll, "you." Then she grabbed the stop sign lying next to her and walked back toward the hulking beast, dragging the traffic sign along the pavement and sharpening its edges.

CHAPTER FIFTY ONE

Pee Break

ARTEMIS AND CATHERINE THE GREAT LXIX RETURNED to the idling SUV, buttoning her pants and cinching down her skirt, respectively.

"We're good to go, Ra," said the former Greek Goddess of the Hunt, wiping her hands on her jeans.

"Finally," he replied, leaning against the hood of the vehicle and shaking his head. "Maybe next time you will listen to me when I tell you not to drink all the water."

"What are you, my dad?"

Ra gave Artemis a weird look.

"Hey, where's Vulcan?" asked Catherine the Great LXIX, looking around at the vast expanse of desiccated earth and alligatored pavement surrounding them.

"Is he not in his trailer?" asked the Egyptian god-king.

Artemis walked to the Airstream being towed by the SUV, opened the door, and looked in.

"Completely empty," she said.

"Then where …?"

CHAPTER FIFTY TWO

One Is the Loneliest Number

VULCAN WALKED OUT OF THE REST STOP, SLIGHTLY MORE THAN one hundred miles north of his friends.

"Oh, man, guys, sorry about that. I fell asleep on the crapper. You would not believe …" The Roman god, finally sensing something was amiss, spun around on the cracked asphalt, looking everywhere. Seeing no one in the parking lot, or on the abandoned road, or anything at all for miles, he said: "Guys?"

CHAPTER FIFTY THREE

Coping Mechanisms

CATRINA DALISAY DROVE THE ARMORED TANK-CAR slowly down Las Vegas Boulevard, the street littered with bodies of all kinds. The Filipina woman was careful to avoid anything that looked like it could have been human, plus the larger chunks of dismembered monsters and the piles of cryptid corpses, lest they gum up the tank's undercarriage and force her to have to walk through the mess in her sandals.

As she and her passengers neared the bubbling, molten clay ruins of the Mos Eisley Casino, William H. Taft XLII appeared from a side street, jogging towards them and absolutely covered in gore. Catrina put the car into Park and she and Thor got out.

"Thor," said William H. Taft XLII, running up to him, "Thank Cumberbatch. I need your help." The mayor-king of Las Vegas pointed toward the enormous mukade still wrapped around the west side of the city. "We got everything else, but that thing does not want to go down."

"Like yo' momma," replied Thor.

"Dude."

"Sorry."

"How did we not see that?" asked Catrina.

"There is a *lot* of smoke over there," replied Thor.

"So," began the president, "can you, you know ..."

"Oh, right."

Almost immediately, the sky turned dark, clouds tumbling in like shoppers to a Walmart on Black Friday. Thunder rumbled loud enough to shatter windows across the city. Then a blinding bolt of horizontal lightning tore through the sky and straight through the mukade, absolutely obliterating the creature, electrocuting the centipede so thoroughly that its component molecules evaporated.

"All set, buddy," said Thor, clapping William H. Taft XLII on the shoulder. "Is that burger place I like still here?"

The cloned president, turned and crouched away from the monster, unturned and uncrouched, looking at the empty, misty section of sky where the centipede had been.

"Oh," he said. "I expected that to get all explodey and gross."

"Me too, actually." Thor shrugged. "What are you gonna do? Now, about that burger place?"

"Uh, yeah," replied William H. Taft XLII absently, "Cows 'R' Us is still here. There's a second one in the Super Miragio now, too. I think they're both still standing."

"Hot damn," said the thunder god. "Hey, how's Cherri[9], by the way?"

"Up yours, Thor."

"If that's what she's into …"

The hulking presidential clone grabbed the thunder god by the collar of his flannel shirt and slammed him against the bulletproof siding of the tank.

"You think this is funny?" he roared.

"Well, I thought *that* was funny."

"Do you have any idea what happened here? How many people died?"

"A lot? I don't think you'd be this angry if it wasn't a lot."

"Bo's dead, Thor. And Marty. And hundreds, if not thousands of civilians," he said absently. "And at least three of the Lincolns … I didn't even know they were here, I just found a pile of stovepipe hats …"

"Oh. Oh, shit. I … I didn't know, Billy."

"Yeah, I know you didn't know. You never know. Get your head out of your ass sometime."

"Hey," replied Thor, grabbing William H. Taft XLII by his bloodied lapels and swinging him into the side of the car, "watch it, man."

The cloned politician's hands fell to his sides as his back hit the tank, then immediately balled into fists.

"Why don't you guys take a breather?" suggested Catrina, her hands outstretched. "You're probably both hungry."

"No," replied the president, seething, staring at the Norseman. "I'm sick of this shit. You guys are always running around like you're the center of the world and nothing else matters. Well, guess what? You're not and things do."

"You think we don't know that, Billy?" shouted Catrina, tears forming in her eyes. "You think we don't care? That we don't lose people too?"

"*You* might," replied William H. Taft XLII, before grabbing Thor by the collar again and pushing him backward. "But not him. Or Vicky or Charlie. Boudica was murdered and he's talking about hamburgers."

"Hey, I didn't know, all right?" Thor let go of the mayor-king's lapels. "I didn't mean anything by it."

"Didn't know," scoffed the fat man, pulling the thunder god closer. "You couldn't have figured it out? Asked? Look around you, Thor ..." He nodded toward the ruined city. "You really think there weren't any casualties here?"

"I don't know ..."

"For fuck's sake," spat the clone, shoving the Norseman away. "I don't even know why I'm bothering. You don't care. You've never cared."

"Yeah, well, when you don't care about anything," said Thor, standing up straight and stretching his neck, the flatness of his voice betraying him slightly, "you can't get hurt."

The Norseman put a hand on William H. Taft XLII's shoulder again. "Now, come on, let's go get something to eat," he said, pulling the clone to his side. "It's what Bo would've wanted."

"Actually, yeah," replied the president, deflating and putting his arm across Thor's back. "It probably is."

The mayor-king of Las Vegas and the former Norse God of Thunder walked off across the entrail-strewn boulevard, the cracked casinos of the strip crumbling and billowing dust before them.

"So are we hanging out here or ...?" asked Mark Hughes, leaning forward and popping his head out of the driver's door of the luxury tank. "I mean, I could probably eat."

"I don't ..." began Catrina, slumping against the side of the car and sliding downward into the chupacabra residue. "I don't know what's going on anymore."

CHAPTER FIFTY FOUR

We Are All On Drugs

THOR ODINSON CARRIED TIMMY, THE COMATOSE SUPER-SQUIRREL, through the sliding doors of Sergeant Major General Hospital while William H. Taft XLII finagled Mark Hughes out of the armored car and into a wheelchair.

"Fucking hospitals," grumbled the bed-and-breakfast owner, shoving and fighting against the cloned president and generally not making anyone's life easier.

"No, it's cool, man," replied William H. Taft XLII. "We have the best hospital in the world. With actual trained doctors and everything."

Mark looked at the heavyset man dubiously. "I'm holding you personally accountable if something goes wrong."

"Well, yeah," replied the mayor-king, knitting his brow. "That's how it works here. I'm responsible for the well-being of every patient who goes in and out of this place, financially, legally, and otherwise."

"Seriously?"

"Yeah."

Mark paused a moment, then said, "Why aren't you running the world?"

"I'm working on it."

"You're … Is that something we need to be worried about?"

"No, it's all perfectly aboveboard. I swear."

"Look, I know I just said you *should* be in charge of everything and all, but –"

"Hey, let's get you some morphine!"

William H. Taft XLII quickly wheeled Mark Hughes into the emergency room.

CHAPTER FIFTY FIVE

Like, Really Old

"EMAIL'S READY TO GO, BOSS," SAID STEVE CAREERS, staring intently at the screen of his laptop.

"Hit Send," snarled the devil.

The tech entrepreneur did as instructed and slammed his pinky on the Enter button. The email was sent.

Satan stood behind him, arms folded across his chest, his foot bouncing up and down like a tap-dancer after several lines of cocaine. Eventually he said: "So …"

"So now we've got to wait."

"How long?"

"I don't know," replied Steve Careers with a shrug. "Depends on how often they check their email, if it's on their phones. Plus we don't even know if they can all read English or if they're going to have to run it through a translation app or their wives or something."

"Who doesn't have email on their phone?" asked Persephone.

"Some of these guys are pretty old."

"Well, yeah, but —"

"I don't think you understand how old I'm talking about."

"I don't think I do," replied the goddess of Ancient Greece.

CHAPTER FIFTY SIX

A Better Mousetrap

LOKI LAUFEYJARSON WALKED THROUGH THE DOORWAY and into the very white office of Walt Sidney, the door sliding shut behind him.

"I know, sir, they're still alive," said the trickster god with not a small amount of exasperation. "I'm working on it, Mr. Sidney."

"What?" said the frozen head. "You're not done with that yet?"

The slender Norseman cocked a slender eyebrow. "Isn't that why you called me in here, sir?"

"No. I wanted your opinion on coffee mugs for the annual town hall meetings coming up next month."

"Oh. Huh."

"How are you not done with them yet?" boomed the cryogenic CEO, veins popping across his expansive forehead.

"They killed the first team I sent to kill them, sir," explained Loki. "And the second team has failed to check in, so they're either dead too or took off with our money. You know how it is with professional liars, Mr. Sidney."

"You're trying my patience, Loki, on a level I wasn't sure even existed." The jarred head of Walt Sidney shook himself. "*You* were the one who kept pushing to kill them. Now I give you the go-ahead and you're just screwing around?"

"Sir, I am not screwing around, I swear. I'm doing my best."

"Then your best is terrible. If you don't get this done – get that vigilante cyborg and his marmot sidekick and all of their friends killed and get the information they've got on us out of the world – in the next forty-eight hours –"

"Don't worry, Mr. Sidney, I've got a plan."

"And I've got a better one," rumbled Walt Sidney. He wiggled his tongue around inside his jar, pressing a few buttons. Loki's phone beeped in reply and he pulled it from the pocket of his jacket.

"Call those people," explained the frozen CEO, "and have them murder the ever-loving shit out of all of them. Bring Bamapana, too; he's being wasted behind that desk. And he's got so many complaints filed against him ..."

"Most of these 'people' aren't even fallen deities," replied the trickster god, looking at his phone and scrunching up his face. "That's a little inelegant, isn't it, sir?"

"This isn't some fancy dinner party, Loki," barked the jarred head, turning back to his computer screen. "Now get the fuck out of my office. I'll figure out these coffee mugs on my own."

"But, sir," stammered the man in the green suit, "I love picking out coffee mugs."

"I know," snarled Walt Sidney.

CHAPTER FIFTY SEVEN

Menage a Knock It Off

IN THE BACKSEAT OF THE RENTED SUV, ARTEMIS, the former Greek Goddess of Hunting, and Catherine the Great LXIX, the last-surviving clone of the longest-reigning Russian empress, were absolutely going to town on one another. Hands were on things, tongues were in places. There were noises.

Amen-Ra, former Egyptian God-King, fists clenched around the steering wheel, looked into the rearview mirror.

"Girls, come on."

CHAPTER FIFTY EIGHT

You Raised My Hopes and Dashed Them Quite Expertly, Sir

HAVING ONCE MORE BEEN MIRACULOUSLY SNATCHED AWAY from Death's cutting board while the Grim Reaper was turned around and waiting for something to defrost, Chester A. Arthur XVII – his face heavily bandaged, his nervous system heavily drugged, and still wearing an orange paper hospital bracelet heavily around his wrist – was lounging precariously in an ill-fitting bathrobe on the couch in one of William H. Taft XLII's collectible-adorned living rooms, surrounded by expensive toys and obscure movie posters, as well as the aforementioned mayor-king himself, Queen Victoria XXX, Thor Odinson, and Catrina Dalisay, all of them sharing what they knew and trying to figure out just what in the bacon-wrapped hell was going on.

"Someone's trying to kill us," Chester A. Arthur XVII gravely explained.

"We've already established that, Charlie," said William H. Taft XLII, rolling up his freshly laundered shirtsleeves as he paced back and forth behind the couch.

"You've said it, like, three times," added Thor.

"Plus, you know, *someone's been trying to kill us*," clarified Queen Victoria XXX, before inching down the absurdly short leather miniskirt she borrowed from the closet of the late Boudica IX. "How in the fiery fjords of Finland did she walk around in this?" she mumbled.

"That's what I've been saying," replied the Frankensteined president – to the first part, not the dress thing.

"For the love of Kung Lao, will you just pass out already?"

"Yeah, sure," answered the swaying president, before tumbling off the couch and onto the carpet.

"Should we –" began Catrina.

"Just leave him," ordered the queen.

"He's lying on the part of his face they *just* fixed."

"He'll be fine."

"To his credit," began William H. Taft XLII, looking at his friend drooling onto his carpet, "he is kind of right. Someone is trying to kill *us*, the people here, in this room. There don't seem to be any other reports of this kind of thing going down anywhere else."

"That's assuming it's all related," said the cloned monarch.

"It has to be, doesn't it?" said Catrina. "They killed the scientists *knowing* we were going to go out there. They were waiting for us."

"But the lady with the guns and the magic went after Timmy and Mark specifically," added Thor, "because of what they did to WANG."

"And we don't know why Las Vegas was targeted," explained the cloned president. "None of you were here until well after it started."

"Maybe it *is* WANG then," postulated Queen Victoria XXX. "Or, given the enormously expensive scope of things, Walt Sidney. Maybe all that crazy paranoid nonsense Mark and Timmy were spouting back after we fixed Montana was right."

"That *was* the last – and really only – thing we were all involved in," said William H. Taft XLII. "Other than the Quetzalcoatl incident a couple years back[10]."

"And he's pretty categorically dead," explained Catrina. "Thor and I hung around a while to make sure. He even kicked up the corpse a little."

"I kicked up the corpse *a lot*," clarified Thor. "But, yeah, that settles it then, right? Walt Sidney and his infinite piles of money and resources are out to murder us all?"

"I don't know," muttered Queen Victoria XXX. "Something about that doesn't feel right. I'm pretty sure we'd already be dead if that really was the case."

"I wish we were," mumbled Catrina. "At least then maybe I'd get to see Ali again."

"That is incredibly morbid," replied the hefty president.

"You've got tons of pictures of him on your phone," added Thor.

"I don't know why you're taking his death so hard," said Queen Victoria XXX, shaking her head. "Billy lost *two* people, at least, and he's not complaining. And Bo and Marty didn't have souls so they can't even come back as ghosts."

"But Ali was an atheist ..." said Catrina, sniffling.

"Really?" said the thunder god incredulously. "He kept doing that? Even after he met me?"

"That doesn't actually matter," slurred Chester A. Arthur XVII from the floor, raising a pointed finger into the air. "Souls have been scientifically proven by sciencetists. Religion's got nothing to do with it."

"We had lunch together, like, all the time," mumbled the former Norse god.

"So we can still find him?" asked Catrina, sitting up straighter in the armchair, something like hope once again in her chest. "We can track down Ali's ghost?"

"Uh, no, actually. Something's fucking with the phantasmagraphic spectrum," explained William H. Taft XLII. "IGDB is down, and all other online communications are sketchy at best. No one's sure what it is yet."

And with that, Catrina's heart collapsed in on itself again.

After Santa's workshop self-destructed at the conclusion of the Torrent War, ending the world for the fifth time and burning down what little was left of the internet – the network already having burned down once before, during the bidding war between Starbucks and Walmart for the metaphorical soul of America – Japanese scientists immediately got to work trying to rebuild the World Wide Web from scratch. In the process, they discovered ghosts and, rather than ponder the philosophical implications or try to solve the existential crises that have plagued mankind for generations, the scientists harnessed the electromagnetic properties of these disembodied souls and used them to power their new internet.

As a result, all ghosts everywhere were automatically catalogued in what came to be called the Internet Ghost Database. If someone wanted to know what Great Aunt Esther was up to, all they had to do was go online and type in her name. The website would immediately give up her current location, the best times to contact her, and her relationship status. This, invariably, was some version of "it's complicated."

"What do you mean, 'no one?'" asked Queen Victoria XXX. "Someone always knows something."

"I've got my best people on it," explained the mayor-king, "but the Japanese scientists who invented ghosts took their secrets with them when they sank."[11]

"Then let's go dig up their graves!" shouted Thor.

"That really wouldn't solve, like, any of our problems. The whole 'taking their secrets with them' thing was a metaphor. It's not like they put everything they knew into a box and held it tight while they drowned," said William H. Taft XLII. "And, anyway, there's nothing there now but irradiated super monsters."

"Now I want to go *more*," whined the Norseman.

CHAPTER FIFTY NINE

Enemy Mine

MARK HUGHES SAT IN HIS WHEELCHAIR AT THE BEDSIDE of Timmy the super-squirrel. Though freshly mended, Mark couldn't walk just yet as his new, neptunium-powered leg was still calibrating. Timmy, meanwhile, was hooked up to an intravenous drip of rejuvenating liquid from the Fountain of Youth.

Discovered shortly after a megacryometeor shower rained icy balls of death on the planet and destroyed the world for the fourteenth time, the Fountain of Youth turned out not to be a mystical pool of otherworldly magic water, but a busted fire hydrant in Mumbai mixing with the septic runoff of trailers for Bollywood movie stars and collecting in a large sinkhole where the National Stock Exchange of India used to be. The combination of high-priced organic dookie and all the cocaine and dead stockbrokers in the sinkhole somehow managed to imbue the water collecting there with regenerative powers.

Why anyone saw a hole full of drowning assholes and shit and decided to first drink that water is lost to time. Why that individual chose to let the stock exchange guys drown is not.

"Hang in there, buddy," said Mark, putting a hand on Timmy's tiny paw.

***

The buildings of Sergeant Major General Hospital stood towering and radiant in the crispy brown sunshine. Beyond the hospital's elegantly manicured campus, the city-state of Las Vegas could be seen, jagged and crumbling and smoking, looking for all the world like the teeth of an old man who spent the last hundred years living off of nothing but coffee and cigarettes and bourbon. As a result, the hospital looked even shinier, even more inviting – a bright, antiseptic symbol of hope and rebirth for the shattered city.

Which is precisely why it was so worrying that two groups of heavily-armed thugs were ascending the hospital's hilltop from two different sides.

From the east came the hulking Sumerian demon Asag, deformed and angry, leading a small army of stony asakku, the lesser rock demon offspring from all the mountains Asag had humped back in the day. He walked side-by-side with Arawn, a hooded Welsh god, six hell hounds leashed to his waist. Behind them, mixed in with the demons, were clurichauns – surly, drunken cousins of the leprechaun – and wayward satyrs[12], all of them carrying clubs and chains and a genuine contempt for pretty much everything.

From the west, Bamapana – the twitchy, bug-eyed Aboriginal god of foul language – and Ogoun – a heavily-armored Haitian Voodoo deity – followed an inhumanly tall shishiga, a pale, naked, Russian wood goblin, with long, brambled hair falling to her knees. Beyond them were wooden, white-barked leshy – shapeshifting tree spirits – and cloudy shaytan jinn – smoke genies – pushing and shoving one another as they neared. A gang of very angry fairies, wearing leather jackets, and with bandanas tied around their tiny heads, flitted back and forth between them.

As the two opposing groups cleared the rise of the hill, they locked eyes almost immediately, Asag and the shishiga stomping toward one another with determination and fury. Their followers followed, as followers are wont to do. Eventually the two sides met, sneering and snarling and flipping each other off – Bamapana showering everyone individually with filthy insults about their mothers – standing in the crowded parking lot in front of the entrance to the hospital lobby.

The Sumerian demon and the wood goblin each stepped forward, posturing and stretching to their full, intimidating heights, shoulders pulled back, teeth bared, their noses nearly touching.

Then Asag, a stupendous pile of boils and ugliness, with a club the size of a small tree resting over his shoulder said: "What you here too for? Not was expecting that."

"Da, I vas not expecting you either," the shishiga answered, freeing an arm from the tousled hair falling over her body and rubbing the back of her neck. "Ve vere sent here by the Loki. He … did not mention there being anyone else …"

"Oh. Huh. We ordered by Satan."

"Oh, no vay."

"Yes."

"Vell, this is awkvard."

"Yes. Bosses ours super hate each other."

"Huh."

The Russian wood goblin put her hands on her hips and bit her lip. The Sumerian absentmindedly scratched at his crotch.

"Hurry the fucking fuck up already!" shouted Bamapana, hopping up and down.

"Hush," barked the shishiga. She turned back to Asag. "So … vhat should ve be doing about this?"

"Satan need kill man and prairie dog to get back in Sidney good graces, get his job back."

"Da … That is vhat Loki needs too, actually."

"For serious?"

"Da, he pissed off the Valt Sidney something fierce. If he does not get this murder done then he is all but dead himself."

"Position bad be in."

"Da …"

"So … we fight each other?"

"Yes!" shouted Bamapana, possessed by a manic fury. "Fuck yeah!" The elderly Aboriginal man decked a satyr. Immediately, two other satyrs jumped at the Australian man, swinging thick chains. The fairy gang swarmed into the horde of clurichauns and asakku. Arawn, quietly, deftly, unhooked the hell hounds from his belt.

"Enough!" shouted the naked lady, her voice an otherworldly howl, like wind down a canyon. Everyone stopped mid-fight, fists raised and weapons drawn.

"Vhy in the vorld vould ve fight each other?" asked the shishiga, scrunching up her ashen face. "Even assuming ve all do not just murder one other —"

"Odds do seem good that happen," said Asag.

"Tell me about it," added one of the fairies, spiraling to the ground, a particularly large sliver of stone stabbed through her chest.

"– the survivors vould have to deal with the Satan, the Loki, *and* the Sidney, and that is not a something I vant to do."

"No," agreed the Sumerian demon, shaking his head. "Not good outcome."

"It would be much easier," suggested Ogoun, his voice an octave below a bass, "to kill the man and the rodent as a group."

"Point. They have only end up dead for get paid."

"Exactly," replied the shishiga. "Let the suits figure the rest of it out."

"Yes. They no need know who kill what how, long as dead."

"God, I love the freelancing," said the shishiga, clenching her fists in front of her chest.

"You go first?" offered the hulking Asag, stepping aside and gallantly pointing his malformed arm toward the hospital entrance.

"Oh, no. I vould not vant to overstep …"

"Insist me do."

"I could not …"

"Why don't we go in two-by-two?" suggested Arawn.

"Da. That sounds delightful." The shishiga turned and, cupping her hands around her mouth, called out: "Everyone, find a murder buddy!"

CHAPTER SIXTY

Make a Crack About Not Having a Doctorate, I Fucking Dare You

MARK HUGHES THREW THE WHEELS FORWARD as hard as he could, speeding his wheelchair down the hallway, Timmy the still-unconscious super-squirrel and his IV bag resting in the man's lap. The pair flew past the nurses' station, a handful of dozens of assorted demons and fairies and goblins not far behind them.

"oh shit oh shit oh shit"

"Hey, no running!" shouted the charge nurse, leaning over the station counter to glare at the man in the wheelchair.

"I'm not!" shouted Mark over his shoulder. "Technically!"

The nurse gave the man a look, then turned and looked back down the hallway. She saw all manner of angry and homicidal sprinting toward her.

"Slow down!" she ordered.

"Screw you!" bleated one of the satyrs, pulling a knife from his bandolier and throwing it at the woman.

The charge nurse caught the knife with one hand and, in a single movement, tossed it back, square into the satyr's face. The goat-man fell backwards, taking a few of the clurichauns down with him.

"What the hell, lady?" gasped one of the leshy, lifting a log-like leg to avoid the tumbling corpse. "You killed my buddy!"

"No. Damn. Running," snarled the nurse.

She hurdled the counter of the nurses' station and stood in the hallway before the demons, one hand outstretched like a very determined crossing guard. The goblins and genies and what-not staggered to a halt, staring incredulously at the woman in the light blue scrubs standing before them. Many brows were furrowed, heads were tilted. Clurichauns turned to jinn turned to asakku, mumbling in confusion. Arawn signaled his hell hounds to sit. Cramped together in the hallway, shoulders to kneecaps to stomachs, the motley assortment of fallen gods and spirits all looked at the single, solitary middle-aged woman standing unarmed before them.

"What the shitting fuck do you fucking think you're arse-ing doing, you buggering fuckwit?" asked Bamapana, literally as politely as he was able.

The nurse simply lowered her eyes and stared back at them. A few of the smaller asakku and satyrs took a step backward.

"No time this have!" bellowed Asag, hunched, the back of his head and shoulders pressed against the ceiling. He smashed his club into a nearby cart and scattered supplies everywhere.

"Make time." The charge nurse leaned back over the counter and hit a button. Immediately, a claxon sounded and a recorded voice began repeating "Code Orange" over and over. Orderlies, phlebotomists, and nurses, both registered and technicians, began spilling out of patient rooms and into the hallway – syringes, scalpels, and skin-shredding medical tape at the ready.

"You have got to be the kidding," said the shishiga.

"I don't kid," barked the woman. "I am a motherfucking *nurse*." Then she pointed to the cloudy jinn in the back of the pack. "And what the hell do you think you're doing? You can't smoke in here. This is a hospital, for Rumpelstiltskin's sake."

CHAPTER SIXTY ONE

The Straw That Turned the Camel into an Unstoppable Killing Machine

MARK HUGHES ROLLED HIS WHEELCHAIR INTO THE LIVING ROOM of William H. Taft XLII, his shoulder aching, his arms burning and his chest heaving. Everyone that wasn't sleeping face-first on the carpet or moping in the corner turned to look at him.

"How did you get in here?" asked William H. Taft XLII, quite sincerely. "It's all stairs."

"We … need … help …" gasped the man with the comatose squirrel on his lap.

The mayor-king of Las Vegas grabbed a tablet from the nearest side table and tapped a few icons. A security feed of his front lawn popped up on the television. A bruised and bleeding horde of ancient ogres and woodland spirits – remarkably thinned out from earlier – were limping their way across his yard, frothing and snarling and stamping on his petunias.

"Oh, come on," said the clone, "do you have any idea how hard it is to grow those in the desert?"

"This is getting old," said Thor, shaking his head.

"Is that … a Sumerian rock demon?" asked William H. Taft XLII, raising an eyebrow and looking intently at the screen.

"Where are these guys coming from?" asked Queen Victoria XXX.

The copy of the United States' fattest president sighed.

"I guess I'll call what's left of my security team."

"Don't bother," said the thunder god, jumping up from the couch and cracking his neck to either side. "I think you were right before. I've got some issues I need to work out. Through clobbering."

"I'm coming with you," said Queen Victoria XXX, picking up one of the orcs' spiked whips from the coffee table and snapping it in the air. "Let's go hurt some motherfuckers."

"Damn it, Vicky," said William H. Taft XLII, "careful with that thing. Some of these collectibles are worth a lot of money."

"You're kidding me, right?"

"One-sixth scale replicas of Marty McFly don't come cheap."

***

Two clurichauns, one standing on the other's shoulders, heaved and pulled at the enormous, solid gold front door of the mayor-king's solid gold mansion.[13] The fairy gang flew up to them, latching onto the Irish sprites' clothing and pulling backward. The door began to ever-so-slightly squeak open, before being kicked down on top of them and squishing them into paste.

"Damn it, Thor."

"What?"

Standing in the entryway – and backlit by a spotlight William H. Taft XLII had installed for just such an occasion – were Thor Odinson, Queen Victoria XXX, and the cloned man-mountain himself.

"It's about fucking t–" Bamapana was cut off by a tremendous crash of thunder and then immediately turned into jerky by the fissure of electricity that followed. The Haitian god in the metal suit of armor standing next to him suddenly regretted everything, then fell to the ground, twitching.

The remaining leshy and asakku began lumbering forward, the wraith-like shaytan jinn winding between them. Arawn, smiling beneath his cloak, released the hell hounds. The enormous dogs – built like brick shithouses, with short fur as black as obsidian, eyes like burning coals, and teeth as pointy as a killer rabbit – charged at the trio, snarling and frothing and making it very clear that they intended to eat them.

"Aw, look at the puppies!" lilted the queen, clapping her hands together in front of her chin.

CHAPTER SIXTY TWO

Dave's Not Here

FROM DEEP WITHIN THE TINY BACK ROOM OF AN OLD BARN passing itself off as an art gallery with what was pretending to be a coffee bar, somewhere in some part of the cow-ravaged wastelands that used to be Wisconsin,[14] Steve Careers sat on a folding chair, a laptop carefully balanced on each knee. He tabbed through a few screens, then made a face.

"They're, uh, they're all dead, boss," he said.

"All of them?" barked Satan.

"Each and every one of them. They got their asses handed to them. Literally, in one case, actually. A nurse sliced a butt cheek off one of the satyrs and then shoved it down his throat until he choked to death."

"Holy shit," said Persephone.

"I know, right? And then the ones that survived the nurses had a run-in with Thor and the clones of Victoria and Taft and, well, things got even more graphic. I'm not even entirely sure how to accurately describe parts of it. Is it still disemboweling someone if it's through their butthole?"

The devil sighed deeply, with heavy resignation and only slightly less heavy anger, then shook his head.

"Fine," he growled. "I guess we'll have to do it ourselves."

"So, we don't even get a vote in this?" asked the former Greek queen of the underworld.

"Oh. You don't ... you don't want to come with me?"

"No, I do. I'm all for making the robot and the muskrat regret not dying the first time I ran into them. And, by now, their friends should be pretty exhausted. It's just, on principle ..."

"Well, I figured if the answer was yes I didn't need to ask ..."

"You should always ask."

"Honestly that seems like a waste of time."

"What if I had said no?"

"But you didn't."

"You didn't *know* that."

"Clearly I did."

"I'm, uh, I'm gonna stay here," interrupted Steve Careers, still watching video feeds of the massacre.

"Are planes still a thing?" asked Persephone. "Can we steal one of those?"

"So, uh, yeah, like, do you guys want a refill to go or anything?" asked the dreadlocked white guy with mysteriously bloodshot eyes standing next to them.

"God no," spat Satan.

"Are you threatening us?" added the goddess.

"Have you just been listening to us this whole time?" asked Steve Careers.

"What?" replied the counter-monkey, scratching the side of his unshaven face.

CHAPTER SIXTY THREE

What's in the Box?
What's in the Box?!

"THANKS," SAID LOKI LAUFEYJARSON, HANGING UP HIS PHONE. With resolve and trepidation, and just a trace of unbridled glee, the trickster god got up from his desk, walked to a white-framed painting of an albino rabbit in a white-walled sanitarium painting a portrait of an albino seal in a snowstorm in Antarctica, took it down, unlocked the safe that was hidden behind it, opened the door, and stared at what was inside.

"I didn't want it to come to this," he muttered, reaching into the safe, "but that's what I get for dealing with amateurs."

He added: "Plus Mr. Sidney is going to be pissier than a dive bar bathroom if I don't get this taken care of."

CHAPTER SIXTY FOUR

Snuggle Up, Buttercup

WILLIAM H. TAFT XLII, IN YET ANOTHER NEW SUIT, walked back into the living room with a pile of blankets in his arms. He began handing them out to his guests.

"Don't any of your other wives have any clothes?" asked Queen Victoria XXX, trying once again to get one of Boudica IX's microskirts to actually cover things that needed covering. "Bo did *not* have an ass, I can tell you that." She took a blanket and wrapped it around her waist.

"Yeah, you'd probably be better off with Stefani's stuff," said the mayor-king, looking over the queen with the impartial eye of an elderly gay fashion mentor, "but she's in another mansion on the other side of the city."

"You have *two* mansions?"

"Four."

"So *each* of your ladyfriends has a mansion?!"

"Yeah."

"Benedict Cumberbatch ..."

"You know, you could just turn the heat up," suggested Thor, lounging on the sofa in a pair of the mayor-king's flannel pajamas and taking a blanket from the forty-second clone of the twenty-seventh president of the United States.

"The thermostat's set to sixty-eighty," replied the heavyset man.

"That's it? You should at least be cranking that shit up to seventy-two."

"You going to pay my heating bills?"

"No," replied the Norseman matter-of-factly.

"I thought you were a Viking or something," said Mark, now moved from his wheelchair to an armchair, his robot leg resting on the coffee table, "impervious to cold and discomfort. Didn't your people invent snow?"

"That was the Vikings themselves, dude. I lived in Asgard. It was a balmy seventy-five and sunny, all day every day," he explained. "And just 'cause I *can* handle the cold doesn't mean I actually *want* to."

"Sixty-eight isn't *cold*, Thor," said the cloned president.

"If I'm not one-hundred-percent comfortable, it's cold. Or, you know, hot, depending. There's no middle ground for stuff like this."

"There's warm, chilly, brisk, I need a layer, I *don't* need a layer ..."

"You live in the desert," said Queen Victoria XXX, pulling a second blanket tight around her shoulders. "Why do you even have heating bills?"

"Deserts get cold," explained William H. Taft XLII, with no small amount of exasperation. "Especially at night and doubly especially since the sun is as unreliable a source of heat and light as Sylvia Plath's oven. How do you people not know this?"

"Who's Sylvia Plath?" asked Thor.

"I knew that," replied Catrina quietly from her corner, a flowery, pink blanket draped over her head like a shawl. Her eyes began getting misty. "Ali told me all about it last time we were out here."

"Oh, lord, here we go again," mumbled Queen Victoria XXX.

"Hey, just because you're incapable of human emotion doesn't mean you get to rag on Catrina," scolded Mark. "She lost someone important to her."

"I'm not *incapable* of human emotion," replied the cloned monarch defensively. "I just don't like them and think they're a waste of time."

"Except for the ones that involve sex and violence," added Thor.

"Well, yeah, obviously."

"Those ones are awesome."

"Damn straight."

The clone and the god fist-bumped.

"Hey," muttered Timmy the rejuvenated, but sleepy, super-squirrel from where he was huddled under a hand towel and spooning Chester A. Arthur XVII on the carpet, "can you guys keep it down? Some of us are trying to sleep off near-fatal injuries."

"Why don't you use one of the bedrooms?" asked Thor.

"I have, like, six," added William H. Taft XLII. "On this floor."

"And they all have doors."

"Because," muttered Chester A. Arthur XVII, nestling into the tiny squirrel playing the role of big spoon, "that would be weird."

CHAPTER SIXTY FIVE

Flies in the Vaseline

ELIZABETH BÁTHORY, FORMER HUNGARIAN COUNTESS and psychopathic serial killer, then onetime high-ranking demon, and current Executive Vice President of the Walt Sidney Company, walked into Walt Sidney's office looking for the frozen head of Walt Sidney, which was in fact resting atop Walt Sidney's desk, behind a placard that said Walt Sidney. Walt Sidney.

"We have a problem, sir," she said.

"Did Loki get himself killed already?"

"No, sir. It's a new problem. Well, an old problem made new, actually."

"Out with it."

"Right, sir. Apparently, Vulcan and Ra and Catherine the Great LXIX are all alive and on their way here. And Artemis is with them for some reason."

"I was told they were dealt with," he rumbled.

"Yes, well, it appears that diverting their cruise ships to Canada and forcing them all to deal with rental car companies did not, in fact, discourage them into going back to their respective homes and, instead, somehow led to them all meeting up and joining together as one unit," she explained. "Those responsible are being dealt with."

"Is that why you're covered in blood, Elizabeth?"

"Yes, sir."

The head sighed. "Send me a list of their names. We're clearly going to need to fill those positions. I'm assuming."

"No, you're absolutely right, sir," replied the former countess matter-of-factly. "I mean, a few of them are still technically alive, but, in a few days …" She waved dismissively. "Anyway, what should I do about the gods and the clone?"

"Are they attracting the same level of media attention as the ones in Las Vegas? A's been giving me regular updates. It seems like a god damned circus out there."

"Well, Satan *is* involved."

"You know how I feel about wordplay, Elizabeth," he thundered, his voice like the beginning of a landslide.

"Right, sir, sorry, sir."

"Don't let it happen again," growled the floating head. "Now, my question? The media attention on this caravan of gods?"

"There's none, sir," said Elizabeth Báthory. "Ra, Artemis, and the rest are doing this completely under the media's radar. In fact, two of them are still legally dead. No one knows about them."

"Good. Take Set and deal with them." He added, "Quietly."

"Yes, sir," the demon enthusiastically replied, her mouth creaking into a supremely unsettling smile. The erstwhile serial killer skipped out of the office.

"It's a good thing I pay her well," mumbled Walt Sidney.

CHAPTER SIXTY SIX
Feces, Meet Cooling Device

" ... AND THEN," SAID THOR ODINSON, LEANING OVER the coffee table laden with hot chocolates, "the banana goes, 'I don't think this is a tailpipe.'"

Everyone – Chester A. Arthur XVII, Queen Victoria XXX, William H. Taft XLII, Catrina Dalisay, Mark Hughes, Timmy the super-squirrel, and the thunder god himself – burst out laughing. But then, suddenly, mid-chortle, Thor stopped. He seemed to be distracted, staring absent-mindedly at the wall of the mayor-king's living room.

"Is somebody holding something shiny?" asked Catrina.

"Is it gas?" asked Queen Victoria XXX.

"You better not fart in here," said William H. Taft XLII. "I just had this place painted."

"No," said Thor slowly. "I sense something, a presence I've not felt since ..."

The former Norse God of Thunder walked quickly out of the room, the blanket draped over his shoulders swaying behind him like a cape as he exited.

***

Standing on the far side of William H. Taft XLII's body-strewn front lawn, bathed in a brilliant moonlight, was a tall, gaunt man in a bright green, freshly-ironed suit. Hefted upon his shoulder was an ancient and massive short-handled hammer.

The man's name was Loki Laufeyjarson.

The hammer's was Mjolnir.

"Loki," spat Thor Odinson, stepping from the gilded mansion's gilded stoop, and then over the corpse of a rock demon from earlier, and onto the yellow brick walkway. "I thought I told you never to touch my stuff."

"Good to see you again," replied Loki, "brother."

"Up yours. Why are you dressed like the Joker?"

"The Joker wore purple, you fucking half-wit."

"You're wearing a purple tie."

"Lots of people wear purple ties."

"Name one."

"Prince." Then he muttered, "Probably."

The thunder god shook his head. "Why are you here?"

"I was doing some spring cleaning and I found this –" The trickster god lifted the hammer from his shoulder. "– in the garage. I thought you might want it back."

"Well, that's clearly horseshit," replied Thor, crossing his massive arms over his massive chest. "You're here to try and kill me again, aren't you?"

"You know me so well," replied Loki. "Do you remember that one time we dressed you up like a lady and tried to marry you to Thrymr after he stole this?"

"I killed so many giants that day. And I never felt so pretty."

"Good times."

"Why are you bringing that up? Are you trying to get me in a dress for some reason?"

"What? No."

"Then you're hoping that if I remember the not-so-terrible times I might not-so-terribly beat you to death, aren't you?"

"A magician never reveals his secrets."

"Why do you always *talk* so much, man?" asked the thunder god, rolling his eyes mightily. "You can turn into all kinds of crazy shit. All talking ever does is get your balls tied to a goat."

"That was a weird dinner, wasn't it?"

"Verily."

"Why is the Riddler standing in Billy's front yard?" asked Queen Victoria XXX, descending the steps behind Thor, along with everyone else that was inside.

"Do you see any question marks?" snarled Loki.

"Everyone," said the burly blonde man in the plaid pajamas, "this is my asshole brother Loki. Asshole brother, this is everyone."

"Hi," said William H. Taft XLII.

"What's up?" added Mark Hughes.

"I thought you said he was dead?" asked Catrina quietly, stepping to Thor's side.

"He will be soon enough."

"You know I can hear you, right?" said Loki. "This yard isn't that big."

"You try growing grass in the Mojave," replied the mayor-king.

"The yard's pretty big," said Thor.

"I've seen bigger," scoffed Loki.

"An elephant could take a dump on one side of it and we'd barely have to cover our noses at all," explained Catrina.

"That's … kind of a weird thing to say."

"No, it's not," replied Thor. "Elephant shit smells *awful.*"

"But how often does that actually happen? Who says that so matter-of-factly?"

"Shut up."

"*You* shut up."

"No, *you* shut up."

"Thank god we don't have any family," said Queen Victoria XXX to her boyfriend.

"You would be a nightmare to be related to," replied Chester A. Arthur XVII through his bandages.

"I know, right? And imagine the parents that would've created *you.*"

"Thanksgivings would be awful."

Thor, the blanket still draped over his shoulders, uncrossed his arms and began striding purposefully down the walkway, shaking his head slowly, like an angry, disappointed Colossus of Rhodes.

"I should have known you'd be the one to send dragons after me."

"Dragons?" replied Loki, raising an eyebrow. "What are you talking about?"

"The dragons, man, you know …"

At that moment, a small WWI-era Curtiss JN-4D biplane appeared in the distance, making a lot more noise and spewing a lot more smoke than it probably should have, quickly coming closer and closer, before crashing spectacularly into the patch of petunias on the side of the yard.

"What does everyone have against my petunias?" asked William H. Taft XLII.

From amidst the smoke and flames and jagged pieces of metal and splintered wood, out crawled Satan, the Judeo-Christian Adversary, and Persephone, the Greek Goddess of the Underworld, seemingly none the worse for wear. Waving his hands in front of his face to clear some of the smoke, the former Prince of Darkness immediately locked eyes with the trickster god holding the hammer.

"Loki," snarled Satan.

"Lucy," spat Loki. "I like the horns."

"Seriously?" asked Queen Victoria XXX.

"What's going on here?" seconded Chester A. Arthur XVII.

"It's a whole thing," explained Persephone, shaking her head, "but the gist of it is we're here to kill the gerbil and the cyborg so we can get our jobs back."

"I thought you looked familiar," said Mark, his ocular implant flashing red.

"Nice leg," she replied with a smile.

Timmy the super-squirrel, hand towel tied around his neck like a cape, immediately used his scientifically-enhanced brain to grip the goddess by the throat and hefted her into the air, like a tiny, furry Darth Vader.

Satan raised a hand and did the same to the squirrel. Persephone fell to the grass.

"Oh shit," said Queen Victoria XXX.

"This is going to get ugly," muttered William H. Taft XLII.

"Real fucking fast."

CHAPTER SIXTY SEVEN

Surprise!

TIMMY THE SUPER-SQUIRREL DANGLED IN MID-AIR, his tiny arms clutching at his tiny throat, while his tiny legs and fluffy tail thrashed violently. Persephone, meanwhile, picked herself up from the ground, coughing sporadically.

Thor sighed dramatically.

"All right," said the thunder god, shrugging slightly, "if that's how you want to do this."

The dark blue night turned black and bubbling as boiling tar, clouds roiling and thunder rolling. An enormous bolt of electricity tore through the air and ripped down the devil's spinal column.

Satan dropped the squirrel.

"Holy *shit*," said the Prince of Darkness, shaking his head. "That'll wake you up."

"Hey, whoa," said William H. Taft XLII, stepping carefully to the middle of his front yard and standing in a ring of quartered satyrs, his hands and arms outstretched. "Before we get to the murder and the mayhem and the even bigger piles of bodies across my lawn, can you guys please, *please* tell me why you attacked Las Vegas? I know it doesn't make much of a difference and it's not going to change a damn thing right now about the blood feuds or whatever, but I guarantee that not knowing will bug the ever-loving *shit* out of me when I'm inevitably trussed up in the trauma ward for a month."

"You think you're going to make it to the trauma ward?" said Persephone, an eyebrow raised. "Besides, we already told you why we're here."

"To be fair, though," said Loki, "I'm actually here to kill *all* of you, not just the WANG wreckers. But, other than that, yes, it's all essentially the same."

"To … get your jobs back?" said Chester A. Arthur XVII, painfully cocking an eyebrow.

"Well, to *keep* mine, technically," replied the skinny Norseman. "But, again, that's semantics at this point."

"Those must be some jobs," said Queen Victoria XXX.

"The salary *is* pretty great," replied Persephone.

"And the benefits," seconded Loki.

"The break room includes a fully-stocked kitchen," added Satan, "and a personal chef."

"Plus there's a convenience store-sized cooler with every kind of soda."

"Bullshit," said Thor.

"*Every kind,*" replied the trickster god gravely.

"OK, fine, you have jobs good enough to literally kill for, I get it, but why send monsters to attack civilians in my city?" asked the heavyset mayor-king. "I mean, I know you guys are evil and all but, come on …"

"Evil?" feigned the Father of Lies. "Us?"

"Really?" said Persephone. "You're going to go that route?"

"I don't know. I thought –"

"No."

"OK, fine."

"The monsters weren't me," said Loki with a quick shake of his head. "Call me a racist, but I kind of hate all of them: cryptids, freaks, mutants, whatever unicorns are classified as …"

"Racist," muttered Mark, Catrina, Timmy, and Chester A. Arthur XVII.

"You hate unicorns?" added Thor.

"You know what they say: Never work with kids or animals or mythological creatures."

"You're half frost giant, you idiot," said the thunder god.[15]

The trickster god raised his middle finger to his brother.

"Wasn't us either," said Satan, shaking his head slowly. A look of confusion began crawling backward down his face like a possessed child. "We've strictly been fallen gods and owed favors – for non-racist reasons, I promise."

"Uh huh," said Queen Victoria XXX.

"Do you have any idea how hard it is to scheme properly with a laptop, free Wi-Fi, and a *lot* of burned bridges? We're lucky we've accomplished anything at all."

"Have we though?" asked Persephone.

"Then … who sent the monsters?" asked William H. Taft XLII.

"And the dragons?" added Queen Victoria XXX.

"What dragons?" replied Loki. "Why do you keep talking about dragons?"

There was a rustling from the shrubbery on the edge of the mansion's lawn, on the side opposite the petunias and the crashed plane. A figure began to emerge from the hedges. But not before there was some more rustling, some swearing and grunting, more rustling, and then a tumbling shadow. The figure picked itself up from the ground, brushed itself off, and looked at the assembled group of gods and humans and clones.

"Oh, for fuck's sake," said William H. Taft XLII.

"You?" said Mark.

CHAPTER SIXTY EIGHT

You Got Me Monologuing!
I Can't Believe It!

"WAIT, THERE'S A *THIRD* PARTY IN ALL THIS?" asked Loki, cocking his blonde brows and crossing his arms.

"Baldur's brawny balls," muttered Thor, rolling his eyes.

"I don't get it," said Satan, "what's going on?"

"Why is *she* here?" spat Queen Victoria XXX.

"I'm here," said the lady from the bushes, stepping from the shadows and into the prodigious moonlight, "because you ruined my life."

The woman was middle-aged, tall and thin, severe-looking on a good day. She had short dark hair, greying at the temples, pulled back tightly. She wore a skirt of tasteful length and a blazer over a white blouse, all of it made of leather somehow, like a librarian for the Hell's Angels. She also had an older model atomic-powered ocular implant and a titanium-reinforced skeleton, though that last part was less than obvious to the average observer.

"Ruined your life?" parroted Thor.

"You're a fifty-something waitress," said Queen Victoria XXX. "Your life was ruined long before we got there."

"Fuck you," roared the woman, her mechanical eye narrowing and glowing red.

The woman was the old waitress from the now-destroyed diner frequently frequented by Thor and his amazing friends. They had all — separately and as a group — crossed paths with her dozens, if not hundreds, of times. On a good visit, things were forgettable; on a bad one, she tried to kill someone. None of them resulted in a decent tip.

"I always figured you died," said Thor, rubbing his bushy beard.

"I disappear from the diner and you think I died?" shouted the incredulous waitress.

"Yeah."

"It happens all the time," added Queen Victoria XXX.

"You have seen the news at least once in your life, right?" asked Chester A. Arthur XVII. "You've seen the world we live in? A single fire tornado took out all of Kansas just last week."

"There's an earthquake going on *right now*," added Persephone.

"Oh. So there is," said the cyborg, raising a foot and looking at the tremoring ground. "I didn't notice."

"That is exactly the point we were making," replied the Frankensteined president.

"Wait, wait, wait, wait," demanded Loki, walking down the brick walkway toward the center of the lawn, waving his arms in front of his chest in disbelief. "You sent the monsters —"

"— and the dragons —" added Mark Hughes.

"— and you're just a waitress?"

"Just a waitress?" spat the cybernetic waitress. "Just a waitress?!"

"Oh, here we go," muttered Thor, pressing his fingers against his forehead.

"I am a queen of the Cyborg Revolution!" she shouted. "I had money and fame and *power* on a level that would make you, you pathetic fallen gods, *weep*, and then these wretched, unenhanced *humans* took that away from me! Embarrassed me! Stripped me of my rank and my pride and —"

"Yeah, OK, fine, lady," said Loki, rolling his eyes. "We've all been there. But Thor's not human."

"And neither are the clones," added Satan, nodding toward the political replicas, "technically."

"And the weasel."

"Squirrel," thought Timmy, furrowing his fuzzy brow.

"It's kind of shitty for you to pinpoint them if you're mad at all of humanity," said Persephone.

"Yeah," added Mark, his ocular implant whirring, "you're really giving us a bad name."

"That's not why I'm mad at them!" shouted the waitress.

"Then why bring it up?" said Loki.

"I am setting the Benedict Cumberbatching scene!"

"I don't know," said Satan, tilting his head.

"Yeah," agreed Chester A. Arthur XVII, "there is an awful lot of indignation running around in there for someone just trying to get across some basic exposition. And the vast majority of us already know your entire life's story. You brought it up *constantly* back at the diner."

The waitress growled, her fists clenched and shaking, her teeth gritted, the rage indicator within her atomic eye glowing like a firefly in a bug zapper and threatening to burn out.

"Look," said Thor, "she's mad at us because she was a shitty waitress and we were shitty customers. That about cover it?"

"She threw me through a window once," added Mark.[16]

"Can we get back to me beating up my brother now? I'm kinda losing wood over here."

"Are you just bad at metaphors or is there something you're not telling me?" asked Loki.

"After you took out my eye," snarled the waitress, frothing at the edges of her mouth and pointing at Thor,[17] "I developed an intense hatred of the diner's customers –"

"Developed?" parroted Queen Victoria XXX.

"– my patience worn thin as a well-worn sheet, my rage collecting and collecting inside of me, until finally I snapped and drop-kicked a baby across the parking lot. After that, I lost my job, my –"

"You drop-kicked a *baby?!*" asked Loki.

"The thing with Thor was ..." Mark scrunched his face and counted on his fingers, then said, "almost two years ago."

"Weren't you there last month?" asked Chester A. Arthur XVII. "Refusing to get me more grape jelly?"

"You didn't get him *jelly?*" asked Satan. "That's almost your entire job."

"Honestly, this all sounds like it's on you, lady," said Persephone.

"Seriously," added Queen Victoria XXX, "see a therapist or something."

"You're one to talk," thought Timmy.

"Sex addiction isn't a real problem!"

"– my apartment!" shouted the waitress, stamping her foot like a horse counting cards. "I lost my apartment and I had to start living in the *woods*, like some kind of *animal!* Eventually I took up with a group of skunk apes displaced by the flooding of Florida and they introduced me to some of the other cryptids. From there –"

"Do you seriously expect us to keep listening to this?" asked Satan. "I think we've made it abundantly clear that we don't give a shit."

"We were kind of in the middle of something here," said Thor.

"It's rude to just interrupt like that," added Persephone.

"Speaking of," said Loki, "you've clearly been tailing these chucklehumpers. What do you know about what's been going on between these assclowns and the Walt Sidney Company?"

"Think about your answer very carefully," said the devil slowly, lowering his eyes menacingly and somehow making his horns hornier.

"I don't know what you *idiots* are talk–"

"You!" screamed Catrina suddenly, loudly, terrifyingly, like a fire alarm at two a.m., erupting with more pent-up rage and fury than a cancer patient dealing with an insurance company. "You *killed* my boyfriend –"

"– and my wife and my best friend –" added William H. Taft XLII, his voice guttural and bone-chilling.

"— and tried to kill *me* –" continued Catrina.

"— and me –" added Chester A. Arthur XVII nonchalantly.

"— and a whole host of civilians –" snarled William H. Taft XLII.

"— because you're still mad Thor was a dick *over a year ago?!*"

"Yes," spat the waitress, staring dead-eyed at the Filipina woman.

In a heartbeat, Catrina – still wearing sweatpants and a twenty-year-old AC/DC t-shirt Ali had purchased at a garage sale for a quarter – marched across the center of the yard, between William H. Taft XLII and Loki, grabbing Mjolnir from the trickster god's grasp as she passed.

"Hey!" he shouted. "I was using that!"

"You fucking *cunt*," roared Catrina. Then she charged at the waitress with Thor's magic hammer.

"Be careful with that," said the thunder god, half-heartedly throwing out a hand and doing his best Willy Wonka impression.

The hammer came down on the waitress with the force of a thousand men and a couple of hill giants. The cyborg lifted her arm to protect herself, but her bones – titanium reinforcement notwithstanding – shattered into dust, the impact burning her skin at such an intensity that it began to glassify. The waitress – dropping heavily to the earth, her arm wobbling and flaking like a severely charred hot dog – managed to kick Catrina in the gut with a cybernetically-enhanced leg, at which point William H. Taft XLII stepped up and, his own leg like a fire hydrant, kicked the robot-lady flat onto her back.

Towering over the waitress, the mountain of a man, a massive shadow blocking out the moon, pulled his arm back to strike again. The cyborg, inching backward along the ground, fired a laser from her eye, straight through the clone's shoulder. The president clobbered her anyway, knocking loose several circuits. And a couple teeth.

To the mayor-king's right, Catrina had staggered back to her feet, hauling the mighty hammer beside her. She and William H. Taft XLII stood there, hunched, heaving, backlit by the night sky, hate radiating out of them like summer off the hood of a car.

Catrina hefted Mjolnir into the air and, together, the cloned president and the human girl beat the cybernetic woman into a literal pulp. When they were done – and it took a good damn while – the waitress looked like a person Slurpee spilled across the lawn.

"Holy shit, you guys," said Queen Victoria XXX, her eyebrows reaching for the sky.

"I'm … I'm feeling a little sick," seconded the devil, swallowing back bile.

CHAPTER SIXTY NINE

Scenes from an Italian Restaurant

ELIZABETH BÁTHORY PULLED HER HUMMER INTO THE empty interstate rest stop and threw the gearshift into Park. Through the windshield, she could see Vulcan kneeling next to the ice machine, attempting to construct a vehicle out of ancient vending machine parts and crap he found in the garbage.

"Sic 'im, boy," said the erstwhile Hungarian countess.

Throwing open the passenger door, Set, the red-furred dog-man and former Egyptian God of Chaos, leapt from the vehicle with abandon and began loping on all fours across the cracked parking lot toward the fallen Roman.

Vulcan, seeing the snarling, angry deity approaching him, said: "Hey, man, think you could give me a jump?"

Set tore the old man's head off.

CHAPTER SEVENTY

Hell Hath the Fury

"NOW ..." BEGAN CATRINA, STILL HOLDING MJOLNIR and pointing it back and forth between Satan and Loki. She and the weapon were both dripping with pinkish globs of waitress. "... which one of you assholes fucked with the ghost spectrum?"

"Uh ... Yo," replied the devil, timidly raising a finger into the air.

"Why are you answering that?" hissed Persephone.

"Why would you do that?!" shouted Catrina. "Why would you ruin my one chance of seeing Ali again?"

"Because I didn't know anything about him? I'm only after the middle-aged robot and the chipmunk. When I get revenge, I get motherfucking revenge. I didn't want the two guys who ruined my life pulling any shenanigans from the hereafter."

"He's a squirrel," said Mark.

"What?"

"You called Timmy a chipmunk. He's a squirrel."

"OK, sure. *That's* the point you should be arguing here." Satan shook his head. "Look. I have no grievance with the lightning god and the cloned presidents-slash-trained assassins. And the girl with the magic hammer that just liquefied a cyborg. You guys seem like more trouble than you're worth. Let me just kill ... it's Timmy, right? And you, guy, I don't remember your name, so I can get my job back at the Walt Sidney Company, and Loki can get his stupid, scrawny, meddling ass fired. It's win-win-win," he explained. "Well, except for Loki, and the Cylon and the capybara."

"Squirrel," said Timmy.

"It's like your purposely being a Belgium about it," added Queen Victoria XXX.

"Language, lady," lilted Loki.

"You really think we're *not* going to get involved with your trying to murder our friends?" asked Chester A. Arthur XVII, his bloodied bandages speaking volumes.

"Maybe?" said Persephone, shrugging her shoulders slightly.

"We don't know your situation," explained the devil. "Maybe you guys don't get along that well or someone slept with someone else's someone and there's still issues."

"Man, I wish," muttered Thor.

The tiny Filipina woman who had been shaking slightly for the last few moments was once more overcome with righteous fury. Her knuckles were white around the hammer. Thunder rumbled overhead.

"She shouldn't be able to do that," said Thor, looking up.

"Oh shit," said Persephone.

Catrina ran screaming toward the devil, Mjolnir hefted over her head. Before he had a chance to react, the woman brought the hammer down on Satan, cracking his skull and sending the fallen angel's body sprawling to the ground. She hit him again, and again, and then, somehow, struck the devil with a tremendous bolt of lightning. The devil's body spasmed from the strength of the electrical discharge, twitching violently on the grass, as Catrina stepped backward, catching herself by surprise.

"Holy shit," she said. "Was that me?"

"Verily," replied Thor, knitting his brow. "How do you keep doing that?"

"I don't know, dude. It's your hammer."

Persephone, standing beside the bleeding former demon, rage and grief churning beneath her face, began to glow slightly, her heavy coat and dark hair fluttering, the grass surrounding her withering and dying. Catrina stumbled quickly backward, barely a step ahead of the greying vegetation.

"If that's how you want to do this," said the goddess coldly, raising her hand toward the woman with the hammer. Catrina dropped Mjolnir and fell to her hands and knees, suddenly struggling for air.

"Not a fucking chance, lady," thought Timmy the super-squirrel, grabbing the chestnut-haired woman with his mind, pinning her arms, and lifting her several feet into the air.

"Catrina!" shouted Mark, running across the lawn to help her.

Loki, knowing a good distraction when he saw one, turned on his heel and started slowly back down the walkway, whistling quietly, his hands behind his back, away from the mansion and the gasping Greek goddess.

Thor bounded forward and grabbed the trickster god by the back of his suit and shirt.

"Yeah, no," he said, yanking his brother backward. "We've got way too much shit we need to rectalize and –"

"Rectify?"

"That cowboy show?"

"That's *Justified.*"

"What's justified?"

"The show, with the guy …"

"Why are you talking about TV?"

"I'm correcting your vocabulary."

"Which is stupid and obnoxious and one more thing we need to ratify."

"Rectify. The word is *rectify,* you brain-damaged cow sodomizer!"

"That was one time, man! And it wasn't even a real cow, it was Sif in a costume."

"Until I turned her into a real cow."

"Yeah, you did," sneered Thor, grabbing Loki by his lapels and dragging him closer, "while we were mid-doing it."

"You're the one who didn't stop."

"I didn't know!"

"She mooed, Thor."

"I thought she was just really into the costume!"

"You are remarkably stupid."

"This is exactly what I'm talking about: We've got centuries of beef that needs to be wrangled, and not just the stealing my hammer part, although I am super cheesed about that. I'm not about to let you hoof it on out of here without dealing with it. Not this time."

"Are you hungry or something?"

"Well, you started talking about cows …"

"Hey, look behind you."

"Really? That's your best move?"

"No, I'm actually very serious."

Thor looked at his brother, his face inches from his own, and watched Loki's eyes widen in terror. He felt the trickster god's skinny frame start to shake slightly.

"This is a weird time to *start* getting scared, dude." A warmth began to seep into his crotchular area. "For the love of cheeseburgers ..."

As Thor released his grip on his brother and took a step back, he caught something unexpected out of the corner of this eye.

Satan, recently deceased, appeared to be alive after all. And standing. And super pissed off. As Thor watched, the bloody, bespoke devil doubled in height, tearing through his fancy clothes and turning into a twelve-foot-tall monstrosity with pointed black teeth and leathery wings, his skin the color of strawberry Twizzlers. His horns grew and twisted, like a particularly metal ram. His eyes were pitch.

"Boo," said the devil, his voice cavernous and dark.

"That's not good," said Chester A. Arthur XVII.

"Shit," echoed William H. Taft XLII.

"I guess we should probably do something now," added Queen Victoria XXX, getting up from the steps on which she had been sitting.

"Heimdall's herniated discs," muttered Thor. Then he called down an enormous bolt of lightning, straight through the devil's skull.

Satan knit his brow and casually raised a hand. Thor went sailing backwards into a bush of man-eating roses on the far edge of the lawn. The roses immediately began eating the man.

"Why do you even have these?" shouted the Norseman, punching flowers in the teeth.

"For security," shouted William H. Taft XLII in reply. "Sorry!"

Satan looked to his right and saw Persephone still struggling against the squirrel's psychic embrace. He squinted his eyes and stared at Timmy. Timmy squinted his eyes and stared back.

Then Persephone exploded.

"Lando crappin' Calrissian," grumbled Queen Victoria XXX, turning her head as bits of Greek goddess rained down over her.

Timmy the super-squirrel attacked the devil with the full power of his chemically-experimented-on-brain, lifting and twisting and pulling and pushing, but all he managed to do was tear off one of the devil's arms.

The archfiend did not look impressed.

"That wasn't very nice, *hamster*," grumbled the devil.

"I. Am. A. God. Damned. *Squirrel!*"

Staring at the psychokinetic rodent – and having only newly appropriated his own arsenal of superpowers – the devil could only then, in that very moment, fully appreciate how terribly shitty his life had been without them. The agony of going from everything to nothing, to depending on being a subordinate to Walt Sidney for even a taste of his former glory.

"Yes," snarled Satan, "yes, you are."

The Prince of Darkness snapped the fingers on his severed arm. Timmy the super-squirrel was just a normal squirrel again.

"Timmy?" asked Mark, kneeling over Catrina as she lay on the steps, slowly de-greying, but still breathing shallowly.

The little animal flitted his head back and forth, then scampered up the steps past Mark and Catrina and into the mansion, the hand towel cape falling from his shoulders.

"You uncircumcised dick!" shouted Mark, storming from the girl's side, grabbing a flail mace from the corpse of something unidentifiable at his feet, and charging headlong at the demon.

Satan snapped his fingers again and suddenly Mark Hughes, the cybernetic war veteran and bed-and-breakfast owner, was also just a normal squirrel. The creature ran around in a few circles and then scampered away. Then the devil looked at the politicians, the way a sociopathic tiger looks at an underfed tourist lost on a safari.

"Oh shit," said Queen Victoria XXX wearily.

"Hey, Thor," called William H. Taft XLII, "buddy …"

"I'm *working* on it," replied the thunder god, nearly out of the rosebushes, but still with some teeth in his leg. "In case you haven't noticed, I'm kind of busy with these fucking *plants* …"

"I said I was sorry!"

Chester A. Arthur XVII took a deep breath and exhaled, then stepped forward from his contemporaries.

"Satan," he began, pulling loose the bandages around his mouth, "Mr. Scratch – sir – if I may?"

"Knock yourself out." The devil shrugged.

"Given this recent turn of events," orated the mangled president, straightening his bathrobe like it was a suit, and gesticulating in a way meant to indicate both the horns and the squirrels, "I think it's safe to assume that your value as an employee to Walt Sidney has risen dramatically in these last few minutes. I'm sure you and your former colleague, Loki, could work out some kind of arrangement wherein you are brought back into the Walt Sidney Corporation fold with full benefits and the like, wouldn't you agree?" He motioned toward the mischief god.

"I am one hundred percent on board with that," said Loki, still shaking in his urine-soaked pants.

"And as that was your primary goal, along with the squirrelification of my friends, I see no reason why –"

"Fuck Walt Sidney," snarled the devil.

Jets of hellfire burst through the ground. A pair burst on either side of Loki, forcing him to find new sources of liquid to excrete. Chester A. Arthur XVII took a column of supernatural flame directly in the face – and chest and groin and inner thighs. He screamed in agony and collapsed to the ground.

"You fucking prick," murmured the president, trying to stand, his torso and face bubbling or altogether seared away, muscles and bone exposed. Again. Parts of his skull glinted in the moonlight. "That was brand new skin."

Satan hit him with another jet of hellfire. Internal organs became visible.

"We weren't even … going to do anything with the WANG/Sidney information," he sputtered, struggling again to his feet. "We were … willing to just let things –"

The cloned politician was interrupted by another blast of hellfire.

"This … was … exactly … why I … didn't … want to get … involved …"

He collapsed fully into the scorched earth. This time Chester A. Arthur XVII didn't get up.

Queen Victoria XXX, having watched her boyfriend die several times before, wasn't terribly worried or even all that upset by this current turn of events. Then she remembered that all the scientists of Las Máquinas were dead. Then she got angry. Then she saw Catrina, nearly her own age again, stumbling to retrieve Mjolnir, and suddenly sympathized with her loss, which made her angrier. Then the queen realized she had been acting like kind of a tool to her friend and got even angrier. Then she realized how angry she was and figured, fuck it, and leaned into an absolutely apoplectic fury.

The queen's fists were balled so tight that her nails cut into her skin. Her teeth were grit so hard that a few were beginning to crack. William H. Taft XLII grabbed the cloned monarch by the waist, throwing his substantial weight backward and struggling to keep her from stomping forward to her own death.

Wrestling against the mayor-king, Queen Victoria XXX stared at the devil with a wildness that almost intimidated him.

"Let's make this fun," roared the devil in response.

"No," said Thor, finally pulling himself free from the rose bushes. "Let's not. Let's just fucking fight." An interstate map of lightning tore through the night, merging and bottlenecking straight into the boogeyman. Satan ignored it.

Across the yard, the piles of dead demons and spirits began to twitch and reassemble and rise.

"Benedict Cumberbatch," said Queen Victoria XXX. "You can raise the dead?!"

As if in reply, a gaggle of zombie mobsters and their victims began crawling out from under the grass, a hundred years of top soil and sewage sliding down their rotting – yet stylishly dressed – frames.

"Seriously, Billy?" asked Catrina, slightly woozy but nonetheless hefting the enchanted hammer onto her shoulder.

"I didn't know they were there," he replied with a shrug.

"Yes, you did."

"Yeah …" The fat man sighed. "It's Las Vegas. Those assholes are buried literally everywhere."

"This is bullshit," grumbled Thor, watching as everything he had worked so hard to murder just hours before reassembled in front of him.

The massive devil shrugged, a shit-eating grin on his gnarled face.

"I hate you fucking sandbagger gods," said the Norseman.

"Technically, he's not a god," offered Loki. Thor, stomping past, immediately punched him across his stupid mouth.

CHAPTER SEVENTY ONE

The Hurt Locker

CATHERINE THE GREAT LXIX WAS HUNKERED DOWN beside the rear left tire of the rented SUV, finessing what passed for a spare tire back onto the studs.

"Hand me the lug nuts," she said to Artemis, the former Greek goddess, one hand out and open, the other holding the wheel steady.

"Are those the things in the dish or the dish itself?"

"Look, I get that you don't know much about cars, but come on."

"Cut me some slack, Cathy," said the goddess, "I am a *lot* older than I look. Certainly older than this automobile fad."

"What? This isn't – It's not a car thing, Artemis. That's just basic *life* right there."

"Knowing the difference between nuts and … the other thing?"

"Yes!" replied the Russian replicant. "'Nuts and bolts' is *literally* a term people use every day!"

"I wouldn't say *every* day," countered a voice.

Without a second thought – or even a first one, really – Artemis grabbed the bow slung across her chest, wheeled around, and fired three arrows directly at the sound. The woman who made the sound – tiny, wearing a red trench coat and tilted fedora, and with three arrows sailing straight for her face – did not seem concerned. And for good reason. The arrowheads lodged themselves deeply into the chest of a large, furry man-dog in a leather thong and not much else, who stepped in front of the woman.

"Damn, girl," said Catherine the Great LXIX.

Set, the furry former Egyptian god, looked down, confused and unimpressed. He grabbed the arrows and snapped the shafts, leaving the pointed heads fixed in his chest. Elizabeth Báthory stepped out from behind him, drawing two axes from within her trench coat and spinning one in each hand.

"That was a bit of an overreaction, don't you think?" said the Hungarian serial murderer. "I mean, 'nuts and bolts' is common, sure, but every day? Come on. I'm not wrong here."

"Who are you?" demanded Artemis, her hand moving toward her quiver.

"I get the feeling you're not with AAA," added the cloned empress.

"Nope." Elizabeth Báthory threw an axe at the clone. Deftly, the Russian woman lifted up the hub cap, the blade lodging itself in the center of the metal disc.

"What the crazy, shitsnack?" asked the empress, titling the hub cap and looking at the axe.

"Set," replied the Hungarian woman.

The Egyptian god howled and sprinted toward the women, fangs bared, claws out, gaining ground fast. Artemis threw down her bow, grabbed the tire iron from beside the clone, and charged headlong at Set.

"Set!" barked a deep, bass voice from behind the car.

The dog-man stopped abruptly and looked around, trying to find the speaker, his countenance suddenly changing from murderous fury to that of a masturbating teenager walked in on by his father.

Artemis, meanwhile, dropped her shoulder and collided hard with Set, knocking him backward, before clobbering him across the face with the tire iron. Shaking his head, the chaos god threw out a hand and grabbed the moon goddess by the throat.

"Set …" repeated Amen-Ra, Egyptian god-king, walking back to the rental car from a nearby convenience stand, his arms full of snacks and maps and tampons.

"Oh, uh, hey, great-gramps," replied Set, his speaking voice remarkably less terrifying than his appearance would suggest. In fact, the Egyptian God of Violence suddenly became altogether goofy and harmless, like Zach Braff dressed up as a wolfman.

"Down, boy," demanded Ra.

"But, great-gramps —"

"I am not going to ask again, young man."

"But —"

Before he could finish, Artemis rammed her knee into the dog-man's solar plexus. Set dropped immediately. The Greek goddess, gasping, lifted the tire iron again.

"There will be no need for that, young lady," said the older Egyptian man. Then, his voice changing slightly, he said, "Set, come here, boy. Now."

The ferocious dog-man sighed. "Yes, sir." He began skulking toward Amen-Ra, his fangs back in his face where they belonged.

"What in the sweaty farts of Jabba the Hutt, Set?" shouted Elizabeth Báthory, her hands in the air. She hurled another axe half-assedly at Catherine the Great LXIX, who, also half-assedly, swatted it away with the hubcap. "Come on, man! We have a job to do!"

"He's my great-grandfather, Beth! And the creator of the *universe!* What am I supposed to do?"

The fallen demon shrugged and said: "Die, apparently."

She pulled open her trench coat, flashing them with an extraordinarily expansive exhibit of explosives. She slid a detonator into her hand from inside her sleeve. Setting her eyes, the erstwhile countess glared at them, the hint of a smile climbing the sides of her mouth like a ninja.

Then Elizabeth Báthory pulled off the explosive-laden coat, threw it at the gods and Catherine the Great LXIX, and ran the hell away.

Bolting down the highway toward her Hummer, the Hungarian countess pressed the button. A tremendous explosion erupted in the distance behind her.

CHAPTER SEVENTY TWO

The Walking Dead

"WE CAN'T GET ANYWHERE NEAR HIM," grumbled William H. Taft XLII, staring as Satan, laughing, spread his wings.

"Right …" replied Queen Victoria XXX, her battle axe pressed against her chest, holding back a trio of diabolically zombified satyrs trying to eat her face off, "but you do see the horde of undead orcs, twenty-foot tall homicidal wood nymphs, ancient rock demons, and all the other crazy shit between him and us, right? All the other crazy shit *that we already killed* coming back to try and kill us again?"

"Yes, I see them."

"OK, just checking." Queen Victoria XXX managed to free the axe and beheaded all three satyrs in a single swing. "You're also aware, then, that things don't get less murder-y after they've died, right?"

"If anything," added Thor, tumbling backwards into the conversation, a half dozen resurrected chupacabra clambering all over him, "they get a lot *more* murder-y." One of the zombie goatsuckers scrambled up his chest and gnashed at his chin. "And bitey."

"I am aware," replied William H. Taft XLII, gritting his teeth as he wrenched the head clean off a reanimated asakku.

"OK," replied the cloned monarch, bringing her axe blade up through the crotch of an orc. "Because, the way you were talking, you seem to be concerned with the only person here who isn't currently trying to eat us."

"If we can take out Satan, we can stop the undead hordes."

"Are you sure?" asked Thor, slamming two of the chupacabra into one another in a meaty explosion. "I mean, it's a solid theory, but do you actually know that's how the devil's magic works?"

"Well, look at Persephone and Catrina," said the cloned president, shrugging, and then punching another asakku in the face. He nodded toward the Filipina woman scrumming with a pack of boraro. "She seems fine now. I mean, that's usually how these things work."

"Usually, sure. But, take a look, Billy." Thor pointed a finger toward Satan. "It's not like he's standing over there strategizing and actively moving these reanimated husks around, like some kind of puppeteer who only had rotting meat products to work with. He's throwing fireballs at Loki and laughing his ass off."

"Yeah," added the queen, the axe blade getting caught in the lumpy body of the shuffling, brainless Asag. "I'm pretty sure bringing these buttholes back to life was a one-time party trick. Then he just stands around and watches them chew people."

"That seems like a gross misuse of superpowers," said the president. "I don't buy it."

"Yeah? Twenty bucks says you're wrong."

"You're on," replied William H. Taft XLII. "But, uh, how do we figure that out?"

"Give me a second," grunted Thor, the undead shishiga clawing at him. A dozen reanimated biker fairies came to back her up.

"OK, maybe a couple seconds," he added, the fairies pulling him down by his hair. Behind him, the reanimated giant centipede burst from beneath the lawn, rocketing dirt and grass and zombified clurichauns into the air.

"Oh, for fuck's sake," said the president.

"Don't sweat it, guys," said Catrina, shattering a rock demon with the magic hammer. She set her sights on Satan. Above her the sky turned black as obsidian. "I got this." Mjolnir glowed in her grasp.

"Seriously," said Thor through the wood goblin pummeling him, "how are you doing that?"

CHAPTER SEVENTY THREE
Goodnight, Sweet Prince

"It's done," said Elizabeth Báthory into her cell phone, casually starting up her Hummer. In the rearview mirror, plumes upon plumes of black smoke billowed into the air.

"You're sure?" replied Walt Sidney.

"Totally," replied the cocksure countess. "You would not believe how many explosives I packed into that coat."

CHAPTER SEVENTY FOUR

No, Wait, Nevermind

"I CANNOT BELIEVE HOW MANY EXPLOSIVES SHE PACKED into that coat," said Catherine the Great LXIX, hunched together with the Egyptian gods and the Greek hunter, all of them simultaneously poking their heads out from behind the SUV and looking with awe at the substantial fire burning away slightly more than a hundred feet in front of them.

Everything in front of them was in flames – the grass, the asphalt, a couple of birds, a turtle – and everything else was shrouded in a wall of thick, black smoke. Everything except the SUV.

"*That* is why I bought the premium package," said Amen-Ra.

"Oh, you, uh, you heard that?"

"You were not that far away. Two, maybe three parking spaces?"

"Yeah, but the trash matrix was running …"

Set, putting a paw on the shoulder of Artemis, said: "It sure was lucky you were able to shoot an arrow into her coat and get it away from us before it exploded."

"Luck had nothing to do with it, Fido," replied the huntress, standing up and slinging her bow across her chest. The sun slid sideways, sluicing through the smoke and illuminating the Greek goddess majestically, as a suspiciously specific wind picked up and blew through her long, dark brown hair.

"Now let's get out of here," she said, pulling open the driver's door of the rented SUV and climbing inside.

A moment later, she leaned her head back out.

"Who has the keys?"

CHAPTER SEVENTY FIVE

Don't Whiz on the Electric Fence

CATRINA CHARGED AT SATAN, MJOLNIR GLOWING, lightning exploding all around the monstrous demon. She swung the hammer at him with all of her strength, plus some. The devil caught the hammerhead with one hand, then put the other straight through Catrina's chest. She didn't even have time to scream.

Watching in slow motion as the archfiend's fist erupted through Catrina's back, something inside of Thor Odinson snapped. Whatever miniscule shred of logic was keeping him tethered to the mortal realm, handcuffing his powers, vanished in a 'roided-out fit of ancient, unrestrained, archaically awful wrath.

Thor threw off the shishiga that was attacking him, hurling her literal miles away.

The thunder god got to his feet, growing six inches in the process. His sandy blonde hair became golden, radiant. His scruffy, mountain man beard turned into something that someone might grow on purpose. His pajama top exploded off his chest, his rippling muscles oiling themselves in the process.

The devil saw this. He shook Catrina off his fist and tossed her body to the side.

"Let's dance, motherfucker," he roared, flashing his razor teeth.

Thunder rumbled so loudly it cracked open the earth at the devil's feet, swallowing him up to his waist. A light so bright and hot that it blinded the politicians burned through the night for a sustained sixty seconds.

When it stopped, Satan, charred and smoking, spat: "Is that all you've got?"

"You have no idea," answered Thor, his voice rumbling across the sky, the very thunder itself.

The sky exploded like the invasion of Normandy. Hundreds of thunderbolts burning like supernovas blazed downward, into and through the archfiend, lighting him up like an x-ray, over and over and over, melting away his skin and boiling the ground around him.

Eventually Thor stopped. His body stooped. He looked spent. Slowly, though, he walked toward the smoking villain, his gaze never wavering. He walked, and then he stopped, the thunder god standing over the demon, exhausted, his chest heaving.

And then the devil began laughing.

"Don't you know who I am?" Satan barked. "You can't kill –"

In a fraction of a second, Thor's hammer ripped itself clean from the fallen angel's grasp and into the Norse god's hand. Thor swung Mjolnir upward, catching Satan by the chin and sending his head – and the first few vertebrae of his spine – spiraling several hundred feet into the black night. Lightning like cartoon sword slashes once more sliced through the darkness, exploding both the devil's head and body before branching like spider veins and burning away the satanic chunks into a rain of glowing cinder.

"Sweet Christmas," said Queen Victoria XXX, blinking through her blindness and marveling at the blurry yet spectacular sight. She was hit across the face by the reanimated corpse of a walking tree.

"Oh, right," she said, shaking her head. The man-made monarch flipped backward, bicycle-kicking the leshy in what passed for a face. "You owe me twenty bucks, Billy."

"OK, fine," replied the cloned president curtly, stuck in a headlock from the undead cave troll that had made its way over to the mansion from downtown.

The leshy tripled in size, grabbing the queen by the waist and hefting her into the air. Its knobby hands squeezed, cracking Queen Victoria XXX's ribs like a Styrofoam cup. The reanimated skeleton of Chester A. Arthur XVII began scaling the tree, a large knife between his teeth.

"You know I won't hesitate to kill you, right?" shouted the replica royal, struggling in the tree spirit's wooden grasp. "We've gone over this exact situation, in detail, many times."

"Hey, Thor," called the mayor-king, kicking at a trio of orcs that had joined the troll, "we could use some of that divine wrath over here."

"One second," was the reply.

Peering out from the troll's armpit, the president could see Thor standing over the pile of infernal ashes and undoing his fly.

"For real, man?"

"I had a lot to drink." Thor unleashed a mighty stream onto the powdered remains of Old Scratch. "Plus, you know, he was a dick."

CHAPTER SEVENTY SIX

Kabong!

THOR ODINSON TUCKED AWAY HIS WIENER and zipped up his jeans. He turned to his surviving friends, currently beset by all manner of monstrosities.

"So … you guys want me to take care of this for you?"

"Yes, please," replied William H. Taft XLII, tossing the cave troll's intestines to the side and backing up as several rotting gangsters approached him.

"Sure thing," replied the thunder god, spinning his hammer in his hand. "You may want to close your eyes. And curl up into the fetal position. And maybe pray."

"To who?" asked Queen Victoria XXX.

"Me," rumbled the sky.

Thor lifted Mjolnir into the air, funneling lightning into it from seemingly everywhere. Then he slammed the hammer into the ground with the force of a hydrogen bomb.

CHAPTER SEVENTY SEVEN

So Much for Job Security

STEVE CAREERS SAT IN THE DARKENED COFFEE SHOP, looking at his laptops.

"Huh," he said. He looked up and around the café. "Hey, are you guys hiring?"

CHAPTER SEVENTY EIGHT

Collateral Smiting

"HOLY SHIT," SAID QUEEN VICTORIA XXX, STANDING UNSCATHED – from the lightning anyway – on the arid remains of William H. Taft XLII's lawn and looking out over the smoking wreckage that used to be Las Vegas. Behind her, the golden mansion sparked and crackled with residual electricity.

"How are we not dead?"

"I know what I'm doing," replied Thor Odinson defensively.

"Are you sure? Because you just murdered soooo many people, dude," rumbled the mayor-king, clutching his broken arm. "And more or less burned my city from the face of the Earth."

"They were already dead," replied Thor.

"Not all of them."

"Most of them."

"You do hear the screaming, right?"

"OK, fine. *Maybe* I misjudged and got a little carried away." The thunder god shrugged. "I tried, though. That's got to count for something." Then, abruptly, he asked, "Where's Loki?"

"I assume you obliterated him from this plane of reality," answered William H. Taft XLII flatly, staring at what used to be his city.

"But did you see it happen? I feel like that's the kind of thing we can't just assume."

"Really?" spat the clone. "'Cause ..." In the distance, the skeletal frame of the Palazzo casino collapsed in a heap of destruction. Dust and smoke plumed upward into the night.

"OK, maybe I did," replied the god.

"So ... you're OK now?" asked Queen Victoria XXX, putting a hand on the thunder god's shoulder. "Got that all out of your system?"

"No," said Thor, the sky rumbling.

"Right, no, obviously," said the queen, taking her hand away. "But the unbridled psychopathic homicidal rage, though. That's at least down to 'bridled?'"

"Yeah. I guess." The Norseman slumped down to the ground, sitting with his arms around his pajama-ed knees. "I'm too sad to be homicidally unbridled."

"OK, good. 'Cause holy motherfucking fatherbanging *shit*, dude." The facsimile of the woman for whom the Victorian era was named once again looked around at the untold miles of vaporized death and electrocuted destruction surrounding them. Fires were everywhere. Entire floors continued to slide off buildings. A thick cloud of smoke and chemicals and particulates hovered over the city like it was a Chinese playground.

"This is a mess."

CHAPTER SEVENTY NINE

Always Look Both Ways

"YOU GAVE HIM HIS HAMMER BACK?!" Walt Sidney shouted over the phone.

"I didn't *give* it to him, sir," replied Loki, limping his way along the boulevard, the collapsed and collapsing remnants of the Las Vegas strip surrounding him. His suit was tattered, his hair was mostly singed off, he was bleeding from places he didn't know could bleed.

"The girl took it, sir," he continued. "It wasn't part of the plan."

"What in the seven-thousand fucks of Liu Kang, Loki? I thought you said you could handle this."

The trickster god squinted his way through the drifting dust, his face and his phone huddled in the crook of his arm. Carefully, he picked his way onward.

"I thought so too, sir. But it turns out I was wrong," he explained. "I knew they had powers, that I thought I could handle, but these guys … they were next level, Mr. Sidney. They –"

"That doesn't concern me," rumbled the frozen head. "You had a single task and –"

"Thor turned Satan into atomized confetti, sir. What was I –"

"You should have been prepared for that eventuality, Loki. You should have done your research and brought more tangible resources instead of relying on your hammer gambit."

"I don't think you understand, sir. No amount of additional resources would have helped. I mean, it's not like we have nukes."

"The Walt Sidney Company has multiple stockpiles of nuclear warheads, Loki. There are three in Nevada alone."

"Oh," said the god of mischief, pausing. "Wish I had known that."

"So do I."

"Sir, once I get back to the office, I can –"

"No. You're fired, Loki. I'm done with your scheming bullshit," roared the floating head on the other end of the phone. "I'll take care of them myself." Then he added, "Even though I'm *supposed* to be starting on performance reviews ..."

"At least I got rid of the cyborg and the hedgehog, right, sir? Doesn't that count for –"

"Your things will be waiting for you in reception," boomed Walt Sidney. "Goodbye, Loki."

There was a lot of sloshing on the other end of the phone and then a brief pause.

"I can't believe the one I fired turned out to be the competent one ..." mumbled the jarred CEO.

"I can, uh, I can hear you, Mr. Sidney. Your phone's still on, sir." "Fuck you."

There was more sloshing and then the line went dead.

"You don't have to be a dick about it," muttered Loki.

The scrawny Norseman squinted forward again, then he took a few steps and squinted behind him. He was completely turned around. Everything was a dense, grey cloud.

And then out of that cloud came an enormous black armored tank, something that looked like the Batmobile and a stretch limo had a baby.

The luxury vehicle plowed straight into Loki's back.

The grille shattered his spine in several places, flipping his torso backward against the hood. His legs, meanwhile, buckled, caught between a chunk of asphalt and the underside of the car. The cowardly and conniving chaos god was torn in twain.

The luxury tank skidded to a stop, partly because it had hit something and it was the right thing to do, but mostly because Loki had a lot of blood and most of it was covering the windshield.

Carissa Gonzalez-Patel stepped out of her car.

"Shit," she said, looking at the lime green corpse halves in front of her.

"I think we just killed Lex Luthor," added her wife Amber.

CHAPTER EIGHTY

The Home of the Braves

AMEN-RA, FORMER EGYPTIAN GOD-KING, STOOD ON THE SIDE of the battered interstate, smoothing out a paper map on the hood of his rental car. He stared at the map for a moment, then looked up to the enormous sinkhole swallowing everything he could see before him.

"That is not on here at all," he muttered.

Behind him, Artemis and Catherine the Great LXIX ran off into a patch of high grass, holding hands and giggling in a way the sun god felt was wholly inappropriate for their age.

"Are you two not going to help with this?" he called after them. "Do you no longer care about our divine retribution against this Belgium of a man?"

"We will in about twenty minutes, Ra," shouted the Greek goddess, briefly bobbing her head above the grass.

"There are probably ticks in there, girls."

Catherine the Great LXIX tossed her bra into the air in reply.

"This is unbelievable." The sun god shook his head, then, noticing something off in the distance, he squinted and looked down the highway they had just traversed.

A small speck on the horizon, trailing columns of steam, quickly grew larger. In a matter of moments, the dot revealed itself to be an enormous gallimaufry of a war machine, cobbled together from the remnants of other, smaller war machines. Enormous treaded triangle wheels took up most of the rear of the vehicle, with smaller caterpillar treads in the front. Several helicopter wings, laden with missiles, thrust out asymmetrically from the sides. An antique and filed-down snow plow tore up any exposed greenery before the machine, and serrated spikes covered almost every other surface.

"Not again ..." Ra braced himself, repositioning the sun directly above him, the orb burning with wicked intensity.

"Set," called the god-king, without breaking his gaze, "come here, boy ..."

As the armored vehicle neared, though, gently slowing, the sun god could see that the machine's prodigious quantity of weapons was clearly disarmed, cannons and guns tucked away or otherwise disabled. The targeting apparati seemed to be minding their own business.

The war machine stopped and a hatch in the center popped open. A tall, middle-aged man with white hair and a terrible mustache clambered out and stood atop the towering vehicle for a moment, before climbing down and then down some more. He stepped to the asphalt and Ra noticed a container of fluid strapped to the man's back, a series of thick intravenous tubes running the liquid from the plastic canister and into his arms.

"Hi, Ted Turner," said the man, walking over and extending his hand. "What the hell is this sinkhole doing here? I'm trying to get to Sidneyworld."

"Amen-Ra," said Amen-Ra, shaking the erstwhile media mogul's hand, "CEO of Heliopolis, creator of the universe. Did Walt Sidney destroy your company too?"

"Not exactly," replied Ted Turner.

After the United States of America was auctioned off in lots following the fourth end of the world, Starbucks and Walmart engaged in a literal bidding war for chunks of the country, utterly decimating the city of Atlanta in the process and destroying most of Ted Turner's media empire, as well as everything else that he held dear. Walt Sidney, up until that point a fierce frenemy of Turner's, offered to buy the totaled remains of his Atlanta holdings, to help get him back on his feet and because that wasn't the way Sidney wanted to win and blah blah blah. Ted Turner, not exactly having a lot of options, agreed, with the stipulation that the Walt Sidney Company not do anything terrible with the biohazardous land.

Walt Sidney built Western Atlanta Natural Gas and Electric directly atop the ruins of TBS and CNN, not even removing the bodies in some cases, before paving the whole of what was once Georgia, South Carolina, and Florida, and turning the city-state of Atlanta into the industrial hellscape Turner had specifically requested he not. Ted Turner went to Walt Sidney's office to complain, paperwork in hand and lawyers in tow, only to find himself launched – via an officially licensed Lindsey Louse Lil' Lapidator Trebuchet – into the mesosphere for his troubles. As luck would have it, Turner collided with the shuttle launching Richard Branson's orbiting space station. The lawyers, meanwhile, ended up somewhere in the irradiated badlands of Eastern Europe.

Richard Branson, former CEO of Virgin All the Things Unlimited, and also screwed over by Sidney, peeled Turner from the side of the shuttle, taking him in and rehabilitating him in the station's highly-advanced med-lab. By the time Turner was functional again, the space station was crazy in orbit, so the two executives settled in, living in the luxurious, well-supplied satellite for quite some time, circling the planet and plotting their revenge. Also, catching up on *years* of television.

Hearing about the decimation of WANG, the pair decided the iron was heated to a high enough degree that striking would be optimal. Turner and Branson gathered up what they needed, made some calls, and prepared to return to Earth. Sadly, Richard Branson died along the way, attempting to parachute back to the planet from the fringes of space. Ted Turner, piloting the space station back to the planet like a sane person and taking the whole of the revenging upon himself, picked up some military-industrial materials at auction, harnessed what was left of the quickly depleted Fountain of Youth to regain some of his youthful vim and vigor, and set out to right some wrongs.

The grass beyond the men began moaning and shaking vigorously.

"Do you have room for one more in there?" asked the sun god, motioning to the war machine. "These two ... They are not much help. And they keep making me feel like a third-wheel. It is not fun."

"Yeah. Sure."

"And my great-grandson."

"Your ... great-grandson?" Ted Turner motioned to the nobody standing next to or around the god.

"Oh," said Ra, turning in place. "I ... I could have sworn he was ... right here ... but clearly he is not." The Egyptian creator of everything deflated. "Nevermind, I suppose."

Then, giving the TBS namesake a brotherly nod, he said: "At my age, the mind, it goes on you."

"Tell me about it."

"Well, if I am being honest, it all started about five hundred and twelve years ago …"

CHAPTER EIGHTY ONE
Waffles Waffles Waffles

WILLIAM H. TAFT XLII WAS NOT A SMALL MAN. As a clone of the fattest president of the United States, he never would be. After years of being bullied about his weight, he had come to terms with that. So the replica politician began working out, turning shame into fury and fat into muscle. The duplicated president was still not a small man. But now his stature was more like that of a half-giant, towering and intimidating and not someone about whom fat jokes would ever be made without grievous bodily harm befalling the one making the jokes.

Judging by the stacks of waffles and ice cream and disco fries before him, the mayor-king was trying to undo all of that in one meal.

"Billy, you're not going to be able to eat her back to life," said Queen Victoria XXX.

"Blow it out your ass, Vicky," countered William H. Taft XLII.

The president and the queen were seated on either side of Thor Odinson – the shirtless thunder god wearing the president's blazer so he'd be let through the doors – in a circular booth in the corner of a facsimile diner trying and failing to replicate the spirit of the 1950s, on the outskirts of Area 51.[18] They had driven to the nearest extant restaurant, an hour and a half away, while they waited for the mayor-king's golden mansion to ground itself. The trio was tired and angry and sad and covered in the blood and guts of a dozen dismembered creatures and smelled like burnt pork.

"I am trying to be polite, god damn it," the replicated royal replied.

"Which god?" asked Thor.

"Please don't start with that again."

William H. Taft XLII slammed his fist against the table.

"Why did Charlie get to survive? Why didn't Bo?" he grumbled. "His fucking *skin* came off."

"He was kind of an arrogant motherfucker," said Thor.

"I did also have his brain scooped out and on ice within thirty minutes," explained Queen Victoria XXX.

"Yeah …" said the big man slowly. "That was … weird."

"It worked, though, didn't it?"

"But you didn't know that. For one thing, we had no idea any of my scientists survived, much less if any of them could do anything with a cooler full of the innards of Charlie's skull. For another, brains shouldn't operate under the same rules as pizza delivery."

"But it turns out they do, so there you go."

"Shit is so fucked up," he mumbled, burying his face in his hands.

"How is Charlie, by the way?" asked Queen Victoria XXX, stealing one of the mayor-king's waffles.

Begrudgingly, and delicately, his broken arm hanging limply at his side, William H. Taft XLII pulled his phone from his vest pocket, shaking off clumps of clurichaun innards, then thumbed around a little.

"His brain's successfully in the new body," he said eventually. "My guys aren't Arahami, though, so don't expect much."

"Does he at least have a dick?"

"No."

"Does he have a waist?"

"Kind of?"

"Good enough. We've got a couple strap-ons. We'll be OK."

"Could you put Catrina's brain in a robot, too?" asked Thor softly.

"No, man. Weren't you listening?" snapped William H. Taft XLII. "Aside from the fact that you would've had to desecrate her corpse within thirty minutes of her dying –"

"'Desecrate' is a little strong," said the queen.

"– Catrina was human, she had a soul. It wouldn't be right to bring her back without it. It wouldn't be her."

"Well … what about those old lady ghosts we fought in Montana?" grasped the thunder god. "Can't Catrina do something like that? Or come back as her own zombie?"

"Souls can't possess their own corpses," explained the large man, "it's too traumatic. Death creates an irreparable schism between body and soul, between the physical and metaphysical."

"Well, what about just the ghost thing then? Or what about someone else? Can she come back as some random corpse? I know where there's a ton of 'em."

William H. Taft XLII seethed for a moment, then answered: "Ghosts – assuming the phantasmagraphic spectrum wasn't borked, which I already told you it *is* – *can* possess other people, but it's never really them. For one thing, they're rotting, shambling cadavers, first and foremost. For another, even if you do recognize them somewhere in there, it wouldn't be all of them. It's *never* all of them. Every time they possess a corpse, they lose a part of themselves. And it gets worse over time. Layers get stripped away until there's only vague notions of the person left, one-dimensional sketches of who they were, forever drifting aimlessly or sobbing or making toast or whatever."

Thor grumbled. The restaurant shook slightly.

"Look, I'm sorry," said the cloned president, softening. "I really am. About her, about barking at you just now, about the rules of the metaphysical world." His voice resolidified. "But don't forget that I have just as much reason to be pissed off about the way this all shook out as you."

The brawny Norseman angrily shoved an entire pancake into his mouth.

"I still don't get why Catrina did that," said the queen. "That wasn't really her style, right? She was never a 'hit first' kind of girl."

"She was angry. She felt justified, emphasis on the justice. Plus, the hammer," the thunder god replied, chewing loudly. "It's power incarnate. You feel invincible. You guys have to get that. You're engineered to be stronger and better than most mortals."

"You're damn right we are."

"But *how* did she do that?" asked the robust politician.

"Honestly, I don't know." Thor gulped down a cup of coffee. "I've got theories. I didn't get my powers back for real until I was protecting you guys from Quetzalcoatl. Until I was overcome with actual righteous fury, using my anger for good. That was kinda my whole deal back in Asgard, and the hammer was built for me specifically, so … I'm assuming that's how Catrina was feeling. She was legit avenging Ali and helping the rest of us. The hammer amplifies that a thousand-fold."

"Well then that explains how you *became the fucking sky*," said Queen Victoria XXX.

"Yeah, about that …" said William H. Taft XLII.

The Norseman shrugged his massive shoulders, the borrowed blazer threatening to tear itself apart. "There must be two levels of god powers or something."

"Like *Dragon Ball Z*."

"Exactly like *Dragon Ball Z*," replied Thor, pointing a fork at the president. "Except less confusing. And there's only the two levels. I think. I'm pretty sure I'm tapped out. I feel exactly like I did before those stupid scientists disproved me."

"But why now? Why wait until something terrible happens? Why not get all your powers, you know, the *first* time you got your powers?" asked Queen Victoria XXX.

"'The power comes in response to a need, not a desire,'" explained the mayor-king.

"Yeah, that might be it," replied the god.

"That was a quote from the show."

"Oh. Right." He paused. "So … I'm a super saiyan?"

"Pretty much," replied William H. Taft XLII. "Your hair did get more yellow."

"Is it pointy?"

"No. Sorry, man."

"You fucking nerds," said the queen, stealing another one of the simulated president's waffles.

CHAPTER EIGHTY TWO

That's Some Inscrutable Logic There, Sir

"CONGRATULATIONS, A, YOU'VE BEEN PROMOTED to Chief Operating Officer," said Walt Sidney, leaning back in his jar.

"Thank you, sir," replied Ah Puch, the former Mayan God of Death, standing before him and smiling unsettlingly. "And who will be taking my position as Director of Public Relations?"

"No, you're still doing that job too."

"Oh. OK. Well, it's still an —"

"I don't care. What do you think we should do about Thor and whichever of his friends lived? I'm honestly a little torn on this one. On the one hand, they have information about the company I don't want released, and it would bring me extreme amounts of pleasure to watch them all die screaming, but, on the other hand, hunting them down is starting to feel like a tremendous waste of resources."

"Well," said the skeletal old man, still smiling, "after extensive research into the issue, I think it would be in the company's best interests to sit back for the time being." Ah Puch slid a number of photos and print-outs onto the desk next to the frozen head. "The Las Vegas Massacre has been well publicized, covered by almost all major news outlets, social media sites, and office cafeterias, with William H. Taft XLII, Queen Victoria XXX, Chester A. Arthur XVII, and Thor Odinson coming out as the heroes, righteously defending the city from evil, despite the fact that the thunder god had a higher body count than any of his opponents, plus all the *Expendables* movies, all twelve of them, combined."

"You're sure about this," rumbled Walt Sidney, his voice like an unbalanced dryer.

"I'm positive," replied the manically grinning former god. "Going after Thor and his friends right now would be disastrous for the Walt Sidney Company image. Currently, public opinion seems to be that the entire massacre was little more than a spat between a tempestuous Satan and them, independent of us. No one knows Loki was there. We recovered his corpse, removed the credentials from both his top *and* bottom halves, and threw him into the mass funeral pyre with the rest of the city's citizens. And while the media's research does show Satan as the former director of Western Atlanta Natural Gas and Electric, they believe he was fired after an industrial accident under his watch. Your ties to him are clean. No one is aware of your proposition to rehire him if he got rid of the cyborg and the squirrel. Which, for the record, he did. Sort of."

"And sending our special ops dragoons ...?"

"Out of the question, sir. With the level of scrutiny and media attention currently on the Vegas Four, someone would undoubtedly catch something. Especially since our special ops dragoons are, in fact, branded with the Lindsey Louse logo."

"You don't think that's a good idea?"

"Well, the point of special ops is stealth, isn't it, sir?"

"That's why the logo is black, on black armor."

"But it's two different shades of black, sir ..."

"Because I want the people we go after to know we went after them."

"But you also *don't* want them to know that," continued Ah Puch, "am I correct? Which is why we send in the special ops units instead of the Louseketeers?"

"Exactly."

"I ..." The underworld god finally stopped smiling. "I'm really not sure how to respond to that, sir."

PART THREE
The Big Get Even

CHAPTER EIGHTY THREE

The Beeps Are Short, The Boops Are Long

"SAY HELLO TO THE NEW CHARLIE," EXCLAIMED William H. Taft XLII, one arm in a sling, the other holding open the door to his guest bedroom as a commercial blender hot-glued to a Roomba rolled in unsteadily.

"Oh, this is not good," said Queen Victoria XXX from where she was sitting on top of the bed. Gingerly, ice packs duct-taped over her midsection, she slid the scrapbook off her lap and her legs off the bed, then approached the robot. Tentatively, she put out a hand.

Nothing happened.

"Does he even know I'm –"

"beepbeepbeepbeep   beep   boopbeepboopboop boopboopbeepbeepboopboop beepbeepbeep beep boopbeepbeepboop boopbeepboopboop boopboop beepboop boopboop beepboop beepboopbeepboopbeepboop," said Chester A. Arthur XVII.

"Shang Tsung's stanky sharts, Billy. Seriously?" inquired the cloned head of state. "Morse code?"

"beepbeep boop beepboopboopboopboopbeep beepbeepbeep boop beepbeepbeepbeep beep boopbeepbeepbeep beep beepbeepbeep boop beepbeep boopbeepboopbeep boopboopboop beepbeepboop beepboopbeepbeep boopbeepbeep boopbeepbeep boopboopboop boopboopbeepbeepboopboop boopboopbeep beepbeep beepbeepbeepboop beep boopbeep boop beepbeepbeepbeep beep boopbeepboopbeep beepbeep beepboopbeep boopbeepboopbeep beepbeepboop boopboop beepbeepbeep boop beepboop boopbeep boopbeepboopbeep beep beepbeepbeep beepboopbeepboopbeepboop"

"This is going to make pillow talk exceptionally terrible," she said, tilting her head and sizing up the robot. "Not to mention, you know, everything else terribly wrong with this situation."

"beepbeep   boopbeepboopbeep   beepboop   boopbeep beepboopboopboopboopbeep   boop   beepbeepbeepbeep   beep beepboopbeepbeep   beepboopboopbeep   boopbeepbeepbeep beepbeepboop boop boop beepboop boopbeepboop beep boopboopboop beepbeepboopbeep beepbeepboopbeep beep boopbeep beepbeepbeep beep boop boopboopboop boop beepbeepbeepbeep beepboop boop beepbeepbeepboop   beepbeep   boopbeepboopbeep   boopbeepboop boopbeepboopboop"

"You seriously couldn't get a translator on there?"

"They're working on it," replied the mayor-king.

"I guess it's a good thing I'm leaving then," said a butt-naked Thor, brushing past William H. Taft XLII and ransacking the guest room's many, many closets in search of a duffle bag and a couple changes of clothes.

"What does you leaving have to do with Charlie?" asked Queen Victoria XXX, taking a long, languished look at her boyfriend, before sliding back onto the bed and crossing her sweatpanted legs. "Also, where are you going?"

"And why are you going through my shit?" asked the president.

"It was a convenient segue to getting my revenge," replied the Norse god. "Because all of my clothes are missing."

The queen knit her brow. "That doesn't – What?"

"Huh?" replied Thor. Then: "Oh. No. I hear it now. Those were three separate answers. My leaving has nothing to do with Charlie, I just saw a good segue and segued with it."

"Since when do you know what 'segue' means?" asked William H. Taft XLII.

"I know things. Sometimes."

"And the other two questions?" asked the queen.

"Right. I'm leaving to go get revenge. And I'm going through Billy's shit because all my clothes are missing."

"They're at the dry cleaners," explained the exasperated president. "I left a note on the refrigerator."

"beepboop   boopboopbeep   beepboop   beepbeep   boopbeep beepbeepbeep boop beepboopboop beepbeepbeepbeep boopboopboop

boopboop   beepboop   beepboopbeep   beep   boopbeepboopboop boopboopboop beepbeepboop boopboopbeep beep boop boop beepbeep boopbeep   boopboopbeep   boopbeepboopboop   boopboopboop beepbeepboop beepboopbeep beepboopbeep beep beepbeepbeepboop beep boopbeep boopboopbeep beep beepbeepboopboopbeepbeep"

"I have no idea what that was," replied Thor.

"Against who ... are you ... revenging?" translated Queen Victoria XXX, adding, "You killed everyone."

"Not yet I haven't," answered the former Norse god. "I'm going after Walt Sidney. If he wasn't such a good boss, those two assholes wouldn't have come after us and Catrina would be alive."

"That makes no sense whatsoever, Thor."

"You have a better idea, Vicky?"

"Many."

"I ... I can't sleep." The brawny blonde nudist closed his eyes, exhaling through his nose. "I feel ... off, wrong, all the time. I have all my powers back but all I keep thinking about is ... Catrina's gone, and Ali and Bo and that black dude that saved me from the old lady ghosts but then I never really saw again but Billy was all torn up about, and all the random mortals that got mauled and chewed up by monsters ... I should have done more." He shook his golden head. "So now I'm going to. For her, for them. I need to do ... *something* and killing Walt Sidney seems like the something to do."

"It's a fucking suicide mission," said William H. Taft XLII.

"Maybe for you." Thor Odinson smiled a swaggering smile and the building rocked, the lights flickered. "But I'm invincible," he said.

"boop beepbeepbeepbeep beepboop boop boopboop beepboop boopbeepboopboop   beepboopboop   beep   beepboopbeepbeep beepboopbeepbeep   boopbeepbeepbeep   beep boopboopbeepbeepboopboop boopbeepbeepbeep beepbeepboop boop boopbeepboopboop boopboopboop beepbeepboop boopbeepboopbeep beepboop   boopbeep   boop   beepboopboopboop   beepbeepboop beepbeepbeep   boop   boopboop   beepbeepboop   beepboopbeep boopbeepbeep beep beepboopbeep beepboopboop beepboop beepboopbeepbeep boop beepbeepbeep beepbeep boopbeepbeep boopbeep beep boopbeepboopboop beepboopbeepboopbeepboop beepboopbeepbeep   beep   boop   beepbeepbeep   boopboopbeep boopboopboop beepboop beepbeepboopbeep boop beep beepboopbeep

beepbeepbeepbeep beepbeep boopboop boop beepbeepbeepbeep beep
beepboopbeep beepbeep boopboopbeep beepbeepbeepbeep boop
beepboopboop beepboop boopbeepboopboop
boopboopbeepbeepboopboop beepboopboopbeep beepboopbeep
boopboopboop beepbeepbeepboop beep boop boopboopboop boop
beepbeepbeepbeep beep beepboopboop boopboopboop beepboopbeep
beepboopbeepbeep boopbeepbeep beepbeepbeepbeep beep
beepboopboop beepboop beepbeepbeep boopbeepbeepbeep beep
beepbeepbeepbeep beepbeep boopbeep boopbeepbeep beepboopboop
beepboop boopbeep boopboopbeep beepboop boopbeep boopbeepbeep
boop beepbeepbeepbeep beep boopbeepbeepbeep beepboopbeepbeep
beepboop boopbeepboopbeep boopbeepboop boopboopboop
beepbeepboop boop beepbeepbeep boopboopbeepbeepboopboop boop
beepbeepbeepbeep beepboop boop beepbeepbeepbeep beep
beepbeepbeep beep boopbeep boop beepbeepbeepbeep beepbeep
beepbeepbeep beepboop beepbeepbeep beepbeepbeep boopboopboop
boopbeepboopbeep beepbeep beepboop boop beep beepbeepbeep
beepboop beepbeepboopbeep boop beep beepboopbeep beepbeepboop
beepbeepbeep beepboop boopbeep boopbeepbeep beepboop boop boop
beepboop boopbeepboopbeep boopbeepboop beep boopbeepbeep
beepboopbeepbeep beepboop beepbeepbeep beepbeepbeepboop beep
boopboopbeep beepboop beepbeepbeep beepboopbeepboopbeepboop
beepboopboop beep boopbeep beep beep boopbeepbeep boop
boopboopboop boopbeepbeep beepboop boopboop beepboop
boopboopbeep beep beepbeepbeepbeep beepbeep beepbeepbeep
beepboopbeep beep beepboopboopbeep beepbeepboop boop beepboop
boop beepbeep boopboopboop boopbeep boopboopbeepbeepboopboop
boopbeepbeep beep beepbeepbeep boop beepboopbeep boopboopboop
boopbeepboopboop beepbeepbeepbeep beepbeep beepbeepbeep
boopbeepboopbeep boopboopboop boopboop beepboopboopbeep
beepboop boopbeep boopbeepboopboop boopboopbeepbeepboopboop
boopboop beepboop boopbeepboop beep beepbeepbeep beepbeepboop
beepboopbeep beep beepbeepbeepbeep beep boopbeepbeep
boopboopboop beep beepbeepbeep boopbeep boop boopbeepbeep
beepbeep beep beepboop boopboop beepboop beepboopbeep boop
boopbeepboopboop beepboopbeep beepboopbeepboopbeepboop"

"I can't understand a single damn thing you're ... saying? Is that
the right word?"

"Sure," said William H. Taft XLII.

"You can't just up and murder Walt Sidney," began the exasperated queen, sighing heavily. "You have to … prove to the world that he was behind WANG and the blackouts, and that he sent his henchholes after us and took a big, bloody dump all over Las Vegas. You need to … fuck up his reputation, bankrupt his megalomaniacal ass, and make sure no one wants to so much as be seen at the funeral of such a colossal jack-off."

"She's paraphrasing," explained the cloned man-mountain.

"Yeah, I figured," replied Thor. He shook his head. "We don't have proof for, like, any of that."

"We can get it."

"He'll buy his way out of a trial."

"His public image will be ruined."

"No, it won't," said Thor. "And if I know that, then you totally know that. Plus I really, *really* want to hit him myself."

"boopboopboop   boopbeepboop   boopboopbeepbeepboopboop beepbeepboopbeep   beepbeep   boopbeep   beep boopboopbeepbeepboopboop boopbeepbeepbeep beepbeepboop boop boopbeepboopboop   boopboopboop   beepbeepboop   boopbeepbeep boopboopboop boopbeep boop boopbeepboop boopbeep boopboopboop beepboopboop beepboopboop beepbeepbeepbeep beep beepboopbeep beep beepbeepbeepbeep beep beepbeep beepbeepbeep"

"You won't be able to find him," translated the cloned lady. "Wait, no, that's dumb." She glared at her fifth-grade science experiment of a boyfriend. "He'd obviously be holed up somewhere in Sidneyland headquarters on his private island."

"Finally, someone being useful," said the thunder god.

"You won't be able to get in there," countered Queen Victoria XXX. "And, no, not even you. Sidneyland is the single most heavily-fortified location in the known universe. And that's not hyperbole. They've done studies."

They had. Even before Walt Sidney had started hiring fallen gods and demons cast out of the various hells, he wasn't someone to be trifled with. As a holdout from the American 1940s and '50s, he was a staunch advocate of the "men were men" philosophy, as well as the "the Russians are going to bomb us back to the stone age so get cozy in this bunker" ism and the "sometimes Nazis try to breed man-eating cows so you better be ready" doctrine. And being a cryogenically frozen head didn't exactly make him any less nuts.

Sidneyland's headquarters was designed by crazy people for crazy people – the Walt Sidney Company did most of its headhunting in the less reputable sanitariums available, and a large number of their architects were troubled children – on a private island in international waters, using all of the alien technology collected after the failed invasion that ended the world for the fourth time. The building *itself* could kill people in new and imaginative ways, and that's not even including the security system, the outer security system, or the perimeter security systems. And it's best to not even bring the fence into the conversation.

"I'll find a way," said Thor gravely. The foundation shook again, the lights blinked.

"Stop that," said William H. Taft XLII, "you're going to break something. Again. Also, again, no, no you won't. You'll go bounding up to the front door, throwing lightning around like beer at a kindergarten commencement party, they'll see you, they'll hide him in some other heavily-fortified part of their sprawling, *extraterrestrially-militarized* headquarters, and then they'll kill you. And then they'll kill you again for good measure. And then probably a third time for fun."

"Do you guys not understand who I am?" rumbled the Norse God of Thunder.

"beepbeep   boopbeepbeep   boopboopboop   boopbeep beepboopboopboopboopbeep boop boop beepbeepbeepbeep beepbeep boopbeep   boopbeepboop   boopbeepboopboop   boopboopboop beepbeepboop   beepbeepboop   boopbeep   boopbeepbeep   beep beepboopbeep beepbeepbeep boop beepboop boopbeep boopbeepbeep beepboopboop   beepbeepbeepbeep   boopboopboop   beepboopboop beepboop   beepboopbeepbeep   boop   beepbeepbeep   beepbeep boopbeepbeep   boopbeep   beep   boopbeepboopboop   beepbeep beepbeepbeep beepboopbeepboopbeepboop"

"He's got a point," said Queen Victoria XXX. "Sidney scared the shit out of *Satan*."

"Because he didn't have his powers back," countered Thor.

"And then he did, and then he thought he was invincible, and then you took his literally godforsaken head off. Proving he was not invincible. There's no such thing, dude. You're going to die." Staring at Chester A. Arthur XVII, the queen's eyes became just the slightest bit moist. She turned her head. "And, honestly, I don't know if I can take another one."

"Look, Thor, we get it. And we're not even saying don't go after him. But not now, and not your way. Aside from all the sane and logical reasons, you just won't be able to get it done." Then, putting a hand on the plastic lid of Chester A. Arthur XVII, the mayor-king said: "But we will. Just give us a few days."

"That's too many days," replied the burly blonde god. "Can you get it done before dinner?"

"It's already five o'clock, Thor. No."

"Then I'm going."

"We *just* went over this," said Queen Victoria XXX, hopping off the bed, her hands balling into fists. "You'll be vaporized before you get past the doormat. Again, literally."

"Then I'll make him find me." The thunder god slung a duffel bag full of William H. Taft XLII's clothes over his shoulder and stomped out the door, nuts swinging in the breeze.

"If you're going to take my clothes, at least put them on!" the mayor-king called after him, leaning out of the doorway.

CHAPTER EIGHTY FOUR

Maps

THE CLOSEST SIDNEY STORE TO LAS VEGAS WAS IN RENO, NEVADA.
Then Thor showed up.

***

The closest Sidney Store to Las Vegas was in New Hollywood, in what used to be Denver, in what used to be Colorado.
Then Thor showed up.

***

"Hello?" said the manager of the Sidney Store in Sioux Falls, in the Hyper-Dakota Territories, picking up the phone.

"What was that?" he continued. "There's a what on the way?

"Can you speak a little slower, my Morse code isn't great.

"Look, just … just hold on a second. There's some serious thunder going on and I've got to bring in the outdoor displays."

CHAPTER EIGHTY FIVE

Check the Vending Machines!

WEI AND SHANNON LEBER-ZHENG WERE IN THE CRETACEOUS PARK gift shop, ruffling through t-shirts and fingering coffee mugs. A thick glass wall surrounded the store, showcasing some of the Park's less remarkable flora and fauna – like an aquarium tank, except with a jungle instead of water and tiny dinosaurs instead of fish. Suddenly a tall, Scandinavian-looking man in ill-fitting corduroys and a *Star Trek* t-shirt stormed through the door. Shannon cocked her head.

"Hey, honey," she said, tapping her husband's shoulder, "do we … know that guy?"

The large, blonde man marched up to the front register and grabbed the teenager behind the counter by his red-and-black polo shirt.

"Is it true," snarled the man, "that the Walt Sidney Company recently bought Cretaceous Park?"

"Y-Yeah …"

The man released the clerk. "Then you may want to evacuate."

"What?"

"I think he's Charlie's friend …" said Wei, staring uncertainly at the big man, "from the diner …"

"The guy who fought the dragons?"

"The guy who fought the dragons."

"Oh. Oh shit."

Thunder rumbled from seemingly everywhere, shaking the merchandise and shattering the reinforced windows surrounding the gift shop. Shards of dense Plexiglas rained onto the floor, as herds of tiny compsognathus and microraptors and aquilops swarmed into the store, scrambling across the floor and the racks and the shelving units, chomping down on everything in their way.

One of the chicken-sized carnivores leapt up and latched its tiny claws onto the clerk's face. He began screaming and spinning around behind the counter.

A pack of compsognathus weaved past Wei and Shannon, streaming by like a thick, shrieking river. A few nipped at their calves as they raced past. One jumped at Shannon's midsection. Wei clobbered it with an expensive, giant-sized box of officially-licensed Cretaceous Park Legos.

"That does it," he said, helping his wife up onto the shelves. "We are never leaving the house again."

CHAPTER EIGHTY SIX

He's Wrecked 'em

AH PUCH, THE SMILING GOD OF DEATH, LEANED THROUGH the doorway of Walt Sidney's retro-futuristic office and tapped his knuckles against the white plastic wall.

"Sir," he said, stepping in fully, "we have a problem."

"I've seen the reports," rumbled the frozen head. "This is about that thunder god wrecking up all of our licensed properties?"

"Yes, sir."

"And?" he boomed, his voice like a malfunctioning cannon. "What do you have to say about this that I don't already know?"

"Well, Mr. Sidney," began the former Mayan god, still grinning unsettlingly, "Thor Odinson has now 'wrecked up' very close to the lower threshold amount of retail needed to justify our swift and unceasing retaliation against him – without damaging our own reputation in the eyes of the public in the process."

"Hm …" Walt Sidney, lacking hands, scrunched up his mustache instead and pretended he was stroking his upper lip. "How much more property do we have to let him ruin before we can go completely apeshit bananas on him? I like to think of myself as a consummate professional, but, quite frankly, this Norse knuckledragger is starting to get on my nerves."

"About five more Sidney Stores," replied Ah Puch, "or one more theme park in a highly populous area."

"Let me know when that happens."

"Yes, sir."

"In the meantime, take a seat."

"Sir?"

"It's time for your performance review."

"But ... Sir ... I was promoted less than two weeks ago. I only just this morning cracked Loki's passwords to get most of the files I need to –"

"Sit down, A."

CHAPTER EIGHTY SEVEN

Cue the Stirring Speech

"BOOP BEEPBEEPBEEPBEEP BOOPBOOPBOOP BEEPBOOPBEEP boopboopbeepbeepboopboop beepbeep boop beepbeepbeep boopboop beep boopboopbeepbeepboopboop boopbeepboopbeep beepbeepbeepbeep beepboop beepboopbeep beepboopbeepbeep beepbeep beep beepboopbeepboopbeepboop beepboopbeepbeep beepbeep beepbeepbeep boop beep boopbeep boop boopboopboop boopboop beep boopboopboopbeepbeepbeep boopbeepboopboop boopboopboop beepbeepboop beepbeepbeepbeep beepboop beepbeepbeepboop beep boop boopboopboop beepbeepbeep boop boopboopboop beepboopboopbeep beepboopboop beepbeepbeepbeep beepboop boop boopbeepboopboop boopboopboop beepbeepboop beepboopbeep beep boopbeepbeep boopboopboop beepbeep boopbeep boopboopbeep beepboopbeepboopbeepboop boopbeep boopboopboop beepboopboop beepboopbeepboopbeepboop boopbeepboopboop boopboopboop beepbeepboop beepboopbeep beep beepbeepbeepbeep beepbeepboop beepboopbeep boop beepbeep boopbeep boopboopbeep beepbeep boopbeep boopbeep boopboopboop boopbeepboopbeep beep boopbeep boop beepboopboopbeep beep boopboopboop beepboopboopbeep beepboopbeepbeep beep boopboopbeepbeepboopboop boop beepbeepbeepbeep boopboopboop beepboopbeep beepboopbeepboopbeepboop beepboop boopbeep boopbeepbeep boopboopbeepbeepboopboop beepbeep boopbeepboop boopbeep boopboopboop beepboopboop boopboopbeepbeepboopboop boop beepbeepbeepbeep beep beepboopbeep beep beepbeepbeep boopbeepboopbeep boopboopboop beepboopbeepbeep beepboopbeepbeep beepboop boop beep beepboopbeep beepboop beepboopbeepbeep boopbeepbeep beepboop boopboop beepboop

boopboopbeep beep beepbeep boopbeep beepboop beepbeepboopbeep
beepbeep   boopboopbeep   beepbeepbeepbeep   boop
boopboopbeepbeepboopboop   beepbeep   beepbeepboop   boopbeep
boopbeepbeep beep beepboopbeep beepbeepbeep boop beepboop
boopbeep boopbeepbeep boop beepbeepbeepbeep beepboop boop
beepboopbeepboopbeepboop boopbeepbeepbeep beepbeepboop boop
boop   beepbeepbeepbeep   beepbeep   beepbeepbeep   beepbeep
beepbeepbeep boopbeep boop boopbeepboopbeep boopboopboop
beepboopbeepbeep   beepboopbeepbeep   beepboop   boop   beep
beepboopbeep beepboop beepboopbeepbeep boopbeepbeep beepboop
boopboop beepboop boopboopbeep beep boopboopbeepbeepboopboop
boop   beepbeepbeepbeep   boopboopboop   beepboopbeep
beepboopbeepboopbeepboop   boopbeepboopboop   boopboopboop
beepbeepboop beepboopbeep beep boopboopbeep boopboopboop
beepbeep boopbeep boopboopbeep beepboop beepbeepboopbeep boop
beep beepboopbeep boopbeepboopbeep beepbeep beepbeepbeepboop
beepbeep   beepboopbeepbeep   beepbeep   beepboop   boopbeep
beepbeepbeep   boopboopbeepbeepboopboop   boopbeepboopbeep
beepbeepbeepbeep   beepbeep   beepboopbeepbeep   boopbeepbeep
beepboopbeep   beep   boopbeep   boopboopbeepbeepboopboop
beepboopboopbeep beepbeepboop beepboopbeep beepboopboopbeep
boopboopboop beepbeepbeep beep beepbeepboopbeep beepbeepboop
beepboopbeepbeep   beepboopbeepbeep   boopbeepboopboop
beepboopbeepboopbeepboop boop beep beepboopbeep beepboopbeep
beepbeep boopbeepbeepbeep beepboopbeepbeep boopbeepboopboop
beepboopbeepboopbeepboop   boop   beepbeepbeepbeep   beepbeep
beepbeepbeep   beepbeep   beepbeepbeep   boopbeep   boop
boopbeepboopboop   boopboopboop   beepbeepboop
beepboopbeepboopbeepboop   boopbeepboopboop   boopboopboop
beepbeepboop beepbeepbeepbeep beepboop beepbeepbeepboop beep
boop   boopboopboop   boopbeepboop   boopbeep   boopboopboop
beepboopboop   boop   beepbeepbeepbeep   beepboop   boop
boopboopbeepbeepboopboop beepbeepbeep boopboopboop boopboop
beep beepboopboop beepbeepbeepbeep beep beepboopbeep beep
beepboopbeepboopbeepboop   boopbeepboopboop   boopboopboop
beepbeepboop beepboopbeep beep boopbeep boopboopboop boop
beepboop boopbeep beepbeepboop boopbeep beepboopbeep beep
beepboopboopbeep beep boopbeep boop beepboop boopbeep boop
boopboop   beepbeepboop   beepboopbeep   boopbeepbeep   beep

beepboopbeep   beep   beepboopbeep   beepboopbeepboopbeepboop
boopbeepboopboop boopboopboop beepbeepboop beepboopbeep beep
boopbeep boopboopboop boop beepboop boopboop boopboopboop
boopbeep   beepbeepbeep   boop   beep   beepboopbeep
beepboopbeepboopbeepboop   beepbeep   boopbeepboop   boopbeep
boopboopboop   beepboopboop   boopbeepboopboop   boopboopboop
beepbeepboop beepboopbeep beep beepbeepbeep boop beepbeep
beepboopbeepbeep   beepboopbeepbeep   beepbeepboop
beepboopboopbeep   beepbeepbeep   beep   boop   beepboop
boopbeepbeepbeep   boopboopboop   beepbeepboop   boop
boopbeepboopbeep beepboop boop beepboopbeep beepbeep boopbeep
beepboop boopboopbeepbeepboopboop beepboopboop beep beepboop
beepboopbeepbeep beepboopbeepbeep beepboop beepboopbeep beep
boopboopbeepbeepboopboop boopbeepbeepbeep beepbeepboop boop
boop   beepbeepbeepbeep   beepbeep   beepbeepbeep   beepbeep
beepbeepbeep boopbeep boop boop beepbeepbeepbeep beep
beepboopboop   beepboop   boopbeepboopboop
beepboopbeepboopbeepboop   boopbeepboopboop   boopboopboop
beepbeepboop beepboopbeep beep boopbeep boopboopboop boop
boopboopbeep boopboopboop beepbeep boopbeep boopboopbeep boop
boopboopboop boopbeepbeepbeep beepboopbeep beepbeep boopbeep
boopboopbeep   beepbeepbeepbeep   beep   beepboopbeep
boopbeepbeepbeep   beepboop   boopbeepboopbeep   boopbeepboop
boopboopbeepbeepboopboop   boopbeepboopboop   boopboopboop
beepbeepboop beepboopbeep beep boopbeep boopboopboop boop
boopboopbeep boopboopboop beepbeep boopbeep boopboopbeep boop
boopboopboop beepbeepboopbeep beep beep beepboopbeepbeep
boopbeepbeepbeep beep boop boop beep beepboopbeep beepboop
boopbeepbeepbeep boopboopboop beepbeepboop boop beepbeep boop
beepboopboop beepbeepbeepbeep beep boopbeep boopbeepboopboop
boopboopboop beepbeepboop beepboopbeep beep boopbeepbeep
boopboopboop boopbeep beep beepbeep beepbeepboopbeep
boopbeepboopboop boopboopboop beepbeepboop boopbeepboop beep
beep beepboopboopbeep boopboopbeep boopboopboop beepbeep
boopbeep boopboopbeep boopbeepbeep boopboopboop beepboopboop
boopbeep boop beepbeepbeepbeep beepbeep beepbeepbeep
beepboopboopbeep   beepboop   boop   beepbeepbeepbeep
beepboopbeepboopbeepboop   boopbeepbeepbeep   beepbeep
beepboopbeepbeep beepboopbeepbeep boopbeepboopboop beepboop

boopbeep   boopbeepbeep   beepbeep   beepboop   beepboopbeep   beep
beepboopboop   boopboopboop   beepboopbeep   boopbeepboop   beepbeep
boopbeep   boopboopbeep   boopboopboop   boopbeep   beep
boopbeepbeepboop   beepboopboopbeep   boopboopboop   beepbeepbeep
beepbeep   boopbeep   boopboopbeep   beepboopboop   beepboop
beepboopbeepbeep   boop   beepbeepbeep   beepbeep   boopbeepbeep
boopbeep   beep   boopbeepboopboop   beepboopbeepboopbeepboop
beepboopbeepbeep   beep   boop   beepbeepboop   beepbeepbeep
beepbeepbeepbeep   beep   beepboopbeepbeep   beepboopboopbeep
boopbeepboopboop   boopboopboop   beepbeepboop
beepboopbeepboopbeepboop   beepboopboop   beep   boopbeepboopbeep
beepboop   boopbeep   beepboop   beepbeepbeepboop   beep   boopbeep
boopboopbeep   beep   boopbeepboopbeep   beepboop   boop   beepboopbeep
beepbeep   boopbeep   beepboop   beepboop   boopbeep   boopbeepbeep
boopbeepbeepbeep   boopboopboop   beepboop   boopbeep   boopbeepbeep
boopboop   beepboop   beepboopbeep   boop   boopbeepboopboop   beepboop
boopbeep   boopbeepbeep   beepboopboop   beepbeepbeepbeep
boopboopboop   boopbeepboop   boopbeep   boopboopboop   beepboopboop
beepbeepbeep   beepboopboop   beepbeepbeepbeep   boopboopboop   beep
beepboopbeepbeep   beepbeepbeep   beep   beepbeep   boopbeep   beepboop
boopboop   beep   beepboop   boopbeep   beepbeep   boopbeep   boopboopbeep
beepbeepboopbeep   beepbeepboop   beepboopbeepbeep   beepboopboop
beepboop   boopbeepboopboop   beepboopbeepboopbeepboop
beepboopboop   beep   boopbeepboopbeep   beepboop   boopbeep
beepbeepbeep   boop   boopboopboop   beepboopboopbeep
beepbeepbeepbeep   beepbeep   boopboop   boopboopbeepbeepboopboop
beepbeep   beepbeepboopbeep   beepboopboop   beep   beepboopboop
boopboopboop   beepboopbeep   boopbeepboop   boop   boopboopboop
boopboopbeep   beep   boop   beepbeepbeepbeep   beep   beepboopbeep
boopboopboop   boopbeep   boop   beepbeepbeepbeep   beepbeep
beepbeepbeep   beepboopbeepboopbeepboop   boopbeepbeep
boopboopboop   boopbeepboopboop   boopboopboop   beepbeepboop
beepbeepboop   boopbeep   boopbeepbeep   beep   beepboopbeep
beepbeepbeep   boop   beepboop   boopbeep   boopbeepbeep
beepbeepboopboopbeepbeep   boopbeepboopboop   boopboopboop
beepbeepboop   boopbeepboopbeep   beepboop   boopbeep   boop
beepbeepbeep   boop   boopboopboop   boopboopboop   beepboopboopbeep
boop   boopboopboop   beepbeepbeepbeep   beepbeep   beepbeepbeep
beepboopbeepbeep   beep   beepbeepbeepboop   beep   beepboopbeepbeep

boopboopbeepbeepboopboop   beepboopboopboop   beepbeepboop
beepbeepbeep boop boopboop beepboop beepboopbeep beepboop
beepbeepboop boopbeepbeep beepbeep boopbeep boopboopbeep
beepbeepbeep beep beepboopbeepbeep beepbeepboopbeep beepbeep
beepbeepbeep   beepbeepbeepbeep   beepboopbeepbeep
boopbeepboopboop   boopboopbeepbeepboopboop   beepboopboop
beepbeep   boop   beepbeepbeepbeep   boopbeep   boopboopboop
boopbeepboopbeep boopboopboop boopbeep boopbeepboopbeep beep
beepboopbeep   boopbeep   beepbeepbeep   beepbeepboopbeep
boopboopboop   beepboopbeep   beepboopboop   beepbeepbeepbeep
boopboopboop   beep   beepbeepbeepboop   beep   beepboopbeep
boopboopbeep beep boop beepbeepbeep beepbeep boopbeep
boopbeepboopboop   boopboopboop   beepbeepboop   beepboopbeep
beepboopboop   beepboop   boopbeepboopboop
beepboopbeepboopbeepboop   boopbeepboopboop   boopboopboop
beepbeepboop beepbeepbeepbeep beep beepboop beepboopbeep
boopboop beep boopboopbeepbeepboopboop boop beepbeepbeepbeep
boopboopboop   beepboopbeep   beepbeepboopboopbeepbeep
boopbeepboopboop boopboopboop beepbeepboop beepboopbeep beep
boopbeep boopboopboop boopbeepbeepbeep beep boop boop beep
beepboopbeep   boop   beepbeepbeepbeep   beepboop   boopbeep
beepbeepbeepbeep beepbeep boopboop beepboopbeep beepbeep
boopboopbeep beepbeepbeepbeep boop boopbeep boopboopboop
beepboopboop beepboopbeepboopbeepboop boopbeep boopboopboop
boopbeepbeepbeep beep boop boop beep beepboopbeep boop
beepbeepbeepbeep   beepboop   boopbeep   boopbeepboopboop
boopboopboop   beepbeepboop   beepboopbeep   boopbeepbeepbeep
beepboopbeep   boopboopboop   boop   beepbeepbeepbeep   beep
beepboopbeep   beepboopbeepboopbeepboop   boopbeepbeepbeep
beepbeepboop boop beepbeep boopbeepboop boopbeep boopboopboop
beepboopboop   boopbeepboopboop   boopboopboop   beepbeepboop
beepboop beepboopbeep beep boopboopbeepbeepboopboop boop
beepbeepbeepbeep   boopboopboop   beepboopbeep
beepboopbeepboopbeepboop   boopbeepboopboop   boopboopboop
beepbeepboop beepbeepbeepbeep beepboop beepbeepbeepboop beep
boop   boopboopboop   boopbeepbeepbeep   beep
beepboopbeepboopbeepboop"

"Charlie," replied Thor, his cell phone between his cheek and his shoulder, "for the last Odin-shitting time, I don't speak Morse code. Is Vicky there? Put Vicky on."

CHAPTER EIGHTY EIGHT

Seriously, Why Are You in the NFC East, Anyway? Go to Hell, Dallas

THOR ODINSON STOOD AMIDST THE BURNING REMAINS of the Walt Sidney Smith & Wesson Jerry Jones Presents the Dallas Cowboys Stadium (Brought to You by Remington and Whataburger), the enormous Jumbotron behind him, half-buried in the field and tilted like a drunken monolith, the screen a maze of spiderwebbing cracks and flickering football highlights. The burly blonde man had one foot ankle-deep in the chest of an animatronic Tony Romo replica, sparks snapping and hissing up his leg, high atop a pile of dozens of other dismembered and malfunctioning officially-licensed Dallas Cowboys Mobile Tourist Information Automatons, wires and flames and unending recitations of football statistics flailing and burning and droning on into the smoke-filled sky. In one hand Thor held his hammer; in the other, raised, the head of a Lindsey Louse plush toy, torn roughly at the neck, stuffing raining down like fluffy hail.

"Walt Sidney!" boomed the Norse God, the sky thundering around him, a chorus of bowel-loosening echoes, the rising smoke shivering with each word. "Come and get me, you ancient, frozen, ugly, stupid, incontinent, corpse-humping, bestiality-endorsing, non-consensual anal fingering of a jagweed!"

For good measure – in case his point wasn't made – the thunder god called a terrific tower of lightning straight down through himself, utterly exploding the pile of Dallas Cowbots and sending pieces of Jumbotron into the crumbling heaps of seats and snack bars.

"You see that, you unasked-for rimjob?!" he bellowed. "You –"

"Well?" asked Walt Sidney, flipping off the wall television from a button within his jar and then bobbing around to face Ah Puch.

The Mayan death god scrolled through his tablet. "He's certainly done enough damage to warrant a legal –"

"No," said the frozen head, gritting his teeth. "No, A, now it's personal. That cretinous oaf of a pigfucker called me *incontinent*. Incontinent! You heard that, right? He knows I don't have a large intestine! Everyone knows that! He was saying those things on purpose, to rub his working excretory organs in my face."

"Sir, I don't –"

The frozen head growled like a hundred starving, poorly-trained pit bulls. "Requisition Item YS-97 from the warehouse, and then have everyone –" He stopped, closed his eyes, and took a deep breath. "No, strike that last part, A. I have a company to run. Have Báthory, Ukko, special security, and that big guy from IT meet me at the warehouse. And a couple of the more homicidal imps from facilities."

"Yes, Mr. Sidney," replied the god with resignation.

"And the feral zombies we have caged up in the labs, and whatever werewolves we can spare."

"Yes, Mr. Sidney."

"You're in charge while I'm gone, A," said the cryogenically-preserved CEO. "There's a pile of agricultural land acquisition forms that need to be approved."

"With pleasure, sir."

The frozen head narrowed his eyes. "Don't fuck this up."

"Yes, sir. Although, if I may, sir …"

"Out with it," barked Walt Sidney.

"Well … if I'm being honest …" began the smiling god, "I'm a little perplexed and preoccupied by the fact that you did not seem offended by the corpse-humping, bestiality-endorsing components of the Norseman's insult."

"What? Those?" scoffed the head, a little too dismissively. "How would I even hump a corpse?"

"That seems like a strange answer, sir."

CHAPTER EIGHTY NINE

I Think We're Parked, Man

CHESTER A. ARTHUR XVII, NOW UPGRADED TO A touch-free garbage can full of electronics mounted to a motorized scooter, clicked off the television, dialed a few numbers in his head, and called the only person who might be able to help rein in Thor.

"Hello?" replied Jesus Christ.

"beepboopboopboop beep beepbeepbeep beepbeepboop beepbeepbeep beepbeepboopboopbeepbeep"

"Hello? Is somebody there?"

"beepbeepbeep boopboopboop boopbeep boopboopboop beepbeepboopbeep beepboop beepboopbeepboopbeepboop beepboopbeepboopbeepboop beepboopbeepboopbeepboop"

"Is this my answering machine? How are *you* calling *me,* man?"

The robot, as begrudgingly as a sentient pile of mechanical scraps could, transferred the call to Queen Victoria XXX's cell phone.

"Jesus?" she said.

"Yeah, hi," replied the Son of God. "What's up?"

"We need your help."

Jesus sighed deeply, like a stoner full of Doritos and Mountain Dew getting up from a very comfortable spot on the couch.

"You know my rates, right?" he asked.

"We know."

"And my Hawaiian pizza?"

"Jesus Christ," she replied, rolling her eyes, "you'll have your pizza. Don't you worry your pretty little head about it."

"So you've seen my headshots then?" replied one third of the Christian trinity. "I'm available for, like, anything, man. Commercials, bar mitzvahs, you name it."

CHAPTER NINETY

Quick, Someone Find Some Clay and a Pottery Wheel

THOR ODINSON, COVERED IN HUMAN, DINOSAUR, and robot innards, had pulled the motorcycle he stole from William H. Taft XLII into a truck stop on the outskirts of the Houston Crater, gorged himself on gourmet hamburgers – paid for with the money he stole from William H. Taft XLII – and then stepped into the spotless, gleaming public shower.[19]

As the six-and-a-half-foot tall slab of man lathered up in the lukewarm water, the ghost of Catrina Dalisay appeared behind him.

"Boo," she said.

The thunder god turned slowly, hands lost in a cloud of shampoo atop his head.

"Catrina? Is that you?" He beamed like a flashlight in a deprivation chamber, then immediately squinted as soap dripped into his eye. "What are you doing here? I thought –"

"Billy's guys fixed the phantasmagraphic spectrum," she explained. "Turns out there *was* a box of secrets after all."

"Told you."

"No, you did–" Another droplet of shampoo kamikazed into Thor's eye, sending his head shaking like a paint mixer. "Dude, rinse off. I can wait. I've got all the time in the world. Like, literally."

"Right."

Thor quickly did as instructed. Then he stepped from the shower, dripping, sans towel, and resumed his conversation with the ghost of his best friend in the tiled changing area, which, due to a few unfortunately placed mirrors, placed him in clear view of the rest of the truck stop.

"Freya's freshly-shorn pubic mound," he said, astounded. "I can't believe you're here … What *are* you doing here? And I mean *here* here." He nodded his chin, indicating the men's restroom.

"I told you if I ever died I'd come back and haunt your ass in the shower. You, uh, you don't bathe as often as you probably should, by the way."

"Yeah …" The Norseman hung his head for a moment, then asked: "How's Ali? You guys are together again, right? Are you banging? Can you even do that? What's it like being a ghost? Can you change clothes?"

"He's good." Insofar as a spectral visage can blush, Catrina did. "We're good. Being dead isn't so bad, actually. We can go wherever we want and we never get tired. But, yeah, I am stuck in this –" She indicated her gossamer sweatpants, sandals, and too-large thrift store AC/DC t-shirt ensemble. "– for aaAAaall eteeEEeernity."

The thunder god smiled again, then, abruptly, stopped.

"I should have saved you," he said solemnly.

"It's all right, Thor," she replied. "I'm with Ali, that's what I wanted. And the afterlife is pretty nice. I mean, you know that."

"Yeah, but it's *after* life, a reward, or punishment, a consolation prize for when you're done living. And you didn't get to do that. Live. I should have done something."

"This isn't a kind world, Thor. You're a god. You forget that."

"I've never forgotten I'm a god," replied the legitimately confused blonde man.

"OK, right, let me rephrase: I'm *not* a god. You forget *that*. You and Vicky and Charlie and Billy … you're built for a world like this, with angry leprechauns and lasers and whatever the hell else there is out there. Me and Ali, we weren't. It was only a matter of time before it caught up to us."

"But Ali had a robotic arm … and a robotic leg …"

"Because he kept losing limbs trying to keep up with you guys."

"Oh, right," said the thunder god slowly, thinking, "yeah. I guess that sounds right."

"It does."

"Hey," he said, "can I ask you something?"

"Anything."

"What was up with the Mjolnir thing?"

"That was awesome, wasn't it?" Catrina replied giddily. "I mean, right up until I got myself killed, obviously."

"Yeah, that part ... that part wasn't so great," he replied. "But ... *how* were you using it? Mortals aren't supposed to be able to even lift Mjolnir, much less electrocute the devil with it."

"Couldn't tell you," she answered, shrugging her ethereal shoulders. "Your family could use it, though, right? Maybe that's what it was."

"You are like a sister I spent a lot of time trying to sleep with."

"So, hey, speaking of quickly changing the subject: what's with all the murdering, buddy?"

"I haven't *murdered* anyone," replied Thor, looking around and trying to avoid Catrina's spectral gaze. "We're talking involuntary manslaughter at worst ..."

"You clearly know that's not cool," said his former co-worker, flickering to and fro to match his rambling stare. "Right?"

"I ... I know." The naked blonde man slumped down onto a changing bench. "But ... I need to make Walt Sidney pay for what he did ... I ... *I* need to make up for what I *didn't* do ..." He shook his head. "I'm trying to draw him out from his not-so-secret lair. It's a whole thing, but apparently I can't just go fight him at his house. That's frowned on for some reason. So I've got to keep fucking up his stuff until he comes after me."

"Killing Walt Sidney won't bring me back, Thor."

"But it'll be fun."

"For you maybe, sure," the ghost replied, "but remember the innocent people? They ones you're hurting?"

"They worked for Sidney," he rumbled. "They deserved it."

"No, Thor. Even you know that's messed up. They were college students collecting a paycheck, they were tourists. You can't ... there were kids in some of those stores."

"The, uh, ends justify the means?"

"No, Thor."

"But it'll make me feel better?"

"Will it? Really?"

"Yes," replied the god matter-of-factly. "You know it will. Righteous justice and the relentless slaughter of my enemies is, like, my whole thing."

"It was, Thor, but not anymore. Powers or not, you live here now, on Earth, in the mortal realm. You can't keep pretending you don't. And, more importantly, all the innocent humans caught up in your warpath ... they're not your enemy."

"Even the ones who worked for the Cowboys?"

"Well, OK, maybe them," conceded Catrina. "But when it's all done, even if you take down Sidney, even if you do come out of this the hero, I'll still be gone and you'll still be sad. You're going to have to learn to live with that sadness, Thor. You can't just keep exploding stuff."

"That sounds terrible. Are you sure you got that right?"

"What would Batman do, Thor?"

"Not murder people," he replied sheepishly.

"Exactly."

"But, wait. You murdered the waitress. Like, a lot."

"That's not the point."

"I think it might be now."

"Look, Batman was sad all the time, right? That's why he kept Batmanning every night. And he never hurt any kids."

"Except all the Robins."

"This is proving to be a terrible analogy," she grumbled. "Look, just be the *idea* of Batman. Channel your sadness into something good, not just something violent."

"But I want the sadness to go away. And getting angry and hitting everything helps make it go away."

"So you're planning on forgetting about me?"

"I'll never forget you, Catrina," he said softly.

"Then you're going to be sad sometimes."

"That really sounds wrong."

"That's life."

"That's bullshit."

The ghost shrugged her tiny shoulders. "You're a human being now, Thor, like it ... or ..." Catrina's attention was caught by a particularly attractive young trucker disrobing and heading toward the shower.

"Honestly," she said, drifting through the shower curtain after him, "there are some perks to being a boring-ass mortal."

"Like what? I don't ..." asked Thor. "Does Ali know about this?"

"I'm cool with it," said the ghost of Ali Şahin, appearing next to the naked Norseman.

"Holy crap, man. Have you been here the whole time?"

CHAPTER NINETY ONE

You Don't Know How It Feels

THOR ODINSON – IN A HOODIE AND CARGOS STOLEN FROM A LOCKER when no one was looking – threw his leg over the motorcycle, situated himself, then turned the ignition and prepared to kick down on the starter, only for a beat-up pick-up camper to rattle up right in front of him. The truck rocked to a halt, the front door opened, and an unwound Little Debbie Swiss Roll of smoke curled out, followed by a middle-aged Middle Eastern man, dressed in distressed jeans and a distressing tie-dyed kurta.

"Yo," said the man, squinting behind his large sunglasses.

"Jesus Christ," replied the thunder god. "How's it going, man?"

"Good, brother. Good."

"This isn't about that thing ... with the –"

"Nah, man," answered the Nazarene, "that was ... it's ancient history, brother, don't worry about it."

"It wasn't that ancient, it was only a couple years ago ..."

"But, man, *we're* ancient, right? And it was part of *our* history ..."

"Ohhh ... yeah. That makes sense." The Norseman killed the engine and climbed off the motorcycle. "So, uh, what *are* you doing here then?"

"Your friends and my answering machine hired me to track you down and bring you home, brother. Said you were off on some rampage over the death of an old girlfriend."

"She was never his girlfriend," replied the ghost of Ali Şahin, suddenly flickering into view next to Jesus.

"Oh, whoa, man," replied the Savior of Mankind, stepping back. He pulled down his sunglasses slightly. "I didn't see you there."

"That's because I wasn't." The donut entrepreneur flicked back out of reality.

"What in the final frontier of James Tiberius Kirk?" Jesus Christ began looking around, staggering back and forth and bobbing his head like a pigeon.

The ghost of Catrina Dalisay appeared next to him.

"We're ghosts," she said.

Ali reappeared next to her. "And we get bored."

"Oh, all right. Right on."

"That's Catrina," said Thor, "and Ali. Catrina, Ali, this is Jesus."

"Hey."

"Hi."

"Anyway," continued the beefy blonde man, "she's the girl friend in question, and since it turns out she's a ghost, we were able to talk it all out. I'm a lot less angry now. No more rampaging."

"You sure, brother?" asked Jesus. "I remember your temper."

"All good. I promise."

"Well, then, all right," said Jesus, sliding his sunglasses back up. "All right, all right."

"Should you really have been driving?" asked Ali, floating around the Prince of Peace. "As high as I'm pretty sure you are?"

"Yeah, no. Probably not. But they said it was urgent."

"There's a bar inside if you want to sober up," said Thor, pointing a thumb towards the truck stop.

"Yeah ... all right. That sounds good, brother."

"You can't drink to sober up," said the spirit of the donut maker. "That is, in fact, the opposite of sobering up."

"From being high, I mean," said Thor.

"You can't be drunk and stoned at the same time, man," added Jesus. "That's just basic math."

"What?"

"That makes absolutely no sense, you guys," said Catrina.

Thor shrugged. "You coming with us?"

"Well, yeah," replied the ghost.

"Not like we're doing anything else," replied the other ghost.

CHAPTER NINETY TWO

A Dollar Short

TED TURNER, FORMER MEDIA MOGUL, AND AMEN-RA, former Egyptian God-King, finally arrived at the white picket gates outside the Walt Sidney Company's corporate headquarters. The enormous war machine rolled to a halt.

"Why are you stopping?" asked Ra, turning in his seat and pointing an angry finger at the windshield. "Why are we not driving this mechanical behemoth right over the gates and straight up Walt Sidney's ass?"

"Trust me, this is the way to do it," replied the man for whom TCM was named. "You have no idea the security they have here."

"Security?" barked the sun god. Outside, the sky blazed white, the asphalt began bubbling. "Why are you concerned with security? Do you not know who I am? Do I need to recount my story to you once more?"

"No, we're good," replied Turner. "Three times was enough. Also, can you knock it off with the sun? The AC in here is not the greatest and you are literally baking me alive."

"Oh. Right. Sorry."

The sun returned to its normal, bearable, occasionally cancer-giving state. Ted Tuner opened the door, climbed down and down some more, and then pressed the intercom button.

"Yeah, hi," he said. "I have an appointment to see Mr. Sidney."

The intercom crackled in response.

"Can you repeat that?" asked Turner, furrowing his brow.

The intercom crackled again.

"What do you mean he's gone?"

CHAPTER NINETY THREE

Where Everybody Knows Your Name

THOR ODINSON AND JESUS CHRIST SAT AT THE BAR, nursing a pair of Moscow Mules each. In the room to their left, Ali Şahin and Catrina Dalisay had, with permission and great fervor, possessed the bodies of a couple playing pool and were now doing ... things.

Thor watched them for a moment, then leaned forward, his golden locks falling over his face. He shook his head gravely and turned to Jesus.

"Why are we the ones that lived?" he asked. "We are terrible fucking people."

"We who, man?" replied the Savior of Mankind. "I'm not terrible. You know, relatively."

"We me and Vicky and Charlie," replied the thunder god. "We're not good people, but we keep ending up on the winning end. I mean, obviously except for Charlie – he's died, like, a bunch – but, still, he's here. He's alive." Thor hiccupped. "Alive-ish, anyway."

"Well, brother, maybe that's *why* you guys lived, maybe terrible is what you have to be now," expounded Jesus. "I mean, I tried doing the right thing, right? And look what happened to me, man." He held up a massively scarred hand. "And that was before guns and nuclear bombs and Republicans."

"I killed Satan and peed on his ashes," said Thor.

"Brother, I don't know why you'd expect sympathy for that guy from me ..."

"I beat a waitress's ex-husband half to death for coffee."

"Well, she wouldn't have asked if he didn't deserve it, right?"

"That doesn't seem right at all."

"The right thing doesn't always look right in the moment."

"After I pissed on Satan, when I was trying to help my friends, I may or may not have electrocuted some civilians, civilians who would've already had to survive some messed up stuff. A bunch of people interviewed me about it. They called me a hero."

"Well, they're not calling you that anymore, brother."

"I just …" Thor rested his forehead on the sticky bar top. "I don't understand."

Jesus shrugged. "Shit is fucked up, man." Then he downed the rest of his drink. Then the Son of God belched, loudly.

CHAPTER NINETY FOUR
Turn This Car Around

"AND YOU'RE SURE?" RUMBLED WALT SIDNEY, staring into the video monitor embedded in the dashboard of his heavily-modified Hummer. "Because we would need to go remarkably out of our way to –"

"I'm sure, sir," replied Ah Puch, the smiling death god. "Doing so would, in the parlance, fuck him up real good."

"OK. Thank you, A."

The monitor blinked out. The frozen head turned, in turn, to the corporate vice presidents sitting on either side of him.

"We'll be making a quick detour," said the floating CEO. "Make sure everyone knows." Then he began punching coordinates into the control panel inside his jar with his tongue.

"Yes, sir," replied Ukko, the former Finnish god of storms, and Elizabeth Báthory, the erstwhile Hungarian countess, hopping out of the moving vehicle and racing down the lengthy convoy – so lengthy, their radios could not reach the end – barking orders into their headsets to the fleet of vehicles and thousands of Louseketeers and black-clad dragoons and imps and werewolves marching behind them.

CHAPTER NINETY FIVE

Daddy Issues

"I CAN'T BELIEVE THEY GOT YOU OUT HERE," SAID THOR. The thunder god and the Son of God had relocated from the bar to a booth in the corner and were now surrounded by dozens of pint glasses and a precariously balanced pyramid of copper mugs. Six plates of chicken bones sat between them. Both of the men were swaying slightly.

"I had to lower my rates, man. I mean, you know. God-for-hiring jush ... it ain't what it used to be, brother. I don't know what changed, but things've been pretty chill out there fer a while," explained Jesus Christ. "You know, other than your rampage."

"I *said* I was *sorry* about that." Thor chugged down half of his beer. "Besides, there was that whole Las Vegas thing, too. And that wasn't me."

"Until it was."

"OK, yeah. Fair point."

Jesus began picking through the plates of discarded buffalo wing remains, hoping maybe they had missed one.

"Can't you jush, y'know ..." The Norseman mimed an explosion with his hand. "POOF."

"Bread and fish only, brother," replied the Nazarene, still digging. "And I'm not feeling that right now."

"Really?"

"Yeah. Who wants fishsticks and beer?"

"Well, I do," replied the beefy blonde man, "but I meant, really? You can only change shit into bread and fish?"

"Yeah, brother."

"That seems kinda weak."

Jesus shrugged. "I've always got the wine thing."

Thor audibly scoffed.

"I know, right?" returned Jesus. "I am so sick of wine."

"Why does everyone think wine is so great?"

"I don't know, brother, I don't know."

"You still talk to yer dad much?" asked Thor abruptly.

"My dad? Yeah, here and there," replied Jesus. "He seems t'be keeping himself pretty busy lately."

"Same here. Says he's 'retired' from bein' a god now though."

"Honestly, man, I'm still a little pissed off at 'im about the whole crucifixion thing. I mean, I get it, I understand why he did it, but that'll fuck a dude up, you know?"

"Not really. My dad loves me."

"That's ..." The Savior of Mankind shook his head. "You got that all kinds o' wrong, brother."

"So ... he killed you, even though he loved you? That's what yer sayin' yer saying?"

"Yeah, man," replied Jesus, furrowing his brow. "That's, like, the whole point. Don't you know anything 'bout Christianity?"

"I know throwing your own name into your religion is a little bit shitty."

"That wasn't *my* idea!" The Son of God leaned back into the vinyl bench of the booth. "The guys who wrote the Bible took a whole buncha liberties, brother, editorialized the crap outta, like, everything, man. But you gotta know that. I mean, there's no way they got all your stories right, right?"

"Prob'ly not," answered Thor, signaling the waitress for another round. "Honestly, I never really read any of it. But, I mean, our shit was weird as fuck. Like, *all* the time."

"You Old Testament-style guys had all the fun."

The Norse God of Thunder smiled. "You don't know the half of it. Dad was one crazy motherfucker back in the day. This one time, he traded away his eye – his fucking eye! – fer magic. And not even, like, fun magic. Jush the ability to see a little bit into the future. Heimdall could already basically do that! I don't know why –"

"Wait, man. Wait. Hold up. Yer dad's got one eye too?"

"What're you – Too? Yer dad has one eye?"

"Yeah ..." said Jesus. "I mean, it happened pretty late in the game. He was away for a century or two, then he came back for a bit, only there was a eyepatch strapped across his face. But, like, he kept acting like it wasn't anything, man, never bother'd to explain the thing. Anytime someone asked, he'd just shrug it off."

"That's weird."

"I think it might be more'n weird, brother …" began Jesus, knitting his brow like a grandma with a bunch of grandkids. "So, like, my dad and I were pretty close for a couple hundred years, right? Even after he, you know, let me get murder'd, but then one day he kinda bounced. Came back ev'ry so often, but never stuck around much."

"That sounds really familiar."

"Your dad ever talk about what he did before he was who he was?"

"Well, he used to go on and on about how he created the world from the pieces of a frost giant he hacked up."

"Yeah, uh, Thor, man … my dad created the world too."

"No way."

"Yeah way …"

"You think … are you sayin' what I think yer saying?"

"Well, there's only the one world, right?"

"Oh, holy shit," said Thor. "Man, Mom is gonna be so annoyed that Dad fucked off and boned a human."

"Well, technic'ly, he didn't bone my mom. Don't you know *anything* about Christianity, Thor? How is that even possible? They tricked the world into accepting my birthday as a secular holiday."

"Man," said Ali, blinking into existence next to Jesus, "knowing this a few centuries ago probably would've saved a few million lives."

"I dunno, man," replied Jesus, "we prob'ly woulda found something else to kill each other over."

"People really are terrible," added the waitress, standing unsteadily at the edge of the table and nearly spilling the tray of beers she was carrying.

"Catrina?" asked Thor, raising an eyebrow.

"Yo," she replied from inside the waitress.

"Why're you –"

The server's possessed body shrugged. "She asked."

CHAPTER NINETY SIX

Stop Dragging My Heart Around

THE JARRED HEAD OF WALT SIDNEY WAS BEING HELD by the burly and remarkably hairy Ukko, the former Finnish God of Storms, the two of them peering over the shoulder of Cthulhu, the transdimensional Elder God and head of the Information Technology department of the Walt Sidney Company.

"You're sure this will get rid of the ghosts?" asked the frozen head.

"For the last time, yes," replied the enormous, winged dragon-squid, sprawled on his back beneath a large server cabinet and existing on several planes of reality at once. "Stop asking."

"Taft was able to repair the spectrum last time. I don't want that happening again."

"That's because Satan's guy only sent a virus," replied the otherworldly horror. "I'm physically dismantling the heart of the internet." He tossed a tangle of wires toward his feet.

"Shouldn't that be in Japan?" asked Ukko.

"No, they had it shipped here, to Jackson, Mississippi, after Japan sank," explained Cthulhu. "Thought it would be safer. Because who the fuck would go to Mississippi?"

With a tremendous wrenching and a strange sucking sound, the eldritch terror ripped the main engine of the internet free from its biomechanical harness. He slid out from beneath the cabinet and held up the glistening object.

"What the hell is that?" asked Elizabeth Báthory, sitting on a server tower behind her boss and her co-worker.

"The heart of the internet."

"I, uh, I thought that was just an idiom," replied the murderess, shaking her head slowly. She pointed. "That is an actual heart."

"Well, yeah."

After the internet was destroyed, Japanese scientists altered the sub-theoretical quantum electromagnetic spectrum of the planet, allowing spirits that weren't accepted into any of the various heavens – or who just felt like dicking off for a year or two – to roam like free-range chickens, rather than being forever tethered to their bodies or points of death. The scientists soon realized that these spirits' electromagnetic energies, should they be harnessed, could transfer significant amounts of data significantly faster and significantly safer than the old, flammable, corruption-prone internet.

Scouring the globe, the scientists eventually discovered that the heart of the Loch Ness Monster had all of the metaphysical properties they needed to exploit all that ghost power, and summarily tore it out of her chest, ruining Scotland's tourism industry in the process. They then connected all of the internet's tubes and cables into the massive organ, sealed it in a box, and put that shit to work.

Naturally, PETA threw a fit when they found out about all of this, but, after seeing how much more efficient the new internet was, they kind of let the whole ordeal slide.

"Good job, C," said Walt Sidney.

"It's Cthulhu, damn it."

"I know that, C, but –"

"*Cthulhu!*"

"Look, I'm sorry, I really am," replied the frozen head, "but I simply cannot pronounce that."

The Elder God grumbled his dissatisfaction. A few of the weaker-minded dragoons guarding the door began seeing shooting colors and impossible angles in the air.

"You have tentacles for a mouth," continued the jarred CEO. "How am I supposed to pronounce something spoken like that?"

"You could *try*," replied a wounded Cthulhu.

CHAPTER NINETY SEVEN

Last Dance with Mary Jane

THE GHOST OF CATRINA DALISAY HOVERED IN THE BOOTH next to Thor Odinson, the pair sitting opposite the spirit of Ali Şahin and Jesus Christ. The pile of discarded dishes and empty glasses between them had grown to an alarming height, to the point that the former former hotel employee had to float a few inches higher off the seat just to see over everything.

Jesus, swaying significantly, attempted to stack another empty glass onto the pile, only to send the tower of drinkware cannonballing to the ground, where it exploded in a sublime symphony of smashing and shattering.

"Oops," he said.

"Don't worry 'bout it," slurred Thor. "No one's been by to clean up in, like, a hour. Thash on the waitress, not you."

"Hey, she's got some serious shit going on," replied Catrina. "Cut her some —" The Filipina woman flickered mightily, involuntarily blinking in and out of existence. "Uh oh."

"I think the spectrum's going again," said Ali, before winking away. After a moment, he appeared again, significantly snowier, like a grandmother's television after the kids haven't visited for a while.

"It's Walt Sidney," explained the ghost of the man from Dunkin' Donuts. "He's taken out the heart of the internet, apparently solely to spite Thor."

"Spite me? Why would he wanna spite me?" asked the thunder god. "Thash just gonna make me angrier."

"I didn't ... I didn't ask, Thor. I was kind of busy trying not to disappear out of existence entirely."

"Right."

"So, thish no internet thing," began the Son of God, raising an inebriated eyebrow, "it affec's you guysh ... how again?"

"The entire phantasmagraphic spectrum was tethered to and funneled through the heart of the internet," explained the ghost. "With that gone, the spectrum is evaporating into the ether."

"Shouldn't that, like, *not* be possible?"

"Really?" asked Ali, briefly turning into a Picasso painting. "You want to get into a technical discussion about that n–"

The ghosts shuddered out of reality for a solid three seconds this time before reappearing – long enough for Thor's heart to sober up and sink into his bowels.

"Catrina ..." he began.

"I think this is it, buddy," she replied, her ghost stretching and contorting like a four-year-old's finger painting.

"We can get Billy to fix it again."

"I don't think he can," said Ali gravely.

"It's OK, Thor. We like it here, in the afterlife." Catrina flashed away and back again. "There's no pain, no suffering, we don't pay taxes, there's skeeball ..." Then she smiled and said: "I love you, Thor."

"I love you too, Catrina."

The phantoms of Thor's friends began to totally seriously flicker some more, like an old timey nickelodeon on the fritz.

"Oh shit, here we go," said Ali Şahin, shaking like a computer monitor that needed a good smacking. "See you in a few, Cat." And then he was gone.

Catrina put her blinking, spectral hand above the table. Thor put his hand into hers.

"Is there anything you want me to do for you?" he asked.

"No, we're happier than we've ever been." The ghost smiled serenely. But she could see the hurt on Thor's face, hidden beneath his beard and the buffalo sauce, the final understanding that she was really gone. She could see the desperate pleading of his heart, for one last gift, an apology, a goodbye, something to help ease his pain, something to let her know what she meant to him.

"Well, I guess there's one thing ..." She smiled a little more sinisterly. "... if you're asking."

"Anything."

"AveeeEEeenge meeee!" she said dramatically, lifting her ethereal frame into the air, her arms wide. "But be smaaaAAaart about it!" And, with a wink of shimmering light, Catrina Dalisay vanished forever.

Thor frowned, then smiled, then knocked back the rest of his beer.

"Hot damn."

"Come on, brother," said Jesus. "I thought you shaid you were done with the rampaging."

"I am, I swear," replied the Norse God of Thunder, hustling clumsily out of the booth. "I'm only goin' after Walt Sidney thish time. I'll be super-duper careful."

"I 'unno, man …"

"He's a total dick, dude. I promish."

CHAPTER NINETY EIGHT
Into the Great Wide Open

QUEEN VICTORIA XXX, WILLIAM H. TAFT XLII, and a two-foot-tall animatronic moose containing the brain of Chester A. Arthur XVII rolled up to the east entrance of the Houston Crater truck stop in a pair of the mayor-king's steam-powered all-terrain-vehicles, covered in dust and splattered bugs and radioactive fallout. Staring through the mess of their windshields, they found Thor standing in front of Jesus's camper, jumper cables running from the vehicle's battery to the thunder god's nipples.

"OK, try it n–"

"What in the unpunched balls of Johnny Cage is going on here?" asked William H. Taft XLII, sliding up his round driving goggles before clumsily climbing out of his ATV, his bulk and still-slung arm making things difficult.

"Well, I can't jush electrocute his RV, can I?" explained Thor. "I'd blow the whole damn thing up." Then, proudly, he added: "I know how to learn."

"Not one-hundred-percent sure this counts as *learning*, buddy," replied Queen Victoria XXX, removing her children's toy of a boyfriend from the passenger seat. She had managed to cobble together an outfit from all of William H. Taft XLII's wives' closets, and was now wearing a long duster over a short skirt and a midriff Misfits t-shirt. From where Thor was standing, her ribs still looked pretty messed up.

"Also, are you drunk?" she continued. "You've never been drunk. I mean, we've drank together before, sure, but … how much did you drink, Thor?"

"Why're you guys on scooters?" answered the thunder god.

"They're ATVs, dude," countered William H. Taft XLII. "They have four wheels. And engines."

"Where's is Charlie's Batmobile? And where's Charlie? And why are you wearing Bo's clothes and carrying around a stuffed animal, Vicky? Is it a sex thing?"

"This is me now, Thor," explained the stuffed moose. "This is my new body. I've been upgraded, for lack of a better beep boop searching thesaurus boop synonym. At least I'm autonomous again. I can do everything I used to be able to do."

"Except nowhere near as well and not really," clarified the queen.

"As for my car: I do not know what happened to it. Someone must have stolen it from where you and Catrina left it parked while we were distracted with the maiming and the monsters and the Satan beep boop searching thesaurus boop hootenanny."

The former Norse God of Thunder, making a face, said: "I *guess* thash better than a scrap pile that only speaks Morsh code."

"I'm sure your tank is very happy wherever it ended up," consoled the queen, squeezing the fuzzy Chester A. Arthur XVII tightly.

"grumble grumble grumble," replied the robot.

She held the moose out in front of her. "Did you ... did you just say the word 'grumble' instead of actually grumbling?"

"Blame Billy's airquote scientists airquote."

"Oh my god," she said, burying her face in her hand.

"So, hey, shpeaking of," began the Middle Eastern hippie stumbling over from the camper, slicking back his greying hair and thinking he was attempting to be suave, "hi, I'm Jesus Christ. Savior of All Mankind."

"Queen Victoria XXX, homunculus," the cloned monarch replied, stuffing the teddy bear under her armpit and shaking his hand. "But it's the thought that counts."

"What are you guys doin' here?" asked Thor, removing the cables from his chest.

"We told you we'd find a way to get you to Sidney, right?" answered William H. Taft XLII triumphantly.

"Yeah ... so, did you?"

"No."

"It, uh, it turns out he's on his way here," clarified the non-stuffed presidential clone.

"Oh," said Thor, then, "Wait." A pause. "So … my plan worked?" he asked. "My plan and not yours?"

"You don't have to rub it in, dude," said the mayor-king of the ruins of Las Vegas, starting to cross his arms over his chest and being met with tremendous pain. Trying not to grimace, the president leaned back against his ATV like nothing had happened.

"Yes. Yes, I think I do."

"So, like, when you say he's on his way …" Jesus hiccuped. "How far is his way exactly? And wha'do we do about that?"

"Thish," said the Norseman, plopping his ass down on a nearby parking block. Queen Victoria XXX shrugged and plopped down next to him, leaning her stuffed boyfriend against the concrete at her feet.

"What do you two think you are beep boop searching thesaurus boop engaging in as an action?" asked Chester A. Arthur XVII, toddling away from them and attempting to cross his tiny arms across his tiny chest.

"Waiting," replied the thunder god.

"Shouldn't we, maybe, like, move it on down the road a little?" asked the Prince of Peace, pointing toward the vast expanse of nothing that started at the edge of the truck stop and ran for what seemed like forever. "You know, so no innoshents get murdered? Like you told me and promised your dead friend?"

"Oh. Right. Yeah. That."

"Eh," replied Queen Victoria XXX.

"Vicky," said William H. Taft XLII.

"OK, fine," she relented and very, very reluctantly got up.

CHAPTER NINETY NINE

Meet and Greet

THE VEHICLES CAME TO A HALT IN A GRASSY PATCH OF NOTHING a hundred miles north of the Houston Crater Rest Stop. Queen Victoria XXX and William H. Taft XLII disembarked from their ATVs, the queen taking the stuffed Chester A. Arthur XVII with her. And then ... well, then the clones just kind of stood around awkwardly for a while. And then a while after that. Finally, a couple minutes after *that*, Thor and Jesus stepped out of the rear of the camper, the vehicle exhaling smoke like an oven with an overcooked chicken in it for several minutes afterwards.

"Really, guys?" asked William H. Taft XLII.

"What?" replied the thunder god.

"We were sobering up, brother," explained the Son of God.

"You're high. High is not sober," explained the clone.

"From the booze, I mean."

"That's not ... weren't you *born* a human, Jesus? Shouldn't you know how human bodies work?"

"Yes? Maybe? What's the question?"

The facsimile of the fattest president of the United States sighed. "There is some serious shit about to go down, you two," he continued.

"And you didn't invite me," added Queen Victoria XXX.

"That's not the issue here, Vicky."

"I think it is."

"I've got more," said Jesus Christ, holding back a burp.

"Well, hot damn," said the cloned monarch, casually tossing Chester A. Arthur XVII to William H. Taft XLII.

"Vicky ..." said the stuffed moose, cradled in the large man's good arm. "What are you doing?"

"What?" she replied. "Like you've never gotten high."

"Not when I need to focus on not getting annihilated."

"How's that working out fer you?" asked the Son of God.

Gingerly, Queen Victoria XXX rested an arm across her bare and bruised abdomen. "I am in tremendous pain, Charlie."

"And I'm not?" countered the non-plush cloned president.

"I've got more," said Jesus.

"Wha's going on?" asked Thor, shaking his head and looking up from his sneakers.

"Holy shit," boomed a voice. "Are you guys for real?"

"What was that?"

"Who said that?"

The group spun around, turning their heads back and forth, looking all over the empty expanse of dried-up grass and scrub brush and rocks for the mysterious voice. Queen Victoria XXX looked straight up. Jesus looked behind a prickly pear cactus. Thor lay on the ground and checked under the camper.

"You guys did hear that, right?" he asked, lifting up his goathead-covered face. "I didn't jush hallucinate someone kind of insulting us?"

"No, we heard it."

"Are you on something else you're not sharing?" asked the queen.

"Only the weed," answered the thunder god. "And the alcohol."

"I's really good weed, though," clarified Jesus.

"I can't believe we let you guys drive," said William H. Taft XLII.

"We drove somewhere?"

"Jesus Christ," exclaimed the mystery voice.

"Yes?" replied Jesus Christ, spinning around like a slowing dreidel.

"Found it," said Chester A. Arthur XVII, raising an adorable arm. Everyone turned to where the stuffed moose was pointing.

Just beyond the group was a shining, white, mechanical exoskeleton, ten-stories of post-space-age circuitry and highly-polished nano-diamond thermoplastic polymer, blocking out the sky. The robot suit stood like a hulking rock giant, nearly as broad as it was tall, with wide-set, stubby legs, an obtuse triangle of a torso, and rounded shoulders looming well above its head. All of the suit's angles were clean and curved, with dense ethylene rubber covering the exposed joints. Somewhere near the upper middle of the suit, in the squared head compartment, hidden behind bulletproof glass, inside a jar of cloudy preservation fluid, the group could just make out the bespectacled visage of Walt Sidney.

"How did we not see that?" asked Queen Victoria XXX in awe.

"Cloaking device," explained Walt Sidney.

"OK, yeah, that'd do it."

"You know, all things considered," said William H. Taft XLII, tilting his head and staring up and up some more at the enormous mech-suit, "this isn't so bad."

"I know, right?" said Thor. "You guys made it sound like he ... had an ... army ... or some ..."

At that moment, three thousand heavily-armed special ops dragoons and Louseketeers in full riot gear were fanning out from behind the Sidneytron 5000™, taking up the rest of the horizon on either side. At the forefront of the gathered ground forces were Elizabeth Báthory, Ukko Jumala, and Sidney's special security team of Attila the Hun CXI, Genghis Khan XII, "Bloody" Mary I LXX, Isabella I LII, and the former demons of the actual Attila the Hun, Genghis Khan, Mary I of England, and Isabella I of Spain. Clearly experimented-upon werewolves being dragged by chains could be seen lumbering through the ranks, snarling and shoving stormtroopers to the side. Several dozen blood-red imps – like fat babies with pointed ears and ineffectual wings – squeezed their way past armored calves and stood before the army. In the distance, cages full of feral zombies were being wheeled forward.

"OK, this is more bad," corrected the president.

"Ukko," growled Thor, shoving his way past his friends to the front of the pack. He grabbed Mjolnir from his hip, only to discover he had left his hammer in the camper, and, instead, pointed an empty hand at the other god of storms. "You fucking Finnish copycat!"

"You don't have a monopoly on thunder-godding!" shouted the beefy, bearded Finnish deity.

"Oh, right! And the hammer thing is just a coincidence?!"

"Lots of people have hammers!" he shouted, hefting Ukonvasara, his enchanted stone mallet, into the air. Lightning flashed in the distance.

"Name six!"

"Well, there's you and me and carpenters, and Kathy Bates in *Misery*, and Ben Carson –"

"Who the fuck is Ben Carson?!"

Ignoring Thor and Ukko's ongoing verbal pissing contest, William H. Taft XLII, backing up slowly toward his ATV, said: "Well, it's not like it can get any … any …"

An enormous dragon-squid stomped into view from nowhere and everywhere all at once, approaching Walt Sidney from what seemed like a great distance away but never changing size as it neared. The creature roared, something audible and physical and theoretical all at the same time, and bladders emptied slightly.

"God damn it, Billy," the clone muttered to himself.

"'scuse me," said Cthulhu, shaking his head, "the dust is getting caught in my throat or something." Then: "All the cars are parked, Walt." The Elder God nodded toward a field of shining vehicles a safe interval behind the militant horde. "You do know there are, like, I don't know, a million better uses of my time, though, right?"

"Not now, C," grumbled the frozen head in the giant robot suit, eyes locked on Thor and Jesus and the clones, trying to keep up his intimidating stare.

"For the love of Sonya Blade, boss, it's Cthulhu! *Cthulhu!*"

"This is not the time for this," snarled Walt Sidney. "Do you see what we've got going on here?" The frozen head swiveled to look at the squid-dragon while the mechanical suit gestured toward the amassed army and the cowering clonefolk. "I am trying to destroy my enemies. And, besides, we've been over this: no one from this plane of reality could possibly –"

"Hey, Cthulhu," Queen Victoria XXX shouted, with perfect pronunciation, waving from where she was standing.

"Oh, hey, Vicky," replied the Elder God, squinting and looking down at the cloned monarch. "How, uh, how's it going?"

"Pretty good," she replied with a shrug, "other than your boss trying to murder us all into oblivion."

"Yeah, he does that sometimes."

"You guys know each other?" asked William H. Taft XLII.

"We were sleeping together for a while," explained Queen Victoria XXX.

"What? When?" asked Chester A. Arthur XVII.

"You said you'd never bone a god!" shouted a visibly hurt Thor, turning from where he was arguing with the former Finnish deity.

"I said I'd never bone a *thunder* god."

"What the hell do you have against thunder gods?" shouted Ukko.

"Stay the fuck out of this, Ukko!" answered the Norseman.

"Oh, what? Now you have a monopoly on conversations?!"

CHAPTER ONE HUNDRED

Here Comes My Girl

"BILLY," SAID CHESTER A. ARTHUR XVII, waving over William H. Taft XLII. The man-mountain knelt down next to the animatronic moose and leaned in conspiratorially. "I know it may not seem like it, but I think we have the tactical advantage here. If he's been sitting on this beep boop searching thesaurus boop exterior protective or supporting structure instead of using it, there's a good chance his strategies are subpar compared to our —"

"Well, it's not exactly inconspicuous now, is it?" boomed the frozen head of Walt Sidney.

"What?"

"You, uh, you heard that then?" asked William H. Taft XLII.

"He can hear *everything*," said a Louseketeer, his voice dripping with regret and amazement and at least one demotion.

"The cost to run the suit," continued the jarred CEO, "even for a short while, is simply astronomical. Even by my standards. And do you have any idea how long it takes to assemble this thing?" He had the giant, trillion dollar suit perform an extravagant arm wave to show off the exoskeleton's fluid ranges of motion. "We got here two solid hours before you did, just to set up the Sidneytron 5000™. I lost three men assembling the left leg alone."

The cloned presidents looked at Sidney's army — some were standing around, some sitting, some were turning their stun batons on and off, a few lifting up their helmets and picking their noses. The Genghis Khans were playing living mirror. The cloned presidents looked at one another.

"OK, sure, but why —"

"If you're going to go through the trouble of hauling the Sidneytron 5000™ a thousand miles across swamps and fields and ravaged infrastructures then you're damn well going to make it worth the while."

"So ... why aren't you doing that?"

"Well, it does take the suit a while to power up," said the CEO.

"You're stalling."

A number of dim red lights on the right forearm of the exoskeleton flicked to green.

"I was," spat the frozen head of Walt Sidney.

He raised the robot's arm. A series of plates ejected and unfolded from the wrist, sliding forward and forming a seamless, massive cannon around the hand. The mouth of the cannon glowed red, then orange, then white, then, with a deafening blast, fired a laser as wide as Jesus' camper directly into Jesus' camper, turning the camper into a pile of glowing cinder collecting in the bottom of a small crater.

"What the –" said Jesus Christ, roused from his stupor. "That was my house, you dick!"

A dozen smaller lasers exploded from the robot's arching shoulders, followed by twice as many spiked grenades. The armed forces of Walt Sidney stormed forward – the werewolves unshackled, the zombies uncaged, the genocidal leaders unhinged – while everyone on the receiving end scrambled and ran and dove for cover. Bare patches of ground exploded everywhere, generally just inches behind someone's fleeing feet.

Chester A. Arthur XVII, dozens of stormtroopers rushing past and occasionally kicking him, and not used to his tiny stuffed animal legs, almost immediately stumbled and fell directly onto a cactus. Struggling to pull himself free, he rolled onto his back and suddenly found a spiked grenade – like a tiny souvenir baseball bat with nails hammered through it – stabbing into his chest.

"Not again ..."

Chester A. Arthur XVII exploded.

"Motherfucker," grumbled Queen Victoria XXX, shoving Louseketeers to the side and watching as the severed head of her animatronic boyfriend sailed through the air.

"It's OK, Vicky, I'm still –"

Another laser ripped through the air and obliterated what was left of Chester A. Arthur XVII. Queen Victoria XXX looked quickly behind her, toward the cooler strapped to the back of one of the ATVs. Then she pulled her phone from a pouch on her belt and set a timer for thirty minutes.

Fighting through the neverending surge of Louseketeers and dragoons, the cloned monarch jostled her way forward toward where the sizzling, steaming chunks of her boyfriend were falling into the dirt and getting stepped on, pushing and punching and seemingly not getting any closer. People screamed and shouted, things exploded, but her attention was focused on the stuffed moose remains. The queen was on auto-pilot. She blocked an electric stun baton with her arm, then stole it, then started smacking dragoons around with it. She kicked an imp in its tiny testicles. Stepping into a less dense throng of stormtroopers and seeing several assault rifles pointed at her, she quickly grabbed a dragoon, used him as a shield until he turned into an unappealing block of Swiss cheese, then shoved the corpse at the gunmen and rushed past them while they reloaded, stopping only when she was stabbed through the gut by a longsword.

Queen Victoria XXX staggered backward, her hands clutching feebly at the blade. She looked up with surprise.

"I don't think so, lady," said Elizabeth Báthory, driving her sword deeper into the replicated royal. The Attila the Huns, the Genghis Khans, and the four other queens, all of them smiling cruelly, gathered behind the Hungarian countess, a variety of medieval weapons drawn. The dragoons and Louseketeers stopped, looked at one another, and then cleared the hell away.

"No, you *don't* think, do you?" replied the woman with the sword through her stomach.

Queen Victoria XXX punched the former demon in the face. Elizabeth Báthory keeled backward, blood spurting from her nose, releasing her hold on the sword. The cloned monarch pulled the blade from her abdomen.

"I don't have *time* for this!"

The clone swung the bloodied blade, trying to take off the demon's head. Elizabeth Báthory ducked sideways, the sword slicing through some of her hair. Then she pulled a second sword from a sheath on her back. The Hungarian countess swung wildly at Queen

Victoria XXX, accidentally slicing open "Bloody" Mary I's jugular vein – and several other important blood-moving pathways – along the way. Queen Victoria XXX parried the attack with her sword. Mary I put a hand to her neck and dropped to her knees. Mary I LXX scrambled to her side. Queen Victoria XXX and the Hungarian demon took a few more savage swings at on another, then, the weapons locked against one another, the clone kicked a boot into Elizabeth Báthory's midsection.

As Elizabeth Báthory caught her heaving breath, Genghis Khan XII rushed forward, swinging a sickle at Queen Victoria XXX. The dark-haired double stepped to the side, then pulled a knife from her duster and stabbed it into the back of the clone's head. Then, for good measure, she pulled another knife and lodged it in the face of the actual Genghis Khan. The Mongolian emperor fell dead to the ground, toppling like a tree and tripping up Isabella I as she ran toward the copied queen. The Spanish demon fell face-first into the dirt and slid forward until she was resting at the feet of Queen Victoria XXX. The clone stepped on the former Queen of Spain's neck until she heard a crunch and a pop, then picked up the woman's warhammer.

Holding the enormous hammer in one hand and the longsword in the other, Queen Victoria XXX spit a mouthful of blood to the ground. Then she said: "We doing this or what?"

Attila the Hun CXI, the demonized version of Attila the Hun, and Isabella I LII looked at one another, then back at the queen.

"You know what? I'm out," said the actual Attila, tossing his katars to the ground. "The back half of my fee is not worth this kind of trouble."

"You pussy," spat the other Attila.

"Eat me, Xerox."

"What was that?"

"You heard me."

The clone of Attila the Hun reached over and grabbed the demon by his furry lapels. The real king of the Huns immediately head-butted his unlicensed copy in return, knocking a few teeth out and sending him spiraling into the dirt. Then, after shooting the clone a withering scowl, Attila the Hun began shoving and pushing past the crowds of meandering dragoons and Louseketeers, looking around and muttering: "Where the hell's my car?"

As the warlord walked away, Queen Victoria XXX could see the cannon hand of the Sidneytron 5000™ glowing again. There was another deafening boom, and then the ATVs – and the cooler – exploded into microscopic confetti.

"No!" shouted the queen. "You asshole!"

"What?" asked Queen Isabella I LII. "Was your iPod in there or something?"

The thirtieth clone of the last Hanoverian English queen grabbed the fifty-second copy of the genocide-endorsing Spanish queen by her sandy hair and pulled her closer.

"ow ow ow"

"Listen," hissed Queen Victoria XXX, "I'm running out of time. A detachment this big, you've got to have supplies or something, right? Or at least a craft services tent with water and granola bars?"

"Yeah, there's –"

The queen was interrupted by a snarling, spitting Attila the Hun CXI running towards them with an enormous double-bladed battle axe in his furious hands.

"For the love of Raiden. Can you …?" asked Queen Victoria XXX, releasing her hair-hold and motioning for the other queen to step to the side.

Queen Isabella I LII took a few steps to her left. Queen Victoria XXX swung the massive warhammer into the entire side of Attila the Hun CXI's head, crushing his skull like a cracker and sending his corpse spinning back into the dirt.

"So," began the first cloned queen, shouldering the hammer, "about those coolers?"

"Right, they're –"

Queen Isabella I LII was interrupted again, this time by a laser through her brain. A smoking disaster where her head was, she fell to the ground as Queen Victoria XXX, a fine spray of Spanish queen on her face, turned toward the Sidneytron 5000™.

"What is wrong with you?" she shouted.

"Why is no one attacking her?" boomed Walt Sidney. "There are at least three battalions of expendable muscle here. What am I paying you people for?! Beth? Elizabeth? Where the hell are you?"

"Sorry. On it, boss," said Elizabeth Báthory, standing a few hundred feet to the left of the Sidneytron and tossing an empty water bottle to the side.

"Where the hell did you get that?!" shouted Queen Victoria XXX.

The replicated royal dropped the heavy warhammer and took a step toward the freshly-hydrated former demon, only to be grabbed around the ankles by Queen Elizabeth I LXX, lunging from where she was mourning. Queen Victoria XXX fell face-first to the ground, immediately spinning onto her back. She tried to kick her feet free, but the frantic Elizabethan facsimile was clawing at her legs, pulling her closer. Then Queen Elizabeth I LXX reeled back and punched the other monarch in the boob. Queen Victoria XXX kicked her in the face.

"What the *fuck*, lady?" shouted Vicky, her hand on her chest, awkwardly crab-walking backward a few steps.

The Walt Sidney employee screamed incomprehensibly in reply, picking herself up and charging like a bull at Queen Victoria XXX.

"I'm not even the one that killed her! You know that, right?"

Standing unsteadily, her longsword on the ground halfway between her and the other queen bearing down on her, Queen Victoria XXX peripherally saw another volley of lasers and grenades preparing to launch through the air. As Elizabeth I LXX dove forward, the clone kneed her in the throat mid-tackle, and then, grabbing her by the shoulders, heaved her backward. The seventieth clone of Shakespeare's favorite monarch took a laser straight through her armpit, before it exited out the other side of her torso.

"This is exactly why we were never friends," said Queen Victoria XXX, wiping a layer of blood off her face as several grenades exploded all around her. "You don't punch another lady in the boobs."

The dark-skinned clone turned around and was immediately kicked in the chest by Elizabeth Báthory.

"Who taught you people how to fight?!" she shouted, once more coddling her tits. She took a few uncomfortable steps backward and picked up her longsword.

The Hungarian countess stood before her, her own sword drawn. Behind her was a squad of black-clad special ops dragoons. Each one was carrying an officially licensed Lindsey Louse Merry Medieval Murd'rer Morningstar, fashioned from stainless steel, the spiky bits dipped in a variety of fatal poisons. Most of them also had handguns strapped to their waists, while two had flamethrowers hanging off their backs.

"You guys must *really* be scared of me."

"I just want to be thorough," replied Elizabeth Báthory. "I have a performance review coming up."

"Well –" The queen's extremely loud alarm began beeping. She turned to look toward the brains of Chester A. Arthur XVII, then turned again, only to realize she no longer knew where they were.

And in that moment something inside of her broke.

"'Well' what?" taunted the Hungarian countess. "Run out of quippy things to –"

Queen Victoria XXX grabbed Elizabeth Báthory by the throat and lifted her a foot off the ground. Then, while choking her, she used the demon's body to beat the entire squad of armored dragoons to a painful and messy death.

The replicated royal threw the former serial killer's lumpy, disfigured body to the ground. As dust briefly billowed up around the corpse, the clone thought she could see a few hunks of Chester A. Arthur XVII, scuffed up and filthy and useless. Queen Victoria XXX fell to her knees.

CHAPTER ONE HUNDRED AND ONE

You Can Tune a Piano, But You Can't Tuna Fish

CTHULHU, STANDING SILENTLY BESIDE THE SIDNEYTRON 5000™, watched with a dismayed look on his giant, tentacled face as an already-injured William H. Taft XLII, hiding behind a couple of medium-sized rocks and an upturned ATV, was fired upon by dragoon after dragoon after Louseketeer. As a clearly stoned Jesus Christ was being chased around Benny Hill-style by a horde of speed-walking, brain-starved zombies. As a mourning Queen Victoria XXX had a pot of beef stew dumped on her before being pounced upon by a scarred, two-headed, cybernetically-enhanced werewolf.

"No, this isn't right," the eldritch horror muttered. Then, louder, from everywhere at once, "Guys, Vicky, there's a weakness in the –"

Cthulhu was interrupted by a laser the size of a camper in the general area of his face.

"Great, now I'm going to have to wait another fifteen minutes," said Walt Sidney with a sigh, looking forlornly at his smoking cannon hand.

"What the hell was that, boss?" shouted the Elder God.

"I'm not paying you to betray me, C."

"It's Cthulhu, you arrogant prick, and, you know what? You're not paying me enough *not* to betray you."

"The time to bring that up was *before* we got to the battlefield."

"Fuck you. I quit. Eat my transdimensional poop, Walt."

"You can't qu–" began the head inside of the giant, mechanical exoskeleton, before getting sucker-punched across his bulletproofed face by an extradimensional colossus. The Sidneytron 5000™ toppled sideways, onto more than one-hundred-and-eighty-two dragoons.

Cthulhu stared down at the rest of the stormtroopers, driving at least half of them into a full-on, gibbering madness with his mere gaze.

The loss of more than sixty percent of their handlers was more than enough of a distraction to break the non-human ranks. The werewolves turned on their captors. The imps started demonically humping every leg in sight, armored or otherwise. The feral zombies splintered apart, leaving Jesus be as they chowed down on a buffet of helpless Louseketeers and dragoons.

As chaos swiftly took over, a few of the shuffling dead began clawing and biting at the otherworldly toes of Cthulhu. The interdimensional god furrowed his lizardy brow and stomped down on them like cockroaches, causing a minor earthquake in the process and ruining card houses for hundreds of miles. Then the dragon-squid lifted his foot into the air and began shaking it.

"Ew," he said, shrinking down to a more manageable size and trundling away, dragging his clawed foot against the ground.

"The weakness!" shouted William H. Taft XLII, holding his good hand on the head of an imp with a knife. Somewhere on his left, an explosion exploded all explosion-like and suddenly Queen Victoria XXX came rocketing through the air above him. The cloned president turned after her, but then, hearing the high-pitched whir of high-end servos, he turned back and watched hopelessly as the Sidneytron 5000™ began picking itself back up. Slumping his shoulders, the former mayor-king muttered: "What about the weakness?"

"Give it up," said a dead-eyed Queen Victoria XXX, slowly getting up from where she had landed. She shook her head and watched the titanic eldritch terror disappear into the distance. "He's very temperamental," she explained, dusting off her duster.

"Well, this still gives us a better chance, right?" asked Thor, rising from underneath a nearby pile of dead and maimed Louseketeers, corpses sliding off of him like Hi-C off a freshly waxed car.

"What were you doing under there?" asked the queen, emptying stew meat from her pockets.

"Hiding from Ukko," explained the thunder god, stripping off his soiled hoodie and standing before her in a sweat-stained tank top. "He spent twenty minutes hitting me with a hammer, then things got all spinny so I fell down and pretended to be dead. Next thing I know there's a bunch of bodies on top of me."

"Was the spinning from the drinking or the hitting?"

"Honestly, I don't know. Which, speaking of, does anyone know where Mjolnir is?"

"Can't you just Jedi it with your brain?" asked William H. Taft XLII, raising an eyebrow at Thor while simultaneously – and awkwardly – snapping the imp's neck.

"Not without my gauntlets."

"You mean the bracelets you've been wearing since we met you?"

"Oh, right." Thor held out his hand and Mjolnir, his magic hammer, flew, unscathed, from the ash heap of Jesus Christ's trailer, through a crowd of Louseketeers and dragoons fighting off an atomic werewolf – literally through them – and squished into his hand, dripping with a hodgepodge of innards.

"Right, so, like," began a winded Jesus, stopping next to the group and hanging his head, his hands on his knees, "what d'we do now?"

"We should ask Charlie," said Thor, looking around. "Where is Charlie? Vicky, you know where he –"

"Dead," said Queen Victoria XXX, shaking, holding back tears and a scream that would terrify a Bengal tiger, despondent and furious and heartbroken and lost and homicidal and kind of hungry, all at once.

"What do you –"

"Dead." This time there was a lot more of the furious and homicidal in her voice.

"OK. Sorry," said Thor softly. Then: "Does this mean that I can be in charge now?"

"No."

"No."

"Not a chance, brother."

"But I've got a really good plan," whined the thunder god. "Come on, guys …"

William H. Taft XLII sighed. "OK, fine, what's your plan, Thor?"

"Take down the guy with the murder ray?"

William H. Taft XLII looked around at the scattered army of Walt Sidney employees surrounding them. Those that weren't fending off tortured monsters, or already dead, were busy fighting with each other, or crying, or curled up in the fetal position. A few appeared to be slowly and deliberately pooping themselves. A handful looked like maybe they were thinking about continuing the assault against the clones and the god and the son of a god, but then they had noticed all the horrible wounds and second-degree burns that the clones and religious icons didn't seem to be noticing, and were deciding that maybe it would be better to give up entirely and find new jobs.

Walt Sidney, meanwhile, waiting for his weapons to come back online, looked angrily down at his army, occasionally barking commands or threatening to fire someone, but mostly just scowling with disappointment.

"Seems like a good a time as any," said the cloned president with a shrug. "Knock yourself out."

Storm clouds oozed across the lime green sky like spilled bacon fat into a paper towel. A skyscraper of electricity lit up across the heavens and then collapsed into the Sidneytron 5000™. Nothing happened. Thor knit his brow and tried again, dropping several more buildings of lightning on top of the CEO. Still, the robot suit kept functioning. Walt Sidney, inside the exoskeleton and still trying to remuster his troops, didn't even seem to notice.

"Huh," said William H. Taft XLII.

"Oh, wait, I've got another idea," said Thor, snapping his fingers. "He's a robot, right? Robots hate water." Before he'd even finished talking, a squall of biblical proportions erupted from the gathered storm clouds. Even more immediately, the downpour stopped.

"What the shit ...?" began the thunder god, squinting up at the receding clouds.

"God of Storms too, remember?" said Ukko Jumala, throwing off a crazed dragoon or two as he marched toward the Norseman.

"By the balls of Loki," muttered Thor. "I thought you went home!" Then, hammer raised, he charged at the other deity.

"Bigger picture, Thor!" shouted William H. Taft XLII, watching as their best hope at stopping the massive, getting-more-murdery-by-the-minute Sidneytron 5000™ got into a hammer fight with a Finnish god.

"Don't worry, brother," said Jesus, putting a tie-dye-clad arm on the president's back, "I got this."

Waving his hands like a vaudeville magician, Jesus Christ turned one of the exoskeleton's nano-diamond plastic arms into an enormous grouper. The cold-blooded aquatic invertebrate fell thunderously to the ground, where it flopped and flipped and gasped and knocked over a few stormtroopers. Above the fish, almost as if Walt Sidney had been expecting this kind of thing to happen, another robotic arm unfolded from inside the exoskeleton.

"Holy mackerel," said Jesus, grinning at his own joke.

Queen Victoria XXX, covered in stew and burns and a lot of other people's blood and generally not having a very good day, slapped the Son of God across the face.

"No."

"Wha–"

"*No.*"

CHAPTER ONE HUNDRED AND TWO

We're Havin' a Party

AMEN-RA AND TED TURNER, HIDING BEHIND A LARGE and conveniently placed purple sage bush on the far side of the field, stage-right of the burning vehicles, watched as the righted and recharged Sidneytron 5000™ released another volley of technological death on Jesus Christ and the clones, all kinds of things exploding behind them as they ran, while Ukko and Thor danced and tumbled across the dried-out grass, raining hammer blow after hammer blow on one another. In the distance, several more platoons of reinforcement Louseketeers were running to join the fray, while those already in the fray were slowly returning to a less insane state of being.

Ted Turner took a deep breath. "We doing this?" he asked.

"Let us," said Ra, cracking his knuckles, the sun visibly flaring behind him. "With reckless abandon."

"All right," said the media mogul, "but I'm going to need a minute." He ducked away from the shrub to go and gear up.

The Egyptian god, meanwhile, stepped forward dramatically from his hiding place – fists clenched, chin slightly raised, a sneer worthy of song upon his face – just in time to see a trio of arrows come tearing across the sky, stabbing through the bulletproof shielding of the Sidneytron 5000™ and lodging themselves firmly into the jar holding Walt Sidney's frozen head. The surgically-sharp tip of the third arrow was millimeters from the CEO's eyeball.

"What is this?" barked Walt Sidney, shaking the robotic head like a windshield wiper on High. "What's going on?"

"You, uh, you got an arrow in your face," said a dragoon. "Sir."

"Why is there in arrow in my face?!"

"Nobody ever bothers to make things arrow-proof," mumbled a disappointed Artemis, shaking her head and striding up beside Ra.

The creator of everything turned to find the former Greek Goddess of the Hunt and the sixty-ninth clone of Catherine the Great standing next to him, armed to the teeth and ready to rumble.

"You just ditched us, you asshole," said the cloned empress, shoving Ra backward into the purple sage.

"I did not 'ditch' you," explained the bald Egyptian man, climbing out of the plant. "I simply did not think you were any longer invested in this endeavor."

"Not invested?! What the hell do you think I left Russia for, dick?"

"Lots of reasons, if we're being honest …"

"Well, OK, yeah."

"You kept having sex in the back seat and then, as a steam-powered war machine approached, you ran off entirely and threw your underthings at me."

"Yeah, but that ended up being Ted Turner, right?" said Artemis, nodding toward the elderly man in long johns behind her. "So no harm, no foul?"

"You did not know that was Ted Turner," rumbled Ra. "For all intents and purposes, you left me to face an unknown threat alone."

"You weren't *alone* alone. You had Set."

"Wait, Set *was* there? Where is he now?"

"This is because we're ladies, isn't it?" said Catherine the Great XLIX, shoving the Egyptian god again.

"No, of course not," replied Ra defensively. "Given the circumstances, I merely thought you had given up on our mutual quest for vengeance."

"We *can* do two things at once, you know," said Artemis, glaring at him like a frustrated professor.

"Like drive and get head," explained the cloned Russian empress.

"Or drive and *give* head."

"That sounds extremely dangerous, young lady," boomed the Egyptian god.

"That was weird … you sounded exactly like Zeus right there."

"Who's giving head?" asked Thor, turning and looking into the shrubbery, distracted long enough from his hammer fight to take the heavy side of Ukonvasara right in his ear. The Norse thunder god went sailing backward, through the sage bush and into a lubed and jumpsuited Ted Turner, the two of them rolling a few dozen feet farther, past a staggering, sleepy-eyed Set.

"Are we there yet?" asked the dog-man, rubbing his face. "Who were those guys?" He pointed toward Thor and Ted Turner with his thumb. "And what's the giant robot doing here?"

"Set!" said Ra, running over and embracing his great-grandson. "You are here! I thought maybe I was hallucinating you."

"What?"

"I'm so sorry I left you behind."

"Behind? I've been asleep in the backseat of the SUV. Seriously, what's going on?" He nodded toward the dried-out prairie in front of them. "There are just dead people everywhere out there."

"I vote the old guy's not in charge anymore," said Catherine the Great LXIX.

"I may be OK with that," said Ra, holding Set by the shoulders and looking at him both lovingly and suspiciously.

"What the hell is going on back there?" boomed Sidney from the far side of the field. "Why is that plant shaking and talking? Somebody go look into that."

"Oh, right," said Catherine the Great LXIX, looking to the Sidneytron 5000™, "this bunghole." She slid on a pair of brass knuckles, then pulled a short falchion sword from the sheath on her back. "We doing this?"

CHAPTER ONE HUNDRED AND THREE

Squad Goals

ARTEMIS AND QUEEN VICTORIA XXX, HAVING QUICKLY become fast friends, were rapidly being swarmed by an entire platoon of brisk-moving black-armored dragoons and were promptly kicking their asses, hastily trying to keep up with demand. Unfortunately, there were a *lot* of dragoons and the women were swiftly falling behind. Thor and Ukko, meanwhile, had grown tired of chasing one another around, so the two thunder gods were now standing stock still in an open patch of grassland, taking turns hitting one another in the face with their magic hammers. Everyone else – Amen-Ra, Set, Catherine the Great LXIX, William H. Taft XLII, and Jesus Christ – was gathered behind the quite possibly enchanted purple sage bush, trying to come up with a plan, while the rest of Walt Sidney's army tried and failed to find them.

"Right, so, I guess," began William H. Taft XLII, doing his best impression of Chester A. Arthur XVII, "someone superpowered should probably go help Thor. That other thunder god is probably our biggest threat, outside of Walt Sidney."

"On it," said Set, nodding his furry head. "I've been waiting for an excuse. I don't know if you guys noticed, but Ukko's kind of a dick. He was always making fun of me at lunch for putting mustard on my hot dogs. Like, way harder than you should make fun of someone about hot dogs, too."

"Who doesn't use mustard?" asked Catherine the Great LXIX.

"Right?"

"Kick his foolish ass, boy," thundered Ra.

"Thanks, great-gramps," replied the Egyptian God of Disorder and Violence, before turning and stalking towards the blonde men.

"OK, so that's done," said the corpulent clone, peering out past the plant. "I have no idea how we're going to fight that robot, though."

"Ted has that covered," explained Ra. Then, turning and shooting the struggling media mogul a look, he said: "It's just taking a while."

"Why don't you go see if he needs help?"

"That sounds agreeable."

And off Ra went.

"So, that just leaves the three of us," said William H. Taft XLII, clapping a hand on the back of Catherine the Great LXIX and nodding toward Jesus Christ, "and the entire rest of Walt Sidney's army."

"I like those odds," replied the cloned empress, hopping up and down. "I haven't fucked anybody up in a while and I'm getting antsy."

"Yeah, I've still got a good amount of anger I've got to work through," seconded the cloned president, balling up one of his fists and sort of weirdly clenching the other.

"What?" asked the Christian messiah, cocking an eyebrow. "What the fuck is wrong with you guys, man? Why do you keep wanting to fight, like, all the time?"

"Genetics."

"We are literally programmed to be this way."

"Oh," replied Jesus.

"Why?" said Catherine the Great LXIX. "You have a better idea?"

"You better believe it, sister."

CHAPTER ONE HUNDRED AND FOUR

Thunder Cats

"UKKKOOOOOO!" ROARED SET, SPRINGING FORWARD and tackling Thor knees first. The gods slammed into the ground, sliding several dusty feet, until Thor's back collided with a prickly pear.

"Why the fuck are these things just laying around?!" shouted the Norseman, twisting uncomfortably atop the cactus.

"Wrong one, Set!" shouted William H. Taft XLII as he hustled past the gods toward another appointment. "That one's on our side!"

"Oh," said Set, looking between the blonde man he was kneeling on and the blonde man coming toward him with a hammer. "Sorry. There was a lot of sun and, honestly, you guys look super the same."

"We are nothing alike!" shouted Thor and Ukko simultaneously. Thor shoved Set to the side and the two thunder gods began thundering it out again.

As they fought, someone, or possibly a couple of someones, exploded off to the gods' side, blood and guts and pieces of armor raining down over them. The hammering ceased as the three deities covered up from the incoming mess, Ukko taking the brunt of it.

"God damn it," said the Finnish thunder god, throwing down his arms and shaking off a motley assortment of pulverized organs.

"Which god?" asked Set.

"Suonetar," he answered, peeling off his canvas work shirt.

"Oh, OK."

Ukko tossed his shirt to the side. The bearded blonde man was now standing before the other two gods wearing a white tank top and khaki-colored khakis. Thor, meanwhile, was also in a white tank top, with khaki-colored cargos. For some reason, they had also both lost their shoes at some point.

"What in the swollen gonads of Jörmungandr do you think you're doing?" asked Thor.

"What?" replied Ukko.

"The shirt, man. Your whole outfit."

"For fucking real, Thor?" countered the thunder god. "A solid nine-tenths of the office wears khakis, and I'm pretty sure that everyone in the world wears a white undershirt."

"Prove it!"

"Prove it? Prove that everyone in the world wears a white undershirt? How hard did I hit you?"

"I don't know," answered the thunder god sincerely. "I really could not feel a lot of it."

"What're you, high?"

"Yes."

"Oooooohhh."

"Oh what?"

"Well, nothing, it just … knowing that, now beating you senseless almost feels like cheating, y'know?"

"So you'll stop hitting me?"

"No, of course not," explained Ukko, hefting his hammer onto his shoulder. "I said 'almost.'"

"Well, you can't say I didn't give you an out," replied Thor, lowering his eyes. Lifting Mjolnir into the air, the Norse God of Thunder called down a tremendous amount of lightning into the hammerhead and then clobbered Ukko with the electrified weapon, sending him sprawling to the ground.

"So we're doing this now?" said the Finnish God of Thunder, shaking his head and sitting up. "If that's how you want it." A thunderbolt like a convoy of semis crashed headfirst into Thor, knocking him to his knees.

"Oh, you dick."

"Yeah? What're you gonna –"

Lightning ripped through the sky and straight through Ukko.

"You cow-fucker!"

"Who told you?!"

Another thunderbolt came tearing down, right into Thor's crotch.

"That was a low blow," whined the Norseman, pressing his hands between his thighs.

"So's your mom."

"You corn-riddled piece of shit!"

The two gods, sitting across from one another in the dirt, continued calling one another names and throwing lightning back and forth a few more times, before, suddenly and unexpectedly, the lightning dried up and the storm clouds receded.

"Was ... was that ...?" began Thor, looking confusedly at the sky.

"No," replied Ukko, doing the same. "Did you?"

"No."

"That was me, guys," explained Set, crossing his arms over his chest. "I'm also a god of storms."

"Are you fucking serious?" said Ukko. "Is everyone just a thunder god now? Is that how we're playing this?"

"Actually, man, I was talking with Jesus," began Thor, "and there's ... well, there's a good chance we're all —"

There was a tremendous sound, everything went white, and then Ukko, the Finnish God of Thunder, was obliterated.

"Whoa," said Set.

"Nevermind then," said the Norse God of Thunder, staring at the smoking crater that used to be Ukko.

"That was Thor, right?" asked Walt Sidney, peering through his arrow-pierced enclosure, his arm cannon raised into the air, strangely-colored smoke twisting into the sky.

"Uh, yeah, totally. Boss," lied the thunder god.

"OK, good. You guys looked so much alike I wasn't sure."

CHAPTER ONE HUNDRED AND FIVE

Prince of Peace

WILLIAM H. TAFT XLII, ALONG WITH JESUS CHRIST and Catherine the Great LXIX, walked out toward the head of what was left of Walt Sidney's amassed army, which was still kind of a shitload of soldiers. The dragoon at the head of the horde – a red stripe down his helmet and deep scratches across his armor – unsure of what was going on, held up a hand, stopping the stormtroopers where they stood. Jesus Christ, sort of on his tip-toes, crept unstealthily to the side of the armored people trying to kill him, grabbed a cooler from their supply tent, and then dragged it over in front of the cloned president.

William H. Taft XLII, stepping onto the cooler and cupping a hand over his mouth, said: "Look. None of us wants to be here. I'm sure that's a given. You're just trying to collect a paycheck, and I get that. But, as I'm sure you are all also well aware, we, the three of us here and the two ladies over there –" The president pointed toward Queen Victoria XXX and Artemis, mid-ravaging of the army's coworkers. "– are almost certainly going to dismember you, with extraordinary violence and speed, or we may set some of you on fire. Or your own boss might blow you up. I don't know. What I do know is, your death benefits can't possibly be worth the trouble and heartache to your families and friends, and –"

"Actually," said a Louseketeer, raising his hand timidly, "they're, uh, they're pretty great. The benefits are why I was willing to put on the armor in the first place. They make the paycheck we get look like the allowance of a crappy child with strict parents."

"Like, how much are we talking, man?" asked Jesus.

"My wife and kids – hell, my grandkids – could retire to a brand new mansion, in the heart of New Hollywood, and never have to work another day in their lives," said the armored employee.

"My husband actually hopes that I die out here," said another Louseketeer. "For the money."

"That seems *really* shitty," said Catherine the Great LXIX.

"He's ... he's not a great guy," he replied. "That's kind of why I'm willing to be out here and away from home so much."

"That's terrible, brother," said Jesus.

"Yeah ..."

"OK, so," began William H. Taft XLII from his cooler, "trying to speak to your wants and needs collectively was probably a bad idea. You're all beautiful butterflies –"

"I am," said a dragoon having an epiphany.

"– and here for your own individual reasons. But, back to the point, if those reasons don't actively involve dying painfully, please put down your weapons and go home."

"We don't want to fight you guys," added Jesus.

"But we absolutely, totally will," said the cloned empress, "if you want us to. And you absolutely, totally will lose that fight and, quite possibly, a limb or two in the process. Definitely at least a finger."

"So, you know, think that over," said William H. Taft XLII. "Pass the word to the guys in the back, I don't think they heard us. And, for what it's worth, if you're worried about your boss's retribution or punishment or whatever, we have every reason to believe Walt Sidney won't be making it out of this fight alive, so, there's that."

The crowd of battle-wearied Louseketeers and special ops dragoons began murmuring and mumbling, heads turning, helmets lifting, chins being scratched. A few had already begun walking away.

"But, again," said Catherine the Great LXIX, slightly desperately, the army becoming less homicidal before her very eyes, "if you are here for the violence, we're OK with that too."

"But, like, also again," added Jesus, "if that is the case, we are going to have to assume you're, like, one-hundred-percent evil, right? So that way if we kill you we won't feel terrible about it."

"*When* we kill you," corrected the cloned empress. "I cannot be more clear about that."

CHAPTER ONE HUNDRED AND SIX

How Artemis Got Her Groove Back

SET AND ARTEMIS AND THOR AND JESUS CHRIST and Catherine the Great LXIX and Queen Victoria XXX and William H. Taft XLII were getting their asses kicked. Jesus literally.

"There were a lot more assholes in that group than I figured on, man," said the Son of God, rubbing his butt with both hands.

"Well, look, you tried," said Catherine the Great LXIX, hopping around on one leg. Her other foot was on the chest of a dragoon, while her hands were wrapped around his elbow, trying to tear his arm out of its socket. The dragoon, meanwhile, was punching her repeatedly in the ribs. "That counts."

"That's of less comfort than I had hoped for."

Jesus got kicked in the rear again. He turned around and was immediately clocked by a Louseketeer. Thor stepped over and punched his friend's assailant, sending the riot trooper rocketing backwards into three other stormtroopers. Six more took their place.

"How the hell were you making more than me when we were hero-for-hiring?" asked the thunder god, holding off the frenzied Louseketeers as they attempted to club him in the head.

"You'd be amazed at what you can talk your way out of, brother," explained Jesus. "Plus, you know, I'll fight if I have to, man. Learned that one the hard way." The Prince of Peace turned a few helmets into record-breakingly-sized carp. The soldiers, their heads now very familiar with the innards of a freshwater fish, began stumbling around, smacking the sides of the carp, trying to lift it off, before eventually running out of air, losing consciousness, and falling to the ground. "I just don't like doing it."

"I thought we decided you went super-saiyan," said William H. Taft XLII, backing up and wrestling a stun baton free from a Louseketeer. "Shouldn't you be, you know, *better* than this?"

"I will be honest," said Thor, ripping the forearm gauntlet off a dragoon and whaling him in the face with it, "I'm still a little spent from wrecking up toy stores and hammer-fighting Ukko. And we're both a little drunk."

"A lot drunk," burped Jesus. "And a little high."

"A lot high," corrected Thor.

"Seriously?" The cloned president grimaced as he took a knife in his already wounded shoulder. "The hours of fighting haven't sobered you up any?"

"Well, they did ..."

"But then ..."

"And, yet again, you didn't invite me?" asked Queen Victoria XXX, lifting up the helmet on a set of dragoon armor she had stolen. "You selfish pricks."

"How long have you been wearing that?" asked the president.

"It's not our fault, Vicky," explained Jesus.

"We were fighting a werewolf and he threw us into a cooler full of champagne," added the thunder god.

"We were saving that!" shouted a dragoon. Thor punched her.

"And then, like, while we were drinking it –"

"Because a bunch of the bottles had opened and we didn't want it all to go to waste," added Thor.

"– I found more weed in my pocket."

"If you two were sober this would probably be over by now," grumbled William H. Taft XLII.

"Oh, I highly doubt that," said Walt Sidney, firing his extraterrestrially-powered cannon into their midst. The heroes dove to the side as a dozen stormtroopers were vaporized.

"Damn it," said the frozen head, pulling a face.

"Wait, I want to go back to this super-saiyan thing ..." said Artemis, picking herself up. "I don't know what the hell a saiyan is, but the super part ... what exactly were you talking about?"

"There's two levels of godding," explained Thor, kicking a Louseketeer into the smoking crater. "The first one, where you can do some of your stuff and take a lot of abuse –"

As if on cue, the Greek goddess was elbowed in the nose. She grabbed the man responsible, twisted his arm behind his back, and then snapped the dragoon's wrist in several places. Then she tossed him into the crater too.

"Right, OK …" she said.

"– and then, when you really hit your old-school groove, there's the next level, where you get everything back."

"Everything?"

The thunder god smiled as lightning zipped down the sky like a hooded jacket in the springtime, then split and snaked through the crowd around Thor, electrocuting a hundred and twenty stormtroopers, but precisely zero of his friends. Seeing a clearing, a baker's dozen of dragoons on the opposite side of the crater unslung their rifles and opened fire on the blonde man, the bullets bouncing off Thor's chest like spitballs.

"Everything," he said.

The barefoot Norseman chucked his hammer across the crater, taking out the gunmen like bowling pins.

"Well, I want to do that," said Artemis, watching as the Norseman's hammer returned to him. Then, "So, uh, how exactly do I …? Do that?"

"Well, what was your, you know, *thing*?" asked Thor, approaching the goddess as more of Sidney's army approached them.

"Women's rights, treating animals with respect …"

"Well, Sidney's probably a dick about that stuff, right?"

"Hey," boomed Walt Sidney from his giant robot. "That's not fair. I take workplace equality extremely seriously."

"Oh, blow it out your –"

"Actually, he really is pretty great," said a lady Louseketeer wrestling with Catherine the Great LXIX. "On-site day care, extended maternity leave, equal pay and promotion opportunities. The Walt Sidney Company and its subsidiaries are consistently rated a great workplace for women."

"Shit," said Thor.

"Well, there's the animals then, right?" suggested Jesus, turning a trio of truncheons into trout. "Look at those guys –" He pointed toward a scarred, chemically-altered werewolf, broken shackles hanging from its wrists. "– there's no way that's on the level, sister."

"Actually ..." said another dragoon. The armored adversary nodded back toward the nearing werewolf. The creature stopped and, throwing back its head, howled with murder and fury and, unmistakably, glee.

"Oh, no way, man ... they actually like being experimented on?"

"Sorry." Then the dragoon punched Jesus across the teeth.

"If it helps," shouted Catherine the Great LXIX from behind the goddess, "I'm a woman and I'm being severely mistreated right now."

Artemis turned to find three imps crawling all over her friend, like kindergarteners on Arnold Schwarzenegger. The goddess fired an arrow straight through each of their eyeballs.

"That didn't do anything. Can you get in more trouble?"

The clone was shot in the shoulder.

"Shouldn't be a problem," she said, wincing.

"Wasn't hunting your thing too?" asked Queen Victoria XXX, tossing her helmet into the face of an advancing zombie.

"Yeah, but I don't see how –"

"Close your eyes."

"What?"

"Seriously."

"All right ..." Artemis closed her eyes. While she wasn't looking, the cloned queen grabbed a white-armored Louseketeer by the neck and scrawled a big ol' X on his helmet with her bleeding palm. Then she told him to run. The Louseketeer did not need to be asked twice.

"OK, open your eyes."

Artemis opened her eyes. "I don't see anything." She began scanning the crowd, looking for anything out of the ordinary. "What exactly did you do?"

"Somewhere in this crowd," began Queen Victoria XXX, "is a terrible young man with a red X painted on his helmet. See if you –"

"Found him."

Immediately, the Greek Goddess of the Hunt pulled an arrow from her quiver and fired it through the teeming crowd, sailing the pointed projectile past countless suits of armor and zombies and werewolves, without so much as nicking a shoulder or wobbling a millimeter off course. The arrowhead planted itself dead center in the X, exactly as the man turned his head to face her, dropping the Louseketeer to his back and sending him skidding through the dirt.

"Oh," said a very surprised Artemis, "I feel … tingly."

"Downstairs, right?" said Thor.

"Yeah."

"Then I think you've figured out your thing."

Artemis, smiling broadly and trying not to jump up and down with joy, closed her eyes. "Do it again, Vicky."

CHAPTER ONE HUNDRED AND SEVEN

I Am Iron Man

FROM HIGH ATOP THE SIDNEYTRON 5000™, as he waited once again for his weapons to recharge, the frozen head of Walt Sidney saw the tide seemingly turning in his opponents' favor. Thor was electrocuting vast swaths of stormtroopers a single thunderbolt at a time. Artemis was hunting down his scientifically-enhanced werewolves while blindfolded. The heavyset empress dual-wielding swords and the dark-haired queen wearing his dragoon's armor and the massive man-mountain with the cudgel had apparently turned into horror-movie villains. Jesus Christ appeared to be selling marijuana to some of Sidney's employees in exchange for their treason. And Set, meanwhile, well, Set was living up to his title.

"Set? Set!" called the jarred CEO. "What the hell are you doing? Elizabeth said you were dead."

"Well, Walt, it looks like she lied." The Egyptian God of Violence dug his claws through the armor of a Louseketeer, disemboweling the woman where she stood.

"Fine," said the cryogenically preserved head, looking once again at the two women who also were not killed by Elizabeth Báthory. "But why are you on their side? Did you hit your head?"

"Why are you asking about that now? You didn't see me fighting Ukko before?"

"I thought that was a small werewolf."

"Benedict Cumberbatch, Walt."

"Do you have any idea how hard it is for me to see from up here, Set? Nevermind the arrows, I'm wearing glasses in a tank full of cloudy liquid. I'm lucky I know what any of you people look like when I'm sitting across a desk from you."

"Sorry …?" replied a confused Set.

"I'm not looking for sympathy," rumbled Walt Sidney.

"Then what are you looking for? In case you hadn't noticed –" The dog-man tore out a dragoon's throat. "– I'm kind of in the middle of some stuff."

"What I'm looking for, Set, is your letter of resignation."

"What? Are you fucking serious?"

"Do you want your severance package or not?"

"Honestly, boss …" A Louseketeer came at the Egyptian god with a machete. Set sidestepped the blade and ripped out the soldier's spine. "I'm pretty good without it right now."

"This is incredibly unprofessional, Set."

Set, blushing in as pronounced a manner as a massive, furry dog-man could, explained: "Look, Mr. Sidney, there were extenuating circumstances. One of the gods you had me hunt down with Beth was Amen-Ra and, I mean, he's the creator of the universe *and* my great-grandfather. That's very clearly a conflict of interests, boss. I wasn't *not* going to follow him here. A lot of this is on you."

"Ra's not dead either?!" boomed Walt Sidney. "So *nobody* died in that explosion where everyone was supposed to be dead?" He paused. Then, sadly, shaking his jarred head, "I had so much faith in Beth …"

"That is because you're an idiot, Sidney," thundered Amen-Ra, former Egyptian God-King, stepping out from behind the magic purple sage bush and clotheslining a zombie.

"Next time," mumbled the frozen head, the lights on the cannon changing color, "I'm hiring nothing but atheists." Walt Sidney fired his giant murder laser at Set. The laser hit, but not nearly with the force he intended. The Egyptian god looked down at his smoking, slightly singed stomach confusedly.

"What the hell?" Walt Sidney lifted his robotic cannon-hand and looked at it quizzically.

"Solar flares, Walt," said Ted Turner, smiling as he stepped out from behind the sage, piloting his own giant robot, transformed from his war machine. "You never did take the environment seriously."

"Ted?!?

CHAPTER ONE HUNDRED AND EIGHT

Robot Fight

TED TURNER SPRINTED ACROSS THE TRAMPLED FIELD toward the Sidneytron 5000™, his mechanical exoskeleton – less autonomous than Sidney's, functioning more as an extension of Ted Turner's own body – a huge, honkin', steam-powered pile of spikes and sharp edges and repurposed steel. The converted war machine wasn't as big as Walt Sidney's exoskeleton, or as pretty, but it was faster, and more nimble, and, more importantly, the Turner Eco-Suit was completely unaffected by the solar flares Ra was calling forth from the sun.

The TES leapt toward the Sidneytron 5000™. Walt Sidney's alien exoskeleton took a careful step forward and then backhanded Ted Turner's robot across the face.

"So that thing *can* move," said William H. Taft XLII.

The TES reeled backward for a moment, then, locking its legs into the dirt and twisting back-and-forth at the waist like a power-walker, the machine drove fists like meat tenderizers into Sidney's plastic torso over and over again. The Sidneytron 5000™ farted out laser dust from its shoulder-guns and vomited out a chunky rain of spikey grenades onto the TES. Ted Turner raised a highly illegal piece of ordinance from his back and fired a laser directly into Walt Sidney's face.

"This is so fucking awesome," said Thor, throwing a Louseketeer to the side and sitting down on top of a fallen dragoon to watch.

CHAPTER ONE HUNDRED AND NINE
Half Baked

THE TURNER ECO-SUIT CAUGHT THE ILL-PROPORTIONED LEG of the Sidneytron 5000™ and flipped the enormous plastic behemoth onto its back. Then Ted Turner extended a serrated blade the size of a large sedan from the back of his hand and pounced on Walt Sidney. The Sidneytron 5000™, rocking like a turtle with terrible luck, did the same, swinging a gleaming ceramic sword through the side of the TES and unleashing a cloud of steam into the air. Ted Turner screamed furiously and unloaded all twelve of his guns into Walt Sidney's robotic face.

"Shouldn't we keep –" began William H. Taft XLII, walking over to his friends and covered in fresh blood, an assembly of armored assholes still marauding behind him.

"*Shhhhhhhhh*," hissed Queen Victoria XXX, passing the glowing joint back to Jesus.

CHAPTER ONE HUNDRED AND TEN

Let's Use Teamwork!

THE ROBOT FIGHT CONTINUED AS IT HAD FOR THE LAST HOUR, the sounds of burning ozone and cracking plastic and rending steel drifting into the background like the white noise of a satellite radio left on after a high atmosphere EMP. Somewhere along the line, the last of the Louseketeers and dragoons had simply shrugged and given up, and now everyone on both sides of the fight was sitting on the sidelines surrounding the warring exoskeletons, catching their breath and stitching up their wounds.

Most of Sidney's former employees had stripped into their underthings, as Ra had briefly increased the intensity of the sun ninefold to dry up the zombies and give heat stroke to the armored stormtroopers that had remained loyal to the Walt Sidney Company. Queen Victoria XXX sat with some of the Louseketeers, smoking the last of the holy weed and thoroughly entranced by the battling 'bots. Set was curled up at Ra's feet, taking a well-earned nap. William H. Taft XLII and Catherine the Great LXIX were raiding the Louseketeers' first-aid tent. And Artemis was popping popcorn over the smoldering ashtray of Jesus' camper.

"This is the perfect temperature," she explained to the former dragoons sitting nearby, shaking the chestplate she was using as a makeshift pan. "You want a nice even heat, not a lot of flames changing direction all the time. You'll never burn a kernel."

"Hey, Ra?" called Ted Turner, his suit picking itself up from the dusty ground, laser holes smoking across the front and side of his robotic exoskeleton. "Buddy?"

"Oh, right ..." said Ra through a mouthful of popcorn. He absentmindedly raised a hand and called forth more solar flares.

"Isn't that gonna fuck up Turner?" asked William H. Taft XLII, walking over with an arm and sling full of Band-Aids and gauze.

"No, he's built dampers into his robot."

"What about the rest of the world?" asked one of the dragoons.

Ra shrugged.

"Oh, come on, man," said the dead president. "We *just* fixed the continental grid."

"Six months ago just," said Queen Victoria XXX.

"Yeah, but how many times a year do you really want to repair a continent-spanning electrical grid?"

"It's highly localized," said the sun god, "I promise."

As they were talking, the Sidneytron 5000™ lumbered up behind the TES, raising both of its massive arms into the air. Walt Sidney brought them down like a crashing satellite, Ted Turner falling out of the way before the arms slammed into the ground and rocketed up all kinds of dirt and dust and small cacti. The Sidneytron 5000™, standing back up, clumsily turned back and forth, waving an arm and trying to look through the cloud now surrounding it. The TES – equipped with heat, electromagnetic, and homicidal douchebag sensors – sprang forward and tackled the other robot by what passed for a waist.

Just then, Thor Odinson and Jesus Christ returned from behind another conveniently placed purple sage, zipping up their flies.

"Did you guys pee together?" asked Queen Victoria XXX.

"It's only weird if you make it weird," said Jesus.

"Anyway, we broke the seal," added Thor, "we're feeling a lot better now. Do they still need our help?"

Walt Sidney walloped Ted Turner with both hands, sending the reinforced cage surrounding his head spiraling around like an astronaut training module.

"Yes, please," shouted the former media mogul.

"You got it then." Tearing off his undershirt and stepping forward dramatically, the wind blowing back his golden mane, Thor was immediately shot in the face by a laser.

"That'll wake you up," said the thunder god, shaking his head.

A few more lasers fired recklessly into the crowd, perforating a couple of Louseketeers and taking off Catherine the Great LXIX's hand at the wrist.

"MOTHERFUCKER!" she shouted, pulling the cauterized stump to her chest, the irony of dropping her much-needed medical supplies in the action completely lost on her.

The sky suddenly resembling a thick stew, thunderbolts burped forth and wove bibulously through the air, down the aluminum shafts of the arrows sticking out of the plastic robot's head and into Walt Sidney's jar. Jesus started turning smaller parts of the exoskeleton into fishsticks and wine bottles. Enough to mildly incapacitate the mech-suit, but not set off its replacement protocol.

"I thought you said you guys were sober," groaned Catherine the Great LXIX.

"Sobererer," replied Jesus.

"You A.D. amateurs," scoffed Artemis, the Greek Goddess of the Wild, glowing slightly and shaking her resplendent head of hair. In a single movement, she grabbed her bow from the ground and fired an arrow into the exoskeleton, the projectile tearing through the plastic and rubber like paper and pushing out the main joint support of the shoulder. The entire weight of the gargantuan arm now pulling down on a missing cylinder, gravity jumped feet first onto all the circuits and plastic shielding, severing the entire arm. Acting quickly, Thor snuck a bolt of lightning into the armhole, electricity flooding through all the exposed wires and shorting out the entire left side of the robot. Jesus, meanwhile, turned all the uncovered ends and innards into catfish, before the suit could regenerate another arm.

The Turner Eco-Suit got in on the action and tore off the other arm of the Sidneytron 5000™.

"I cannot believe this is working," said William H. Taft XLII.

It was working. Artemis was taking out mechanical supports and major control boards left and right, Thor was electrocuting the ever-loving shit out of the exoskeleton, and Jesus had Walt Sidney's suit literally falling apart, fish product by fish product.

CHAPTER ONE HUNDRED AND ELEVEN

The End

EVERYONE STOOD AROUND THE JARRED HEAD OF A HALF-BOILED, clearly brain-damaged Walt Sidney, ten-foot piles of fish and wine as far as the eye could see.

"So … what now?" asked William H. Taft XLII, staring at the blinking, twitching head.

"We kill him," said Artemis, stepping forward, Ukko's hammer over her shoulder.

"Where did you get that?" asked Thor.

"No, man," said Jesus, arms spread, stepping between the goddess and the frozen head. "Hasn't there been too much killing already?"

"I did kinda promise Catrina I'd kill him," countered the thunder god, rubbing the back of his neck.

"But you also promised her you wouldn't kill anyone else, brother, and, well …" The Son of God motioned toward the piles of bodies hidden beneath the piles of fishsticks.

"Hey, none of that was me. At worst, I severely maimed some dudes. I mean, OK, my hammer maybe took out a few once or twice, but not on purpose. That's on them for not moving. Plus, you know, didn't we establish they were all super evil?"

"He killed Charlie," said Queen Victoria XXX coldly.

"You killed Elizabeth," said Set. "And, you know, a lot of others."

"She was a crazy murderer."

"So are you," said Jesus. "You know, technically."

"And, I mean, look, Vicky …" The thunder god put a hand on her arm. "Charlie was pretty much dead already," he said gently. "That robot thing was not working."

"Yeah ..." The cloned monarch deflated, then took a few steps away from the group and slumped to the ground.

"That's not good," said Artemis, looking after the queen.

"I vote we kill him," said Amen-Ra. "He murdered my entire staff and burned down my factory." Then, menacingly: "He killed Bambi."

"OK, sure," said a long-johned dragoon, stepping into the tightening circle, "but he did do a lot of great things too. He wasn't *evil* evil, like you keep saying. He's built orphanages and taco stands and brought joy to millions of people. You just all ended up on the receiving end of some of his more drastic actions."

"I don't know about that, Ash," said Set, shaking his furry head, "slaughtering innocents is more than a 'drastic action.' And he's totally slaughtered innocents. That's literally why I was hired."

"The blonde guy *you're* all palling around with killed a bunch of kids," added a Louseketeer, pointing at Thor. "Like, the day before yesterday. And not even for a good reason."

"I said I was sorry! Benedict Cumberbatch ..."

"So there are good reasons for killing kids?" asked William H. Taft XLII, shoving the Louseketeer. "I don't think you get to have an opinion on this anymore."

"That's not —"

"Ted," rumbled the sun god, "what do you —"

"Hang on," said Ted Turner, fighting with the harness inside his mech-suit, "I'm still trying to get out of this thing. Also, for what it's worth, the homicidal douchebag sensor is going absolutely nuts right now."

"Really, guys?" asked Artemis. "Are we seriously arguing over the moral repercussions of killing a horrible, terrible, no-good asswipe of a severed head like —" She pointed a finger at Walt Sidney. Everyone turned to follow it and found Catherine the Great LXIX hiking up her skirt and squatting over the frozen CEO.

"What?" said the cloned empress. "Do you have any idea how long a drive it was to get here? And then all that running around?"

She dropped a colossal deuce into the jar of preservation fluid.

"Look, let's compromise," she continued. "If he survives this, I vote we let him live. Trust me," she said, grimacing as she squeezed another one down the turdpipe, "it'll be punishment enough."

CHAPTER DOES IT REALLY MATTER AT THIS POINT?

The Diner America Deserves

HAVING BADE FAREWELL TO THE CLONES AND TED TURNER, Jesus Christ and the blood-soaked gods – Thor, Artemis, Set, and Amen-Ra – had assembled at Denny's to discuss some things. No one was happy about it.

"How many apocalypses has it been?" grumbled Ra as the waiter refilled his coffee. "And Denny's is still in business."

"Never underestimate Americans' ability to underestimate what actual food is," replied the slight young man.

"That's awfully cyclical," said Thor.

"Cynical," corrected Jesus.

"That's our motto." The waiter pointed to a large placard mounted on the wall behind them.

"Oh, wow, look at that."

"Well, if it's all the same with you four," began the Egyptian god-king, shooing away the waiter, "I'd like to get this conversation over with. With Walt Sidney dead –"

"That was one hell of a shit," said Thor.

"– I've got to get back to Egypt and rebuild Heliopolis. And the sooner we're out of this ... *restaurant* ... the better." He slid the paper placemat advertising the Coronary Killer – a sandwich made out of fried pancakes, onion rings, bacon-stuffed Twinkies, and triple half-pound meat patties – toward the center of the table.

"All right," said Artemis, crossing her arms over her chest, "then go ahead."

"Oh. So, you just want me to … OK, well," stalled Ra, "as I'm sure you've all figured out by n–"

"So why Ra?" asked Thor. "Why not Odin?"

"Or, you know, God?" added Jesus.

"Honestly, boys," explained Amen-Ra, "I get severe seasonal affective disorder and having control of the sun helps considerably."

"Yeah, man – dad – but, if you, you know, went full God you could do that."

"If I went 'super saiyan?' Is that what you kids are calling it now?"

"Until we come up with something less stupid," added Artemis.

"What's wrong with super saiyan?" asked Thor.

"Vicky told me you stole it from a cartoon!"

"So? Cartoons are awesome."

"Benedict Cumberbatch," mumbled the Greek goddess. "I cannot believe I am related to you."

"Oh, so this is a family gathering?" asked the waiter, dropping off dishes and taking in the variety of ethnicities sitting around the table. "I take it some of you are adopted then?"

"Who fucking says that, man?" asked Jesus.

"Get out of here, dude," added Thor, gently shoving the waiter away and into and over a nearby table. Salt shakers and silverware clattered to the ground.

"Look," boomed Amen-Ra, "you're right, with any of my other identities I could absolutely control the sun, eventually, but do you know how much effort that would take?"

"Yes," replied Thor gravely, his mouth full of Coronary Killer.

"My ground level powers as Ra allow me to control the sun, and that's all I wanted," he explained. "And, I'll be honest, I missed Egypt. It's a lovely country."

"Really, Pops?" asked Artemis. "Laziness? That's your argument."

"Yes. I told you I was retired."

"He is *our* dad, sister," added Jesus, pointing a finger between himself and Thor.

"You're just mad that my version of great-granddad won out," taunted Set.

"I'm not mad," said Artemis, "just confused. It really had nothing to do with who you were masquerading as during The Fall? You were powerful enough to choose who you wanted to be but not actually get your powers back?"

"I'll be honest, honey," explained Ra, "I really did not give it a lot of thought. I'd kind of checked out well before The Fall."

"I'll say," said Jesus.

"It's just, well, I would've went with Zeus is all."

"Well, of course you would've," said Set.

"I still don't see what was wrong with, like, just straight-up being God," said Jesus.

"He is," replied the Egyptian God of Chaos flatly.

"He means Zeus," replied the Greek Goddess of the Hunt.

"No, I mean God."

"So, like, Brahma?" offered the waiter from where he was painfully righting the other table.

"Stop fucking interrupting," said the Greek goddess, flinging a butter knife dangerously close to the waiter's neck. The young man made a face and then turned and limped slowly to the kitchen.

"Thor," said Amen-Ra, putting a hand on the thunder god's shoulder, "you've been awfully quiet, son. Do you have anything you'd like to add? Thor?"

"Sorry," said the former Norse god, "this sandwich is amazing."

"The coffee's pretty good too," added Jesus.

"You guys are still high, aren't you?" asked Artemis.

"God, I love Denny's," exclaimed the thunder god, shoving the rest of his fried pancake sandwich into his mouth.

The preceding chapter has been paid for by Denny's.*
Denny's: "If you're stoned and starving, and manage to avoid the food poisoning, we're actually not that bad."

The preceding chapter was not actually paid for by Denny's. However, if Denny's would like to pay for the chapter retroactively, … well, it would have to be a lot of money.

Like, a lot.

We're talking the GDP of a small island nation a lot.

CHAPTER HOLY CRAP
AM I STILL GOING?

Dun Dun DUNNN

"THEY'RE ALL DEAD," SAID THE GOBLIN.

"All of them?"

"Well, the important ones anyway. Sidney definitely. There were some dragoons and Louseketeers that made it through, but all the survivors have fled, per the terms of their survival."

"OK." Ah Puch, the smiling Mayan god of death and acting CEO of the Walt Sidney Company clicked the window closed. He narrowed his eyes. "This cannot stand."

CHAPTER THE LAST ONE I PROMISE

Waa Waaaa

"ACTUALLY, NO," SAID AH PUCH, SHAKING HIS HEAD, "what am I talking about?" The death god began scrolling through some spreadsheets, mumbling to himself. "I am totally OK with letting this stand. It was idiotic, petty revenge that got Sidney killed in the first place. What was the practical value of going after those guys? Nothing, that's what."

Ah Puch opened a folder labeled Secret Projects.

"Benedict Cumberbatch, Walt," said the CEO. "You can't just label something Secret Projects." He began going through the files within. "We are spending far too much on our security and acquisitions teams. Who needs this large of a nuclear arsenal? If we'd do things legally, people wouldn't constantly be trying to kill us."

"Honestly," he continued, looking at more numbers, "they did this company a favor getting rid of Walt. We've got more money than we could –" He hit a few buttons. "Yup, wow. More money than we could even quantum theoretically spend. I'm going to send them a fruit basket. And who has this many vice presidents? I didn't even know we had an office on Easter Island. That's getting closed …"

The smiling god hit the intercom button on his desk.

"Cynthia, get Makemake on the phone. And prep him for some terrible news." Ah Puch looked around the all-white, retro-futuristic office, then hit the intercom button again. "And then get our interior designers on the line. This office is atrocious."

Acknowledgments

THANKS TO MONICA, MIKE, STEVEN, ALLY, everyone that's purchased an *Exponential Apocalypse* book in the past, everyone that's reviewed or recommended one, and anyone else that wants to be thanked.

I would also like to thank and apologize to the following entities, as I shamelessly stole either ideas or words or ideas about words from most of them: *Futurama*, *Star Wars*, Douglas Adams, Tom Petty, Danger Slater, *Dragonball Z*, *Broad City*, *Bob's Burgers*, Warren Zevon, religion, Benedict Cumberbatch, and *The Simpsons* probably.

And, finally, as always, the only reason I was able to complete this book (and graduate college and work a second shift for the better part of a decade) was because of coffee. So thank you Flying Star and Café Bella and my kitchen coffee maker and my mother-in-law for getting me the coffee maker. This book would have been a Superfund-level disaster without you.

About the Author

EIRIK GUMENY IS THE AUTHOR OF THE EXPONENTIAL APOCALYPSE series, the latest of which you've just read. Congratulations! His short fiction can be found all over the internet and in various anthologies, and he has contributed to Cracked.com and *Atlas Obscura*. In 2014, he received a double lung transplant and may have briefly died. He currently lives in Albuquerque, New Mexico, where he regularly has to fight giant atomic ants with a flamethrower.

Website: www.egumeny.com
Twitter: @egumeny
Facebook: egumeny

Also By the Author

Exponential Apocalypse
Dead Presidents (Exponential Apocalypse #2)
High Voltage (Exponential Apocalypse #3)
Black Hole, Son! (Exponential Apocalypse #5)

Store-crossed
Quintology of Qualms
We're Going to Die Here, Aren't We?
Devil Went Down to Jersey
Screw the Universe (with Stephen Schwegler)

Endnotes

---

[1] During the previous six months of near-utopia, Jesus Christ – bored and antsy from no longer being needed to provide miracles at a reasonable price – held a press conference asking the world to, once and for all, stop using his name in vain. He was totally fine with blasphemy when he was dead, he explained, but since science had made him mortal again five years earlier and he was now actively walking around being a good dude, using his name as a curse word felt like kind of a dick move and it was hard to not take it personally. Plus he never knew if people were actually talking to him or not and it was hurting his self-esteem. So, the world held a vote and "Benedict Cumberbatch" was decided to be the new mild epithet of choice, both because the actor had died twenty years earlier as a megalomaniacal despot (he was so British about it that no one saw it coming) and because Benedict Cumberbatch was really fun to say, especially when you were angry.

[2] The Walt Sidney Company employed a large network of gremlins to spy on pretty much everyone and everything, all the time. Between them and the ability to check on all surveillance cameras everywhere, there was very little that the corporation didn't know.

[3] The dog-man in question was actually Set, ancient Egyptian god of both disorder and violence. Set is perhaps best known as the father of Anubis, one of the playable characters in the 1995 video game *War Gods*.

[4] After Philadelphia was bombed into oblivion during the eleventh end of the world, it was unanimously decided by everyone everywhere that it should be used as a septic disposal ground and compost heap, because, really, who would be able to tell the difference? Seriously, fuck the Eagles *and* the Flyers.

[5] The city of Moscow, Russia, was purchased by the McDonald's Corporation shortly after the Zombie Holocaust decimated the city and

ended the world for the sixth time. It was widely rumored – and eventually proven – that McDonald's chose Moscow due to its proximity to Horsepower!, the vast horse ranch and energy production mill of Catherine the Great LXIX. Per the incriminating leaked internal memo: "After all, those horses have to go somewhere when they die."

[6] A South American forest nymph with backwards feet, an enormous dong, and weaponized acid pee.

[7] After a long and drawn out series of events involving cloned dinosaurs and killer mutant shrimp, the fuel standard of the automotive industry switched from petroleum products to pretty much everything else – garbage included. This was generally seen as a wonderful idea by everyone, except, understandably, sanitation workers and their families.

[8] After a sub-tectonic magma extravasation caused a global earthquake and jammed the continents of Europe, Africa, and Asian into one another like a bunch of leftover dough being rolled into one misshapen sugar cookie, ending the world for the twenty-first time, the handful of governments that survived decided to lean into their calamity and the super-continent of Eurasica was born.

[9] Cherri was one of the merry wives of William H. Taft XLII. She was also a stripper. She also slept with Thor on a previous occasion. She also had many other merits and hobbies unrelated to men in any way, none of which, though, were relevant to the story at hand.

[10] Quetzalcoatl was an Aztec god, expelled to the mortal realm along with all the other gods when science disproved religion. He got really drunk and crazy, fell in with the Hobo Empire, and tried to take over the world. He was stopped when Thor crushed his skull with a sledgehammer. Along the way, though, he became the first god to figure out how to get his powers back. (*Exponential Apocalypse*)

[11] Growing tired of the constant armageddons plaguing the planet, the United States of America created robotic centaurs to kill the Four Horsemen of the Apocalypse, hoping to save the world for all time. They failed. Hard. The centaurs went homicidally bonkers and started killing everyone and everything. Ultimately, Japan created a team of super robots of their own to fight the kill-happy horse-men. And while they successfully destroyed the centaurs, they also accidentally sank the entire island of Japan into the sea.

[12] Goat-men of the classical tradition. They had hooves and horns, and, while not intrinsically evil, this particular batch was a bunch of dicks.

[13] After Donald Trump's disastrous first – and only – term as President of the United States bankrupted the country to such a degree that it was forced to auction itself off to the highest bidders following the fourth end of the world, the converted White House – now the solid gold Trump House – was removed wholesale from Washington, D.C. and buried on a military bombing range in the Nevada desert, where no one would ever have to think about it again. Eventually, after William H. Taft XLII took over the now-sprawling city-state of Las Vegas, he found the Trump

House, melted it down, and used the gold to make several mansions of his own, as well as three orphanages, a velodrome, six Orange Juliuses, a Cinnabon, and a pet shelter.

[14] Taking a cue from the sentient kangaroo uprising in Australia that launched a global chemical war and ultimately ended the world for the twenty-second time, the cows of Wisconsin – tired of being turned into hamburger and sick of the cold, impersonal machines milking their teats – turned on their human masters and rioted, in what would come to be known as the Dairy Revolution. The movement spread worldwide and, before long, cows were the dominant species on Earth. That said, they were still cows; their economic ideas and understanding of proper nuclear disarmament were sketchy at best. Within weeks, things started exploding all around them, both literally and figuratively, ending the world for the twenty-fourth time. The humans began preparing a resistance to overthrow their cow overlords, only to find that the cows willingly conceded and returned to their roles as livestock. Hamburgers have tasted especially delicious ever since.

[15] Loki was the bastard son of Thor's dad, Odin, and an unnamed frost giantess. Because the one unifying trait of all ancient gods was that they liked to get their swerve on.

[16] Mark Hughes had gotten hammered and crudely hit on the waitress, only to be thrown through the diner window for his troubles. All things considered, this was probably the least helpful anecdote to bring up, as, while defenestration may have been an overreaction, she wasn't entirely in the wrong. (*High Voltage*)

[17] After denying Thor pancakes for no conceivable reason, Thor reached into the waitress's skull and pulled out her eye. He then held it for ransom until he got his pancakes. The pancakes were, not surprisingly, poisoned. Neither of them left the diner that day feeling good about things. (*Exponential Apocalypse*)

[18] After a failed alien invasion obliterated itself trying to enter Earth's atmosphere, raining flaming debris across the planet and ending the world for the fourth time, the United States government decided it no longer needed to cover up all the extraterrestrial shenanigans it had been sitting on since the 1940s and opened Area 51 to the public. The "outer spacey jewel of Nevada" was now home to one of the only entertaining museums in the history of ever, as well as a, quite frankly, astounding water park.

[19] Given the precarious nature of roads in a post-post-apocalyptic society, trucking became even more dangerous and lonely than it had already been. As such, truck stops evolved from roadside diners and gas stations into vast, sprawling, heavily-fortified strongholds for cross-country drivers – cities unto themselves – replete with bars and strip clubs and antiques stores and the like. Also, diners and gas stations.

www.ingramcontent.com/pod-product-compliance
Lightning Source LLC
Chambersburg PA
CBHW031024260626
47153CB00017B/2004